Lady Bridget's Diary

His eyes flashed. Had she angered him? How could that have angered him? He took a step toward her.

"I'm nothing like Rupert," he said in a low voice.

"I know," she said in a whisper.

He took another step closer. His chest was inches from hers. She had to tilt her head back to look up at him. She had to, for his gaze had locked with hers, mesmerizing her, and she could not look away.

"You don't know," he said in a fierce whisper. Her heart began to pound, hard. *"You don't know."*

He placed one finger under her chin, tilting her face, her mouth, up to him. "Rupert will never do this."

And then he kissed her.

D1020974

By Maya Rodale

Keeping Up with the Cavendishes
LADY BRIDGET'S DIARY

Coming Soon
CHASING LADY AMELIA

Bad Boys and Wallflowers Series
WHAT A WALLFLOWER WANTS
THE BAD BOY BILLIONAIRE: WHAT A GIRL WANTS
THE BAD BOY BILLIONAIRE'S GIRL GONE WILD
WALLFLOWER GONE WILD
THE BAD BOY BILLIONAIRE'S WICKED ARRANGEMENT
THE WICKED WALLFLOWER

The Writing Girl Romance Series
SEDUCING MR. KNIGHTLY
THE TATTOOED DUKE
A TALE OF TWO LOVERS
A GROOM OF ONE'S OWN
THREE SCHEMES AND A SCANDAL

ATTENTION: ORGANIZATIONS AND CORPORATIONS
HarperCollins books may be purchased for educational, business, or sales promotional use. For information, please e-mail the Special Markets Department at SPsales@harpercollins.com.

MAYA RODALE

Lady Bridget's Diary

AVONBOOKS

An Imprint of HarperCollinsPublishers

This is a work of fiction. Names, characters, places, and incidents are products of the author's imagination or are used fictitiously and are not to be construed as real. Any resemblance to actual events, locales, organizations, or persons, living or dead, is entirely coincidental.

AVON BOOKS
An Imprint of HarperCollins*Publishers*
195 Broadway
New York, New York 10007

Copyright © 2016 by Maya Rodale
Excerpt from *Chasing Lady Amelia* copyright © 2016 by Maya Rodale
ISBN 978-0-06-238673-1
www.avonromance.com

All rights reserved. No part of this book may be used or reproduced in any manner whatsoever without written permission, except in the case of brief quotations embodied in critical articles and reviews. For information address Avon Books, an Imprint of HarperCollins Publishers.

First Avon Books mass market printing: March 2016

Avon Trademark Reg. U.S. Pat. Off. and in Other Countries, Marca Registrada, Hecho en U.S.A.
Avon, Avon Books, and the Avon logo are trademarks of Harper-Collins Publishers.
HarperCollins® is a registered trademark of HarperCollins Publishers.

Printed in the U.S.A.

10 9 8 7 6 5 4 3 2 1

If you purchased this book without a cover, you should be aware that this book is stolen property. It was reported as "unsold and destroyed" to the publisher, and neither the author nor the publisher has received any payment for this "stripped book."

For my readers.

And for Tony, who won't let me read his diary.

Acknowledgments

I would like to thank my editor, Tessa, and the entire team at Avon Books for helping to create this book. I am eternally grateful to Tony Haile for editorial and emotional support and to Lady Miss Penny for being my devoted companion. And most of all, thank you to my readers.

Fashionable Intelligence
By A Lady of Distinction

All of London is talking about one thing and one thing only: the arrival of the new Duke of Durham. His Grace, we are told, hails from America, of all places in the world, which begs the question of how this came to be.

Older readers—or younger readers who bother to visit their aged relatives and actually listen to them speak of scandals from days of yore—will recollect the Great Scandal of 1784 in which the fifth duke's brother, the Lord Harry Cavendish, beloved rake, absconded to America with the duke's prize horse. This horse-thieving younger brother had done a stint in the army, as second sons are wont to do, especially when they are so obviously unsuited to clergy. Whilst stationed in the colonies, he happened to fall in love with an American woman. It was a love so great that he would forsake family, country, membership at White's, and a voucher for Almack's.

After extensive sleuthing this author has been able to determine that Lord Harry Cavendish established a farm in Maryland where he bred and trained racehorses, raised his family, including a son who followed in his footsteps, and refused to use his title.

That is, until the fifth duke died without a son, making Lord Harry the next in line. When Her Grace, the duchess of Durham, finally tracked down that horse-thieving younger brother, it was too late. Unbeknownst to anyone, the dukedom had been passed from one generation to another.

So yes, dear readers, a horse farmer from the colonies now holds one of the loftiest titles in England. His arrival is expected any day now and this author has it on excellent authority that he is bringing three sisters of marriageable age. Let there be no conversations about a dull season, for this one is sure to be most entertaining . . .

Prologue

Oceans crossed: 1
Sisters who plagued me the entire journey: 2
Brothers who suddenly became a duke: 1
Fearsome duchesses: 1

LADY BRIDGET'S DIARY

London, 1824
Durham Residence
The Ballroom

One would think that having one's brother inherit a dukedom was a stroke of good fortune that would transform their lives from ho-hum to utterly fantastic. One would think that until one was on a reducing diet, stuffed into a tightly laced corset, and forced to practice walking backward.

"Once again, Lady Bridget," the duchess said crisply.

She was *Lady* Bridget Cavendish now. Before she had just been Bridget Cavendish of Duncraven farm in Maryland. But then a letter had arrived one day, with the unexpected news that their late father, God rest his soul, had inherited the title and died without knowing it. James was now a duke and they were all to leave everything behind and travel to England, immediately.

"Yes *Lady* Bridget, once more please," Amelia said with a smirk.

"Do shut up, Amelia," Bridget said, under her breath. Younger sisters were quite annoying, on any continent.

"It's 'Do shut up, *Lady* Amelia,'" Claire, the oldest sister, corrected. She found all the formality as ridiculous as the rest of their family, much to the despair of the duchess.

Somewhere about the massive house—probably in the stables, even though the duchess made it perfectly clear dukes were above mucking about in the stables—was her brother, James. Or, as he was now to be known, His Grace, the Duke of Durham. Dukes had many responsibilities, it seemed, but walking backward in a gown with an excessively long train was not one of them.

Before her, with sharp blue eyes and perfectly coiffed blond hair, was Josephine Marie Elizabeth Cavendish, Her Grace, the Duchess of Durham, widow of the fifth duke, and aunt to the Cavendish siblings.

One did not call her Josie. Amelia had asked.

"Remind me why we are learning to do something as ridiculous as walk backward?" Claire asked. From a young age, she had spent her free hours devoted to the study of mathematics, otherwise known as Important Work. Bridget's head ached just to think about it.

"It is for your presentation at court," the duchess replied. "Which is necessary before your debut in society, which you must do in order to find a husband, which a lady must do, lest she become an impoverished spinster."

"What if we do not wish for a husband?" Amelia asked.

"What a silly question," the duchess replied. "Lady Bridget, once again."

At the duchess's request, Bridget sank into a curtsy. They had practiced this extensively on Tuesday afternoon. Then, with as much grace as she could muster, Bridget rose and began to elegantly glide backward. Or so she tried; feats of grace did not come easily to her (a point upon which their dancing instructor would absolutely agree). Nothing about being a True Lady did. Bridget had daydreamt through lessons on the order of precedence amongst members of the haute ton, how to properly pour a cup of tea, and all the other lessons on etiquette and deportment they endured morning, noon, and night.

"Now Lady Amelia, it is your turn."

While the duchess's attention was focused on her sisters, Bridget took advantage of her distraction to continue walking backward until she had crossed the length of the ballroom, then she continued through the large double doors and halfway down the corridor, at which point she turned, lifted her skirts, and proceeded to the kitchens. Reducing diet, deportment lessons, and True Lady-ness be damned.

Chapter 1

Tonight is our grand debut in society. ~~I hope I don't make an ass of myself.~~ I hope that I conduct myself as befitting a lady of my station. (That sounds proper, right?)

LADY BRIDGET'S DIARY

The Americans had arrived. In fact, they had arrived in London a fortnight earlier but the Duchess of Durham had kept them hidden from the prying eyes of society. Tonight, at Lady Tunbridge's ball, they made their debut.

A hush had fallen over the ballroom as the Duchess of Durham appeared for the first time in public with the new Duke of Durham and his sisters, three dark-haired young ladies of marriageable age. The ton craned their necks for a glimpse of them, eager to see what the newspapers had been speculating about for weeks.

The haute ton immediately commenced with clamoring for introductions to the new duke—the ton had already taken to calling him that—and gossiping about the sisters. The duchess and her collection of Americans began to circulate the ballroom. Introductions were made. Polite conversations were had. Some fawning ensued.

Three gentlemen preferred to watch the mayhem from a distance.

"Well, this should liven up the season," Rupert remarked. "Or at the very least, will inspire conversations about how they shall liven up an otherwise dull season."

Beside him, Lord Fox, a good friend, simply said, "They're pretty."

Lord Darcy resisted the urge to roll his eyes and said nothing. That one of England's oldest, most venerated titles was now possessed by a horse breeder from the colonies was surely a harbinger of the downfall of English society. It mattered little if his sisters were pretty when civilization as they knew it was over. It went without saying that as a wealthy, respected, powerful peer of the realm, he was quite fond of civilization just as it was.

"It's a pity the Durham title is going to an American," Darcy said, simply repeating sentiments widely shared by the haute ton and printed repeatedly in a majority of the city's newspapers.

"You're such a snob," Rupert said, laughing at his older brother. He was the only one who dared to speak to him that way.

Somehow, Lord Burbrooke had managed to infiltrate their conversation. Darcy noted the man's red cheeks (from an excess of alcohol, surely) and bright green waistcoat (from a dearth of taste).

"Can't say I didn't thumb through *Debrett's* to see if there was a chance I'd inherit," he said jovially. "I heard that if the duchess hadn't tracked down this fellow, the title would have gone to some distant relation. Pity that."

"Spare us all from distant relations," Fox said.

"Yes, it would have gone to a Mr. Collins." He was one of those distant, imbecilic relations one despaired of. As the head of his own estate, and raised to ensure that it was successfully passed to the next generation, Darcy understood why the duchess had plundered the colonies in search of an heir. Anyone was better than Mr. Collins.

"Say, how do you know that, Darcy?" Burbrooke asked, awed.

"Darcy knows everything," Rupert said, smirking.

"But Darcy," Fox drawled, "did you know they were pretty?"

"Says the man who is betrothed to one of the ton's most sought after young ladies," Darcy remarked, reminding his friend of his impending wedding.

"And who has also landed London's most sought after mistress," Rupert added.

"Right." Fox straightened and looked around, presumably in search of his intended. Spotting her, he strolled away in her direction.

"Half a mind to marry one of them myself," Burbrooke said. "I bet they have very fine . . . dowries." There was no mistaking the direction of his gaze, which was not precisely on their . . . dowries.

"There would be some advantages to wedding one of the American girls," Rupert said, a little too thoughtfully for Darcy's taste.

"Don't get any ideas. I won't welcome any recalcitrant colonists into the family."

"Oh look, one of them seems lost," said Rupert.

Burbrooke wandered off to lose money in the card room while Darcy and his brother stayed to watch the wayward American girl. She had certainly become disconnected from her group. Apparently she had not been informed that ladies did not wander about the ballroom unaccompanied, gawking at this and that. Or perhaps she simply had no regard for etiquette and protocol—a thought that gave Darcy anxiety. Or perhaps—

"Oh dear God." Rupert started forward when he saw what had just happened.

Even Darcy was shocked.

"Did she just . . . ?"

"She did," Darcy confirmed, mouth set in a grim line.

"Well, we had better go rescue her," Rupert said. Darcy protested: "I am not in the habit of rescuing young women."

When they stepped into the ballroom and a hush fell over the crowd, Bridget finally began to understand what the duchess had been trying to prepare them for.

But what could possibly prepare her for this? The ballroom itself was downright palatial (or so she had imagined, not having many palaces lying around in Maryland). And the people within the ballroom . . . a room full of earls and viscounts and countesses, all dressed in the finest, most beautiful clothes, all wearing heaps of glittering diamonds and other jewels, all of them so refined and elegant and . . . staring at the Cavendishes. As if they were some novelty item or the evening's entertainment.

"We're not in America anymore," Amelia murmured.

"Definitely not," Claire murmured in agreement.

"Remember what I taught you," the duchess murmured. *I don't remember anything*, Bridget thought in a panic. Not true: she remembered sipping chocolate in bed and sneaking into the kitchens at midnight. Not helpful now!

Then, arm in arm with His Grace, the Duke of Durham, the duchess led the way forward.

And so began the endless round of introductions and conversations with what seemed like every lord, lady, and right honorable person God ever made and stuffed into one hot, crowded ballroom. Bridget didn't quite seem to understand why everything they said was subject to murmurs and laughter. Was it her accent? Well, these stuffy English folks ought to hear themselves, with their *Loooord* this and *thawghts* about that.

Or was it because they weren't born and raised in a world of privilege? She overheard more than a few snide remarks about the scent of the stables around them, a snub to James's (former) occupation rather than how they smelled. She hoped. More than once she wanted to turn around and say, *I can hear you.*

It couldn't be because of their attire; the duchess had certainly ensured they were turned out in the most beautiful, sumptuous dresses and she'd even dipped into the Cavendish family jewels to find something sparkly for each of the girls. They certainly looked the part. And yet . . .

Whatever it was, Bridget was having a devil of a time keeping up and keeping a smile on her face. And then she fell behind. Literally. In the throng of guests, she became separated and cut off from the duchess and her sisters. And then she got lost. Bridget found herself alone in the ballroom, fighting to keep a smile on her face as if she meant to be strolling by herself, all while craning her neck looking for the duchess's towering hairstyle.

And then, oh God, then.

While Bridget admittedly hadn't been the most diligent student of Josephine's lessons on deportment and such, she was certain that one was not supposed to find herself flat on her back, gasping for breath, in a ballroom.

Yet there she was, having slipped and fallen,

the wind knocked from her lungs, staring up at the intricately painted ceiling of Lord and Lady Something or Other's ballroom. There were big, fluffy clouds swarmed by an army of fat babies, armed to the teeth with bows and arrows. Cupid.

Perhaps if she just squinted a bit and looked very pensive she could pass this off simply as a uniquely American method of art appreciation. In a moment, when she'd caught her breath, she would stand up and declare that the brushstrokes in the clouds were evocative of a wild spirit in the artist, or some other nonsense statement.

Or not. Perhaps she might just lie here and wait for the floorboards to open up. Perhaps the haute ton would just trample her underfoot with their silk and satin slippers.

She imagined her tombstone: *Here lies Lady Bridget Cavendish. She has fallen to her death.*

It would technically be true.

Bridget ought to get up. Really. A lady couldn't just lie there forever, wishing the floorboards would open and shut and whisk her away to a place where corsets didn't dig into one's skin, and reducing diets were unnecessary, and people didn't gawk at her like she was on display at the circus.

And then a head popped into view.

Oh. *Hello.*

A head with a handsome face. And, most importantly of all, a friendly face.

"Admiring the view, are you?" the handsome man inquired, peering down at her.

"You really cannot appreciate the artwork on the ceiling from any other position."

Handsome Man smiled. It was like sunshine. And fireworks.

She accepted his outstretched hand; he helped lift her to her feet as if she were light as a feather. Once standing, she saw someone with him. Tall, dark-haired, a bored expression, and one fleeting, dismissive glance at her.

Well then.

"I've always wondered why cherubs were so plump," Handsome Man said, and Bridget turned to give him her full attention.

"No reducing diets for them. I was just wondering why they are always naked," she added, even though she was quite sure the duchess would frown upon mentioning nudity in mixed company.

"And is it really the wisest course of action to arm small children with weaponry?" he mused, staring up at the ceiling.

"It doesn't seem advisable, does it?" Bridget said, laughing.

"A disaster, waiting to happen." Handsome Man demonstrated his possession of the sort of gorgeous smile that made a girl forget her wits.

His bored, disapproving friend coughed in that discreet way that everyone knows isn't actually a cough but a gentle, oh-so-polite request to cease speaking immediately and quit the scene.

Bridget spared him a brief glance and saw just enough: he was another stuffy, boorish Englishman. This place was infested with them. He could hardly compete with his handsome, charming, and nice companion for her company.

"How remiss of me," Handsome Man said. "We must find someone to introduce us."

Bridget and he looked around at all the finely dressed guests around them. He probably wouldn't find anyone to do the deed. Though the duchess had been introducing them all evening, there was no one she recognized. There had been too many names and faces to keep track of.

Not wanting to find herself left alone with his dark and brooding companion while he sought a mutual acquaintance, Bridget decided to just introduce herself. She stuck out her hand and said, "Bridget Cavendish, of the American Cavendishes."

"I know."

"I suppose everybody knows."

"Mr. Rupert Wright, at your service," he said with a bow. She grinned because his name was actually *Mr. Wright*. It had to be some sort of sign. "And this is my brother, Darcy. He is a stickler for propriety and probably having an apoplexy that we have violated the most basic etiquette by conversing before being introduced by a mutual acquaintance."

"Well aren't we living dangerously," she murmured. Rupert's eyes flashed and a smile teased at his lips.

"Indeed, it's so very thrilling," he murmured. Lord above, he was handsome. She would probably go home and write *Rupert and Bridget* in her diary. Repeatedly.

"I was just saying that an American family infiltrating the English aristocracy will surely lead to the downfall of English society," Darcy said smugly. "As usual, I am correct."

"Is that so?" Bridget inquired. "How exactly does that happen?"

"First, it's an occasional informality; perhaps a conversation without a proper introduction. Then the rules are regularly relaxed, which, over time, leads to a general mayhem. Then we are all no different from the beasts. Or savages. Or Americans."

"You sound like the Duchess of Durham," she replied. "Or one of the conduct books on my bedside table. They are a remarkable remedy for insomnia."

Aha! A flicker of *feeling* in his features! He seemed shocked and maybe, perhaps, a bit wounded to have been compared to one of the dragons of the ton. She felt thrilled to have gotten a reaction out of him.

Rupert burst out laughing. "Finally, Darcy, someone to stand up to you!"

"So happy to oblige," she replied, smiling, because she made Rupert laugh with her instead of at her.

But her smile faded when she caught Darcy staring. Under his gaze, she became intensely aware of her dress, her hair, whether she was standing straight enough, and she involuntarily wondered if he liked what he saw or why she cared if he did. He made her skin feel hot.

Why this man should have such an effect on her was not something she was inclined to dwell on. Not when she could banter with his handsome and *friendly* brother. *Rupert and Bridget* did have such a ring to it.

"Oh, is that a waltz starting?" Rupert asked, groaning slightly. "I promised our hostess that I would dance with her daughter, and I live in fear of Lady Tunbridge's wrath if I don't comply. Lady Bridget, it has been lovely not officially making your acquaintance and discussing art. I hope to see you soon. Do take care for the rest of the evening."

And with that, Rupert flashed her a grin and ventured off in search of Lady Tunbridge and her daughter.

She was left alone with his brother.

His eyes were dark and intensely focused on *her*. His jaw was set. If his brother was sunshine and cupid, this man was dark clouds, thunderstorms, that feeling of electricity in the air before lightning strikes.

They stood there, staring at each other, in an agonizing silence. In her opinion, extended silences were the worst. The longer they lasted, the harder it was to find something to say. And she often blurted out the first thing on her mind to avoid it. This moment was no exception.

"Do you dance, Mr. Darcy?"

"Lord Darcy," he corrected. Of course. Everyone here was Lord or Lady or Your Grace or Your

Lordship. Not only were there rankings, but also different forms of address, many of which changed depending on whether one was writing or speaking. Bridget remembered Josephine lecturing on this—and she remembered not paying attention.

She longed, intensely, for America, where everyone was either Mr., Mrs., or Miss, and that was that.

"I'm ever so sorry, Loooord Darcy," she said, drawing out the sound and imitating his accent. Her attempt at humor was met with more silence. Dreaded silence. "Do you?"

"I do not." Of course he didn't. Because dancing was *fun* and she could already see that this man was where anything amusing and pleasant went to die.

Most ladies would take the opportunity to flee from a man who obviously had no interest in them. But she was not most ladies.

She accepted this Dreadful Darcy as a personal challenge. She *would* make him laugh, or at least crack a smile, if it was the *last* thing she did. Bridget leaned in closer, as if to whisper something scandalous. He stood still, like a statue. Barely breathing.

"Are you not speaking to me because we haven't been properly introduced?"

"No."

"Tell me, Lord Darcy, do you find it amusing, this brooding and striking fear into the hearts of innocent young maidens?"

Was that a twitch at his lips? Laughter? She wanted to crow in triumph. But it was too soon. She was emboldened to continue.

"I wonder, Lord Darcy, if we have not been introduced, then has this conversation even happened?"

She lifted one brow, questioning.

He simply stared at her. Was he horrified by her outspokenness or was he actually considering the question? It was a good question, actually. One she would pose to Josephine tomorrow over breakfast. She was actually curious how this disapproving gentleman would answer.

"I think you will agree that it's best we proceed as if this conversation has never taken place. Excuse me," he said, ever so politely. Then he turned and walked away, leaving her alone in a crowded room.

"Have a good evening," she muttered to his back. Then quietly under her breath, she added on one of the slang words she'd recently learned from a stable hand.

"Did she just . . . *fall*?" Miss Mabel Mulberry said with a shake of her strawberry blond hair.

"I think she just fell," Miss Kitty Montague said, mouth agape.

Lady Francesca DeVere just smiled. "She most certainly did."

When *The London Weekly* broke the news that the new Duke of Durham would be arriving from *America* with not one but three sisters in tow, most of the ton lamented the foreign invasion. A few enterprising mothers began to plot how they might land the duke for their daughters, with the hope that in time his title would trump his past occupation. But Lady Francesca DeVere was nervous about the arrival of three new young ladies.

She had only just vanquished her chief rival and best friend, Lady Katherine Abernathy, who had failed to snare the Duke of Ashbrooke after four seasons of trying. Instead she had married nobody and was now rusticating in the country.

And now Lady Francesca was the reigning beauty of the ton.

Unless those American girls were beautiful, amiable, and charming. They were pretty, but not beautiful. She'd heard they were nice enough. But now that girl had fallen in the middle of the ballroom and nothing else mattered.

Francesca's status as darling of the season would be secured. But wait . . . was that . . . ?

"Is that Darcy and his brother with her?" Miss Mulberry asked.

"Yes," Lady Francesca admitted through gritted teeth.

"Did he propose yet, Francesca?" Miss Montague asked.

No, he had not. Which was fine. Truly. She was still on schedule—the first season was for flirting, the second for entertaining suitors, and in the third she would marry her older brother's best friend, Darcy. She was so certain of it that she'd even spent the earlier part of this season with her aunt and chaperone, Lady Wych Cross, taking the waters in Bath.

She turned to face her silly friend.

"If he had proposed, you wouldn't have to ask. I would tell you." *And the whole bloody town.*

"Why is he spending so much time talking to the American girl?" Miss Montague asked.

Francesca sighed. "The question is why is he talking to her at all? He is probably just being polite. You know Darcy, he is nothing if not perfectly polite."

But she wasn't taking any chances. She would have to go flirt with him immediately. As much as one could flirt with Darcy, anyway.

A short while later, having taken great care when walking through the ballroom, Bridget found her sisters and the duchess.

"Where did you go? We lost you in the crowds," Claire said.

"I hope you didn't get into any trouble," the duchess said, giving her a once-over as if she might detect what Bridget had done and with whom she had done it.

"I took a turn about the room," Bridget said. "In a manner of speaking. What did I miss?"

"We were introduced. To people. A lot of very English people," Amelia said, yawning.

"They are the very best of high society."

"I'm so sorry to have missed that," Bridget said dryly.

"I said, 'How do you do' and 'It's a pleasure to

make your acquaintance' approximately six and twenty times," Amelia added.

"And I thank the Lord that is all you said," the duchess said with a glance heavenward.

"And then we were asked about Indian attacks and bears," Claire said, rolling her eyes, which made Josephine cringe. Apparently proper ladies did not roll their eyes. "Amelia, of course, encouraged them in believing the worst."

"I see I didn't miss anything," Bridget said. "Where is James?"

It was important that they all stay together in this foreign land.

"There." Amelia pointed to the dance floor, and the duchess reminded her about pointing (it was yet another thing that was Not Done). Their brother was waltzing with a very long-faced woman who seemed to smile as much as Loooord Darcy, which was to say, not at all.

James didn't look like he was having much fun either.

"Oh dear," Bridget murmured.

"She looks like a horse," Amelia murmured.

"Lady Melinda Cowper would make an excellent duchess. Her bloodlines are perfect and her manners are exquisite."

"And she is described like a horse," Claire said under her breath.

"She probably never finds herself flat on her back in a ballroom and speaking with gentlemen to whom she has not been introduced," Bridget remarked.

Amelia burst out laughing.

"Why am I not surprised?" Claire asked, sighing. Bridget scowled in annoyance at her older sister.

"I certainly hope not," the duchess said crisply. "And I shudder to think of how such horrific things even cross your mind, Lady Bridget."

"You don't want to know, Josephine. You really don't."

She was given A Look that managed to convey her displeasure with being referred to so informally, that she was above actually *saying* anything about it, and that she was well aware that Bridget knew better and ought to apologize.

"I'm very sorry."

It was an amazing skill, that. One that Bridget would one day like to possess. Perhaps if she stayed with Josephine long enough, and actually paid attention to her lessons, she would pick up the skill by osmorisis or osmosis or whatever it was.

"Come, there are more introductions to be made. Everyone is desperate to make your acquaintance."

And with that they continued their campaign to win over the haute ton. They paused to speak with Lord and Lady Something near the lemonade table. Bridget failed to pay strict attention to the conversation; instead she noticed Darcy. There was a woman on his arm—the sort of tall, sleek, beautiful woman that made a regular woman in her best dress feel the most dowdy provincial spinster.

Theirs was a conversation she strained to overhear and she was infuriated by what she overheard him say.

Lord Darcy knew that there was only one thing to do when one's equilibrium was disturbed, and that was to stand very still and patiently wait for the world to right itself. He stood alone on the terrace, sipping a fine brandy and enjoying a respite. As a precaution, he arranged his features into something that could be described as brooding, the better to ward off anyone who might even consider the foolish notion of trying to converse with him. It was better that everyone thought him in a dark mood, rather than the truth.

And the truth was that he found himself flummoxed.

It went without saying that he was never unbalanced, remotely emotional, or disorganized. He was never flummoxed, confused, or any state other than perfectly calm and collected. He had spent his entire life cultivating the particular talent of suppressing every uncomfortable, wayward emotion.

His father would be so proud. This he thought with a small trace of bitterness.

So it was shocking that *he* found himself flummoxed, and it was unthinkable that the cause was an American woman sprawled on the floor of a ballroom.

He didn't know a world where that happened.

Where women sprawled upon floors in ballrooms, then stood up and made jokes about it and proceeded to tease him.

No one teased him.

No one spoke to him the way she had done—informally, as if they were old mates of the same rank. Did she not know that she was supposed to be afraid of him?

Apparently not.

No one ever left him with a tight feeling in his chest either. Like he couldn't breathe. Like she took his breath away.

But that was preposterous.

Darcy sipped his drink and willed his world to rights. The tension in his chest eased and his breathing resumed. A young woman caught his eye and quickly averted her gaze—ah, that was more like it.

He hadn't seen Rupert since the bounder abandoned him with Lady Bridget—here he took a sharp intake of breath and refused to consider her further—and he reluctantly returned to the ballroom in search of him.

But then there was Fox, heading his way and grinning for having found him. His sister was with him, strolling along gracefully. Lady Francesca DeVere was beautiful, clever, and irreproachable. The perfect wife for a man of his station. He would probably marry her.

"Have you seen my brother?" Darcy inquired.

"I think I spotted him in the card room with Croft," Fox said, referring to an old school friend of theirs. Darcy wasn't surprised; his brother had recently begun racking up gaming debts. "But never mind that. I have made the acquaintance of the new duke," Fox said, falling in step beside him. Francesca did as well. "He's all right."

"Glad to hear it." Darcy would pay call upon the new duke tomorrow—they were neighbors in London after all—because civility and manners demanded it. Therefore, he saw no reason to join the hordes seeking his acquaintance this evening.

They had made it as far as the lemonade table when a crush prevented them from walking further. So the trio stood there and carried on their conversation.

"And I saw you made the acquaintance of one of the sisters. The girl who fell," Lady Francesca said, glancing at him under her thick black lashes.

"Yes. Lady Bridget."

There was a flicker in her eyes; she was surprised he knew her name.

"It's all anyone is talking about tonight. Poor thing."

Darcy tensed, then muttered a vague response. It only occurred to him now that if everyone had seen Lady Bridget falling, then they had undoubtedly seen him conversing with her. He would be an object of gossip. Their names would be linked. How distasteful.

Lady Francesca mercifully carried on. "I heard the other one is a bluestocking. And the third mentioned riding astride. Can you just imagine?"

She laughed lightly.

"They're pretty," Fox said. Again. He wasn't known for the depth or variety of his thoughts. "Darcy, don't you think so?"

"They're not handsome enough to tempt me to overlook their manners," Darcy said flatly, while his gaze strayed to Lady Bridget in particular.

He didn't miss the smug smile on Francesca's lips. And out of the corner of his eye he saw . . . the woman in question. Standing nearby, within earshot, with her family. Had she heard? What did he care if she did?

"Well, I think they're pretty," Fox insisted.

"You're engaged," his sister said.

"So people keep telling me."

"Why can't you be more refined and dignified, like Darcy?"

Francesca gave him a coy smile as she linked her arm with his. He appreciated that they shared the same values. That was why he would marry her. That, and she would never flail about and fall down in a ballroom and ask him inane questions, such as *If they were conversing without having been introduced, did the conversation even happen?*

He wanted to say no. It never happened. But it did. Because he was still thinking about it. And the wicked gleam of amusement in her eyes as she asked.

"There aren't many men like Darcy," Fox said.

"Isn't that the truth," Francesca cooed.

"I would enjoy this topic of conversation more if I were less modest."

"The perfect gentleman, aren't you?" Lady Francesca laughed and brushed a speck of lint from the lapel of his evening jacket. Except he was Darcy, and so never did something as mundane as having lint on his jacket.

"Not always," he replied, thinking about his conversation with Lady Bridget. He'd been aloof to the point of being rude. He'd practically given her the cut direct. And why? An Englishman is never rude *by accident*. But his wits and thoughts had been so tangled up by a woman who fell to the floor, then stood up and proceeded to make conversation and tease him as if no one had informed her that he was to be feared.

"Not always a perfect gentleman?" Francesca laughed. "Pray tell."

"There's nothing to tell."

"Too much of a gentleman, I suppose?"

Hardly, if his thoughts and behavior this evening were any indication. He again became aware of the Americans nearby . . . of Lady Bridget . . . and a disturbance to his equilibrium. Suddenly, he'd had enough of this ball and enough of this evening. Already he'd had enough of *her*.

Chapter 2

Lessons in proper etiquette avoided: 27
Lessons I should not have avoided: 27
Reception in English society: dreadful
                        LADY BRIDGET'S DIARY

The duchess sat at her dressing table, sipping a glass of sherry while her companion, Miss Green, painstakingly removed all the hairpins holding up her elegant coiffure. It was their evening ritual, ever since Miss Green had come to act as companion and occasional lady's maid to the duchess, taking over the position her mother had filled before her.

Josephine took one sip of sherry, then another, before she could bring herself to speak of the evening they had all barely survived. She'd been so certain of success; how wild could her American nieces and nephew be? Surely if anyone could turn them into darlings of the ton, it was she, the esteemed and feared Duchess of Durham.

"How was the ball?" Miss Green asked.

"It was a disaster."

"It could not have been that bad."

Josephine gave her A Look in the mirror, even though it was a requirement of Miss Green's position to say things like that.

"Lady Bridget fell and lay sprawled upon the floor. Lady Claire could not hide her boredom if her life depended on it, which it does, though I cannot seem to impress it upon her. She already has a reputation as a bluestocking, which will hardly serve her well. Lady Amelia mentioned riding astride on their farm, so now everyone thinks her a hoyden at best. That one will be the death of me, I am sure of it. And the duke . . ."

"What about the duke?"

The duchess watched Miss Green closely in the mirror. Had her breath hitched at the mention of the duke?

"You'd think he was being led to the gallows, not waltzing with the finest young women in England."

"And how was the dancing?"

Together they had watched the lessons Monsieur Bellini had been hired to provide. The sisters had eventually grasped the waltz, thank the Lord, with its three simple steps. The steps of the quadrille and other dances had eluded them thus far. Was it really too much to ask that one dance with a modicum of grace?

The duchess took another sip of her sherry.

"They were adequate. They were not ready for society, but if we delayed their debut, everyone would think the worst." At least, that had been her rationale. It pained her to admit even privately to herself that she might have been mistaken. "Of course now they already know the worst."

"They still must be better than Mr. Collins."

"The less said about Mr. Collins, the better."

But the man was never far from her mind, for until James had a son or two, there was a chance that Durham could fall into the hands of a bumbling provincial clergyman who possessed neither wit, taste, nor self-awareness. It was a ghastly combination.

But more importantly, he lacked what it took to run an estate like Durham. And too many good people were dependent upon a duke with his wits about him and heart in the right place.

Which was why she had searched high and low for her late husband's younger brother, only to learn that he'd died in the Americas some years earlier. But he had a son—an heir—and she had, by the grace of God, managed to persuade him to leave the dirt and dust of the stables and assume his rightful place in England.

Now she just needed to ensure that he stayed.

"There is always tomorrow for more lessons with the girls. And there is always you to teach them."

"Thank you, Miss Green. If anyone can mold

them into perfect lords and ladies, it is I. Though I fear for the future of the dukedom if even I cannot manage it. I have had one task in life and it was to secure the Durham dukedom for another generation. Failure is simply not an option I shall consider."

After this disastrous evening, I am resolved harder to become the Woman of Quality the duchess wishes me to be—whom I wish to be. I shall adhere to my reducing diet, become an expert in the order of precedence, distinguish between all the forks at the dinner table, and learn how to waltz without stepping on my partner's feet.

LADY BRIDGET'S DIARY

After their debut in society, each Cavendish sibling quietly retired to his or her bedchamber in the monstrous Durham residence. But one by one, after the maids were dismissed for the evening, the sisters made their way to Claire's bedroom and climbed onto her four-poster bed. It was a habit of theirs from back home. Bridget needed to know that this, at least, had not changed. She had a feeling her sisters did, too.

"Tonight was a disaster," Bridget said flatly. She didn't want to talk about it, but she could not *not* talk about it.

"I wouldn't say that—" Claire began diplomatically.

"Claire, I fell. On the floor."

"And apparently I am not supposed to refuse

offers to dance," Amelia said. "Even from decrepit old gentlemen with lecherous grins. That sort should not be allowed out near young ladies."

"Apparently I already have a reputation as a bluestocking," Claire said flatly. "All because I wear spectacles. And possess a modicum of intelligence."

"You also asked a few ladies which subjects they liked to study and mentioned that you looked forward to meeting the Duke of Ashbrooke to discuss mathematical theories," Amelia pointed out. "Apparently we are only supposed to discuss the weather."

"Well, at least you're not known as the girl who fell."

Amelia giggled. Then Claire. Sisters.

Bridget glared at them. She pretended she was Josephine—no, that dreadful Darcy—and gave them her best death-to-you-insect look.

"Are you ill, Bridget?"

"No."

"Because you were making an odd face."

"It's nothing," she said, heaving a sigh and thinking back *again* to what she'd overheard the Despicable Darcy say. *She is not handsome enough to tempt me to overlook her manners.* He thought her ugly and ill-mannered. A tragic peasant, trussed up in fancy clothes. And he was, in all likelihood, merely echoing the sentiments of everyone they'd met tonight. While Bridget didn't care what he thought, as he was a dreadful human, she did care what the rest of the ton thought of her and her family.

In that moment, it all became very real to her: chances were, this was their home now. This was where they would make friends, fall in love, start families of their own. If they weren't laughed out of town.

She supposed they could go back to America. But now that Bridget thought about it, could she really return to everyone whispering that she just couldn't succeed in England? They would say that she wasn't pretty enough or ladylike enough so the English sent her back to the horse farm from whence she came.

She pictured a look of smug satisfaction on the face of Dreadful Darcy.

"So much for the duchess's plan for us to take the haute ton by storm," Amelia said, lazily twisting one of her long brown curls around her finger. "I hope we have disabused her of that notion so we can cease all those tedious lessons. I couldn't care less how to address the younger son of a viscount. Or whomever."

"Actually, I think I understand the point of all those lessons now," Bridget said softly. They were to *help* her succeed rather than infringe upon her time spent perusing fashion periodicals in bed, sipping chocolate. They were to help her become a True Lady. "And now that I have already ruined my reputation, and made myself a laughingstock, I want to make them all forget." She pictured Darcy, snidely dismissing her looks and her manners. She thought of that tall, beautiful woman being all tall, beautiful, and well mannered. *She* probably knew whether a baron outranked an earl. She probably never fell, not even when learning to walk as a baby.

In that moment, Bridget was resolved. She would silence their laughter. She would earn their respect. She would faithfully attend to Josephine's every lesson. "I will make everyone forget that I am the girl who fell," she said, with a look of fierce determination. "I shall be known as Lady Bridget, diamond of the first water."

Amelia laughed.

"Really?" Claire asked, skeptical. "I would much rather have some complex equations to solve. At least numbers make sense and are what they are, and opinions don't matter at all."

"To you. They make sense to you," Amelia pointed out.

"If you would just apply yourself . . ." Claire replied.

Bridget interrupted a frequently recurring argument. "If we would all just apply ourselves to the duchess's teachings, then we wouldn't be the laughingstocks of London."

"That has quite a ring to it," Amelia said.

"That is *entirely* beside the point, Amelia," Bridget huffed.

There was a knock on the door. James pushed it open slightly.

"Are you all decent?"

"Yes, do come in, Your Grace," Claire called out.

"Oooh, it's the duke," Amelia teased. "We'd better bow and curtsy."

Giggling, she and Bridget slid off the bed and Bridget was, well, Bridget. When she bowed and lifted her arm with a flourish, it smacked Amelia in the nose.

"Ow!"

"Good evening, Your Grace," Bridget said in her most Dignified Lady voice. She might as well start practicing, for she had much catching up to do.

"We are *so* honored to have you grace us with your presence, Your Grace." Amelia tried to curtsy and hold her nose at the same time, which resulted in her tumbling to the floor.

"Do shut up, all of you," he muttered. Then he pulled up a chair next to the bed and took a seat, stretching his long legs out before him. He wore breeches, boots, and just a shirt. The duchess would undoubtedly be horrified by the informality.

"We were just discussing what a disaster this evening has been," Claire told him.

"Living through it wasn't enough? You have to discuss it, too?"

"Was it so bad dancing with all those women?"

"Aye." James made A Face.

"What is it with gentlemen who do not like dancing?" Bridget wondered.

"It's not so much the dancing as it is having everyone watch you do it," James said with a shrug.

"I cannot believe Father never mentioned any

of this," Amelia said. Their parents died, one after the other. First, their mother passed away after contracting a wasting disease. Their father followed a few days later. Everyone said his cause of death was a broken heart.

"Sometimes he spoke of life in England before he came to America," Claire said. She was the oldest and remembered more than the rest of them. "He spoke of foxhunting, cruel schoolmasters, and his time in the cavalry."

"He spoke about Messenger," James added with a fond smile.

They all smiled wistfully at the memory of the family's prized horse, may he rest in peace. Legend had it that their father had absconded to America with the prize stallion—owned by his brother, the duke, Josephine's late husband. He'd fallen in love with an American woman his family forbade him to wed, so he left England and never looked back. When their father needed to find a way to support his new family, he bred Messenger and raised and trained a series of champion racehorses on their farm.

They'd had an idyllic existence . . . loving parents, a beautiful farm to roam, and siblings to either play with or fight with or both.

"But he never mentioned any of this, did he?" Bridget asked softly. She waved her hand at the bedroom, and the house, and the unimaginable wealth they hadn't even set eyes on yet. The duchess had mentioned country estates. Plural.

"He occasionally referenced his brother the

duke but he did not say much. He certainly never mentioned that he or I were in line to inherit. He never even knew that he had inherited. Which is for the best; it probably wasn't the best topic of conversation back home, if you think about it, with all the anti-royalty and anti-British sentiments."

"Vastly preferable to all the anti-American sentiments we encountered this evening," Bridget said.

She thought again of Darcy, standing there so proud and perfect and seeing *her* as the downfall of civilization.

She thought of home, too. She hadn't fit in there either, but at least it was familiar and comforting.

"I wonder if there is a portrait of Father somewhere in this great big house," Amelia mused. "I'd love to see what he looked like as a young man."

"We can ask Josephine tomorrow," Claire said, affectionately patting Amelia's hand.

"Oh good. Perhaps it can distract her from more deportment and etiquette and torture lessons," Amelia said.

"No, we *need* those," Bridget said. All eyes turned to look at her. "If we are going to stay . . . we need to fit in."

"Bridget, that is all part of her nefarious plot to marry us off. We'll be separated," Amelia said, anguished.

"I'm not going to let her marry the lot of you off," James said. Then, with a slight grin, he added, "Much as you plague me and I sometimes consider it."

"I hate to point this out, but Bridget does have a point," Claire said thoughtfully. "If we are going to stay, we ought to make an effort to fit in."

"This is not a temporary situation then, is it?" Amelia asked.

The siblings fell silent. James was the duke. He ought to stay. The sisters could return, of course. They could go back to Maryland and tell stories of their little (failed) foray into English high society. But Bridget, for one, couldn't imagine life without *all* her siblings nearby.

The Cavendish siblings stuck together. No matter what.

It was all becoming clear to Bridget: she would have to start applying herself to becoming a True Lady and ensuring that her sisters did as well. If they stayed, they needed to fit in. If they returned to America, it would not be as failures.

"I don't want us to be apart," Claire said softly.

"So we stick together," James said, leaning forward to look earnestly at his three worried sisters. "We either all stay in England. Or we all return to America. Together."

A short while later, Bridget tossed and turned in her large bed, in her large room, in this large house. She was homesick for her small bed, in her small room, in a smaller house, halfway round the world.

But she knew she couldn't go back.

She might have had one misstep (literally) during her debut tonight, but that paled in comparison to her years back in America. She never had quite the right dress, her hair was never done enough, she always seemed to have mud on her boots, and she always seemed to say the wrong things.

She was so tired of being laughed at and so tired of never quite getting this business of being a woman *right*. She missed her mother, who wasn't here to show her how or to console her and encourage her to try again.

Instead she had Dreadful Darcy. And the way he looked at her with those dark eyes, down the length of his perfect noble nose, as if she were mud on his precious, expensive boots. As if he couldn't believe the riffraff had been allowed in to mingle with the Good and Proper people.

The way he said, in that haughty English voice of his, *She is not handsome enough to tempt me to overlook her manners.*

But she had the duchess to help her.

She would become a Person of Quality and a True Lady, if it was the last thing she did. She would be strict with the reducing diet so she could have a fashionable figure and fit into the fashionable dresses. Somehow, she'd get her hair to be glossy, sleek, and curled. She'd learn all the steps of the quadrille and all the other obscure country dances she might need to know. She would learn how to bite her tongue, unless she had exactly the right thing to say. She would figure out the right thing to say. And she'd never again hear or see condemnation from the likes of Lord Dreadful Darcy.

Tomorrow. She would begin becoming perfect tomorrow.

Chapter 3

Most people I met tonight were horrible, crashing bores, except for one handsome and charming gentleman, Mr. Wright. But his brother Lord Darcy was The Worst.

LADY BRIDGET'S DIARY

Darcy was at work on vital estate business and matters of national importance when his brother strolled into the study and dropped into a chair.

"Did you know that Rothermere lost ten thousand pounds and a hunting box in Scotland over a game of whist last week?"

"I did not." Darcy didn't bother looking up from his paperwork.

"Certainly puts things in perspective, doesn't it?"

"What things?"

"Well, say a person lost just a few hundred pounds . . . It's really not the end of the world, now is it?"

"Should I even bother to ask who lost a few hundred pounds?" Darcy asked dryly, finally looking up from his work. In the past few months, Rupert had begun losing at cards. In fact, he was steadily becoming worse and racking up increasing debts with each game. It should be noted that Darcy wasn't opposed to cards or wagering; he was simply opposed to losing.

"You know, Darcy, you're my favorite brother."

"I am your only brother."

"And brothers take care of each other. Especially when they haven't any other family in the world."

They both happened to glance up at the portrait hanging above the mantel. It was their late father, a beast of a man whose interests included increasing his wealth, spending his wealth, ensuring his heir would not be "a grave disappointment to the family name" and lose all the wealth. He had no time for his spare son, deemed a sissy at a young age and ignored.

Their mother, God rest her soul, has passed away while the boys were young. Frankly, she didn't seem like the warm, maternal sort anyway. Darcy barely remembered her.

"We have Aunt Ermintrude, in Lincolnshire."

She was also as mad as a loon, but Darcy ensured she had a roof over her head, food at her table, and a bevy of servants paid to indulge her belief that she was the Queen of England.

"You know what I mean," Rupert said dryly.

Darcy thought back to the night before, finding his brother in the card room, deep in a game of whist.

"I am not obtuse. I know that you find yourself in need of funds for gambling debts." Here Darcy paused, knowing that an extended silence often conveyed more than a thousand words. "Again."

There was a moment of unease between the brothers. They both knew that Rupert's debts had been increasing in amount and frequency. He had a generous allowance, and yet it was still not sufficient.

"I'll see that you get the necessary funds. But Rupert, this must be the last time."

"Are we broke?"

Darcy gave him A Look. "Do I seem like the sort that would mismanage an estate?"

"Good point."

"No, I have some notion of teaching you responsibility and restraint at the gaming tables."

"Of course."

Again, Darcy became aware of the portrait. Someone had to be responsible for the estate. Someone had to uphold their good name and preside over the family. Someone had to set an example and insist upon discipline and dignity. Someone had to be more like a father when he'd like to be just a brother. But there was no point in railing against the way things were, and Darcy didn't do things that were pointless.

"I do have one condition, though." Here he fought a grin as the condition occurred to him.

It was almost enough to make him glad for Rupert's debts.

"Anything."

"That you join me in calling upon the new duke."

"Afraid to go alone?"

"I am hardly afraid of the duchess and her pack of uncivilized Americans."

"I'll admit it. She terrifies me." Rupert said, grinning. But it wasn't the duchess that Darcy feared. No, it was a different Cavendish woman that he dreaded seeing. "But," Rupert said brightly, "I look forward to seeing Lady Bridget again."

Today we are at home for calling hours. I am given to understand that this means we are locked in the drawing room for a long afternoon awaiting visitors. The number will somehow indicate our popularity, and thus our worth as women, particularly with regards to gentlemen suitors. I am not optimistic, having made the mistake of reading the gossip columns this morning.

I do hope Mr. Wright (1) has not read the gossip columns and (2) comes to call and (3) falls in love with me.

LADY BRIDGET'S DIARY

Darcy and Rupert were not the only ones to pay call upon the new duke. Never ones to miss a spectacle or a subject of gossip, the haute ton was out in force to welcome—or inspect—this newly discovered branch of the Cavendish family.

Their return meant the resurfacing of decades-old gossip—how the duke's younger brother stole the prize stallion from the Durham stables and absconded to America (horse thief!). Or how he had abandoned his family and his country to marry an American woman he'd fallen in love with during the war (traitor to the crown!). And now his son was the Duke of Durham and his daughters were attempting to infiltrate high society.

"Are we really still discussing such old news?" the duchess said witheringly to her guests.

The topic of conversation shifted immediately.

Darcy meant to have a polite, perfunctory conversation with the new duke and take his leave. Instead he found himself surrounded by women, a cup of tea thrust in his hands. Then Rupert acted like . . . Rupert.

It began innocently enough.

"Lady Bridget, I wanted to inquire as to your welfare after last night."

Darcy tensed. What the devil was Rupert up to now? The less said about their scene last night, the better.

"What happened last night?" The duchess leveled a sharp stare at Rupert.

"Yes, do tell," one of the sisters said smugly. She received an elbow in the ribs from the other sister, the one with glasses, and a chilling glance from Lady Bridget.

"Do go on, Mr. Wright," urged Lady Evelyn Fairfax, voicing the sentiments of at least half the people in the room. Beside her, Miss Eileen, her sister, smiled her encouragement and added, "I do hope it's something romantic."

A dozen of the ladies scattered about the room murmured their agreement and faced Rupert expectantly.

And then Rupert, for all he professed to be disinterested in matrimony and terrified of the duchess, launched into an outlandish tale.

"Lady Bridget and I found ourselves trapped in a crush of people trying to make their way into supper," he lied. "The heat must have overtaxed her, and Lady Bridget swooned. I caught her in my arms, naturally."

Here he paused to grin at his rapt but skeptical audience. Those who had been gossiping in the foyer about decades-old horse thievery or a social faux pas committed the previous evening were now glancing at Bridget and her siblings differently because one of their own, the universally beloved and constantly charming Mr. Wright, had taken a genuine interest in her.

Darcy noted that Bridget was beaming—at Rupert. But she would. Not. Look. At. Him. No, she was gazing at his brother with starry eyes and drinking up his every word. Not that he cared. Not that he cared in the slightest.

Bloody hell, he was watching her fall in love with Rupert because he was painting such a romantic tale for all of London to gossip about, when the truth was that she slipped and fell and they happened to be there.

Darcy suddenly found the drawing room far too confining.

"And then," Rupert continued, "she gazed into my eyes and murmured, 'I don't think we have been introduced.'"

Oh for the love of God. Darcy wanted to roll his eyes. But that was the sort of behavior that had been beaten out of him a long time ago.

"That is not quite how I remember it," she said, all flustered and flummoxed and delectably pink, "but I far prefer your version of events."

Darcy could practically see her heart racing and hear the wedding bells chiming in her head. Her every thought and every feeling were so clear for all to see. It made him uncomfortable. Embarrassed. Terrified.

And he remembered, for a heart-stopping second, that he used to be that way.

"I hope there is no cause for alarm," the duchess said. "Or a wedding."

"And here I thought you were trying to marry us off," Durham said dryly. It was the sort of thing everyone knew but no one *actually said aloud*, in company.

A tense moment of silence followed, and Rupert rescued them all with a laugh and a grin, saying, "But not to rakes like me."

Lady Bridget thought that calling hours couldn't possibly improve after Rupert's visit, and thus they ought to send everyone along so she might go and write *Rupert and Bridget* in her diary.

She was already halfway in love with him, and not because he was handsome (he was, oh he was) but because he was kind and he knew just what to say, which was one of those life skills she never quite managed to acquire.

But no, the onslaught continued with the arrival of Miss Montague and Miss Mulberry, with Lady Francesca and her aunt and chaperone, Lady Wych Cross.

One recognized girls like these the world over. Their natural beauty—clear skin, pert little noses, hair that never frizzed—was enhanced by their exquisite sense of style. It didn't hurt either that they possessed the tall, willowy figure upon which even an old bedsheet would look fashionable. They were the sort of girls who never deigned to associate with mere mortals like Bridget and her sisters.

So what the devil where they doing here?

"I was hoping to be one of the first to welcome you to London but I see everyone beat me to it," Lady Francesca said with a smile. "Why, even my dear friend Lord Darcy is here."

Bridget recognized her as such a close friend of Darcy's that he would tell her that Bridget was not handsome enough to tempt him to overlook her manners.

It still stung, that.

But today her manners were very fine. For example, she hadn't accidentally on purpose spilled her tea on him or informed him that he needn't waste his time with the formality of a social call because she already thought he was the worst and nothing he could ever say or do would cause her to revise her opinion.

"I hope you all enjoyed the ball last night," Lady Francesca said. "And Lady Bridget, I hope you have sufficiently recovered from your . . ." And here everyone in the room held their breaths. *Would she say it aloud?* ". . . excitement."

In approximately thirty-six hours Bridget would think of the perfectly polite yet cutting retort. But all she could think to say at the moment was *I do hope you have recovered from being an ass.* She glanced at the duchess, who, apparently able to read her thoughts, simply shook her head no.

"What was so exciting about last night's ball?" Miss Mulberry wondered. Lady Montague whispered in her ear, loudly, that Bridget had fallen.

"You are of course talking about the excitement of Bridget and I meeting," Rupert cut in, saying just the right thing at the just the right moment. "My heart is still racing."

Bridget smiled and glanced around because *was anyone else noticing the romance?* Her brother lifted his brow. Darcy's expression had darkened, if such a thing was even possible.

It was a mistake to look at him, because then their gazes locked. She didn't know why she couldn't look away or why breathing suddenly seemed hard.

"Always such a charmer, aren't you, Mr. Wright?" Lady Francesca said with a laugh.

"It runs in the family," Darcy said dryly. It took a moment for everyone to realize *Darcy had made a joke*, and they all burst into laughter.

Who was this man? Just when Bridget thought she had him figured out as a bore, he went and surprised her. She regarded him for a moment, noting the spark in his eyes in spite of the mouth that refused to curve up into a smile.

But she did not wish to revise her opinion of him.

"Lady Amelia, I heard a rumor that you ride astride," Lady Francesca said, baiting Bridget's younger sister.

"I heard that, too!" Miss Mulberry exclaimed. "Is it true?"

Lady Wych Cross murmured something about not gossiping so obviously.

"Only when I can persuade a stable hand to lend me a pair of breeches," Amelia replied with such a sickening amount of sweetness in her tone, she had to be joking. Of course she was joking. Bridget, Claire, and James knew that, but everyone else in the room gasped. Darcy even raised one brow. Oh, what he must think of Americans—think of them!—now. Not that she cared what he, in particular, thought. But Lord Darcy, dark, disapproving Darcy, was the embodiment of the aristocracy.

And they were not pretty enough to make him—and everyone else—overlook the "fact" that they did things like trip and fall or make rude comments about assignations with stable boys.

They would have to go back to America in shame and explain that even the second (or was it third?) highest ranking title in the aristocracy was not sufficient for them to be welcome in society. How mortifying.

But Bridget had forgotten about the duchess.

One should never forget about the duchess.

"Is it true that you are on your third season, Lady Francesca?" the duchess asked, in a voice that was pure innocence and elegance. "Or is it your fourth? It seems like ages since you've made your debut. And one would expect a wedding announcement, but it seems you're having trouble bringing your suitor up to scratch."

Bridget fought the urge to leap to her feet and shout, *Ha!* Because the duchess had made both Francesca and Darcy turn pale.

"My first season wasn't so long ago that I have forgotten how daunting a debut can be. Which is why I thought I'd extend an invitation to your nieces. Perhaps they would like to join us for ices at Gunther's?"

Bridget sipped her tea and Claire stifled a yawn. Under her breath, Amelia whispered, "I would love to, but I shall be busy sticking forks in my eye," which made Bridget laugh, which made her spit out her tea, which made the duchess close her eyes and purse her lips.

"I'll just take that as a yes," Lady Francesca said dryly.

Chapter 4

On Tuesday we went for ices at Gunther's.
LADY BRIDGET'S DIARY

Lady Francesca was certainly the most beautiful girl in this carriage, not that she would say that aloud to her friends. She glanced out from under her darling new bonnet to see if anyone on the street noticed her and smiled when she made eye contact with a young man, who promptly walked into a lamp pole. She might be on her third season, but she could still turn heads.

"Why did we invite the American girl to join us?" Miss Mulberry asked, confused.

Beside her in the open carriage, Lady Francesca replied, "Have you ever heard the phrase 'Keep your friends close but your enemies closer'?"

"Of course. But what does that have to do with anything?"

"She means, Mabel, that she thinks Lady

Bridget might be an enemy. So we invited her to join us for ices," Miss Montague said.

Her explanation did little to clarify things for Miss Mulberry, but she had the right of it. It all had to do with Darcy. It was one thing to see him conversing alone with Lady Bridget at the ball. Of course he only went to call because good manners dictated he should. But there was no good reason for all those smoldering glances Darcy was giving Bridget during calling hours yesterday. She seemed too taken with Rupert to notice, which Francesca would have to encourage.

Darcy was hers. They'd had an unspoken understanding for years, ever since her brother brought him home during a school holiday. She would not lose him to an American who couldn't even walk across a ballroom without falling flat on her bottom. It was Francesca's turn to be the darling of the season and catch the most eligible bachelor.

The obvious solution to a potential threat was to invite her to ices and to ascertain just how much of a threat she was.

"Is Lady Bridget really an enemy?" Miss Mulberry was still puzzling this out. "But Francesca, you're so much . . ." She paused, tilting her head like a small dog as she thought about it. Finally she settled on "taller."

Francesca gritted her teeth. "You could have gone with thinner, prettier, or richer but you went with taller?"

"My brother says men like women who have a little padding on them," Miss Mulberry said, which didn't help anything at all.

"No more speaking of this. We're here."

Bridget had quickly come to realize a few essential truths: Lady Francesca was a viper. But she was also a popular viper who wielded not a small amount of influence over the collective brain of the haute ton. If, for example, she decided that Bridget should no longer be known as the girl who fell, no one would dare speak of it again.

Or so Bridget hoped.

That was just one of the reasons Bridget had agreed to this outing. Amongst the others: she couldn't think of a good excuse, as Claire and Amelia had done. And there would be ices and she was starving, thanks to the reducing diet.

And there was one other reason: she wanted, very badly, to fit in. And there was no better way to accomplish this than by befriending the most popular young ladies.

Which all brought Lady Bridget here, to this moment: ensconced in the open carriage, nibbling on delicious raspberry ices, and listening to their conversation.

"Did you see what Miss Witherspoon wore last night?" Miss Montague asked.

"That hideous puce dress?" Lady Francesca shuddered. "Yes, I saw it and wished I hadn't."

A conversation on fashion ensued, in which

they ruthlessly critiqued what every woman wore at the ball the previous evening. Lady Something's ruffles were too ruffly. Miss What's-Her-Name's hairstyle did her no favors whatsoever. Another woman's gown was an unflattering shade of white—which begged a question that Bridget didn't dare ask aloud (shades of white, really?).

Bridget decided her best course of action was to remain silent, lest she say the wrong thing, and savor her raspberry ice and generally do her best to seem like she belonged.

Her heart leapt with joy and no small amount of relief when she saw Mr. Wright walking down the street. He was with another gentleman she didn't recognize.

"Oh, look! It's Mr. Wright!" Bridget exclaimed. She did get such a thrill from saying his name. It was too perfect. *Oh, I met Mr. Wright the other night.*

She called his name and waved him over.

"Lady Bridget! What a pleasant surprise to see you." Their eyes met. And she saw what he didn't dare say aloud. He was surprised to see her, here, with these young ladies. She smiled as if to say, *I know!*

"Mr. Wright and Mr. Croft," Francesca said graciously. "So lovely to see you together. Again."

"It is always a pleasure," Rupert said stiffly. Mr. Croft just nodded.

"I don't suppose you could tempt your brother to come join us," Francesca said.

"I daresay only you could manage such a feat, Lady Francesca."

"But why would you want to?" Bridget asked, pulling a face.

Everyone gasped, but Rupert burst into laughter.

"Darcy is a catch," Miss Mulberry explained, as if Bridget were a small child of limited intellect.

Bridget shrugged. "I suppose he is, if you like the dark and broody sort."

"Or if you like the rich, titled, and perfect sort," Miss Montague said with a little laugh.

Bridget fell silent, thinking about something her mother used to say: *Don't be surprised that if you marry for money, that's all you get.* Bridget knew that money wasn't everything and that titles hardly mattered; she wasn't any happier for having landed both. Bridget was a fervent believer in love.

She had seen true love firsthand: her own parents were wildly, madly, catch-them-kissing-in-the-corridor in love. That was what Bridget wanted to find for herself.

And she could hardly imagine Darcy stealing a kiss in the corridor, or a waltz in the rain just because. Ditto for Lady Francesca. And she felt sad for them both. But Mr. Wright, on the other hand . . . He smiled at Bridget and her heart did a little flip. Yes, she could definitely imagine kissing him.

On Wednesdays we are to wear pink.
THE GOSPEL ACCORDING TO LADY FRANCESCA,
AS RECORDED IN LADY BRIDGET'S DIARY

For their visit to Almack's on Wednesday evening, Bridget wore pink because Francesca said that was the done thing. Her sisters could not be persuaded to join her.

"Matching ensembles, Bridge?" Claire asked, wrinkling her nose, causing her spectacles to slide down slightly. "Really?"

"I wasn't aware you had such definite opinions on fashion," Bridget replied, annoyed.

"I hate pink," Amelia said to no one in particular.

Thus, Bridget was the only Cavendish to wear pink and she prayed it was the correct shade, whatever that might be, even though there was no shade of pink that flattered her. She decided that it was more important to be seen with the popular girls than to wear the right thing. Francesca eyed her gown and didn't say anything, and Bridget breathed a sigh of relief, or as much of one as possible, given how tightly her corset was laced.

"Bridget, come over here," Francesca hissed from a mere three feet away. She dutifully stepped three feet to the left.

"That's the Wallflower Corner," Francesca said loudly. "You do *not* want to be seen there."

Bridget glanced over at the Wallflower Corner,

where an assortment of girls stood about, chattering amongst themselves. Some wore an expression she recognized (and may have, once or twice, practiced in the mirror): it was the look of someone pretending that they hadn't just heard the very mean thing said about them. It was quite similar to the look of appearing interested in dancing (so that someone might ask) but not too interested (so she didn't seem tragic if no one asked).

Bridget suspected that she really belonged with those girls.

The evening wore on. Lady Francesca and her vapid friends wore on Bridget's nerves. Bridget was beginning to—shudder—empathize with Darcy. Right now, standing off in the corner alone and not smiling seemed rather appealing after the strain of circulating, keeping up with all the conversations and keeping a smile pasted on one's face.

But then there was Mr. Wright, with that smile of his, bowing before her.

"May I have this dance?"

"Let me check my dance card. Why, yes, I would love to," Bridget said, not even bothering to check her dance card. If there was a name written there, then the gentleman had her apologies.

He swept her into his arms.

She nearly felt like swooning with pleasure.

The music began and they started to move. Mr. Wright was a far better dancer than her brother, but then again, he'd been raised in this world and had probably been waltzing since he was four.

She stepped on his toes.

"Oh! I'm so sorry."

"I don't mind." He smiled genuinely and she believed him.

"I have been led to believe it is a grave faux pas, and that I shall die a spinster if I step on a man's toes during a dance."

"We're a bit silly, aren't we?" he asked.

She knew he was referring to all the rules of the English high society. Because she felt so at ease with him, because she felt like she could be herself with him, Bridget confided in him.

"I'm finding it very hard to follow all the rules," she said. "It's quite exhausting, really."

That was not something she'd dare to say to Francesca or anyone else, other than her sisters.

"Can I tell you a secret?" Mr. Wright asked thoughtfully.

"Of course."

"Me too," Mr. Wright said softly.

On Thursday we discussed Dreadful Darcy.
                              LADY BRIDGET'S DIARY

It was another evening, another ball. The duchess was making every effort to find dance partners for her nieces and nephew. James was off waltzing with a young woman who clearly couldn't stop giggling, but who was a daughter of an earl and thus a suitable bride, according to the duchess's strange logic.

"Is it really necessary to dance every dance?" Amelia lamented whilst she took a much needed break to sip lemonade and stand on the sidelines. "My feet are in agonies."

"Yes. It keeps you out of trouble," the duchess said crisply. "And it keeps you where I can see you."

"You are very clever," Bridget said. The duchess smiled, too polite to say, *I know*, even if she was thinking it.

"We've been trying to keep her out of trouble for years, to no avail," Claire said.

Bridget then noticed Looord Darcy nearby, doing his best impression of the pillar he stood next to. Which was to stay, he stood straight, tall, and still, as if he were a marble statue. She admitted, privately to herself, that he would be a handsome statue. His expression was equally stony; he stared directly ahead.

"I don't understand why Lord Darcy even bothers to attend parties," Bridget said. "He doesn't seem to enjoy them."

"Because it's what one does," the duchess replied, which was her answer to most of the Cavendish questions about why morning calls were done in the afternoon, or why an earl went in to supper before a viscount.

Bridget looked back at Darcy and wondered

what he would do if he didn't have to do the done thing.

He happened to glance at her in that moment, while she was regarding him intensely. Oh, curses! He would think she was interested in him or something to that effect, and she certainly was not.

But then why couldn't she bring herself to look away from those dark eyes? Why did her gaze travel down to his mouth, always so firm and yet . . . No, she did *not* think it was a sensual mouth. And why, then, did she feel a heat start to unfurl in her belly? Why could she feel a telltale blush stealing across her cheeks?

And why wasn't *he* looking away?

By Friday, Darcy had had enough.

The Americans had thoroughly invaded England, the haute ton, and his life, even though Darcy had done his best to avoid them. They were in attendance at nearly every soiree. He saw the ladies at the opera and he frequently saw the duke riding in Hyde Park during the early morning hour when no one was out, save for gentlemen who wanted a good ride and some peace and quiet.

There were endless mentions of them in the newspapers that his butler ironed each morning and placed at the breakfast table.

One American in particular plagued him especially: Lady Bridget. And it was through no fault of her own.

"I quite enjoy the company of Lady Bridget," Rupert said, apropos of nothing, at the breakfast table one morning.

Darcy barely glanced up from the newspaper. There was an important article on a divisive issue in Parliament. He would need to be prepared to speak at length on it today.

"I really feel that I can be myself with her," Rupert continued. Darcy had no idea what that even meant. He sipped his coffee. Black. Unsweetened.

A day or two later, Darcy watched as his brother and Bridget waltzed together at a ball. Rupert was an excellent dancer, for he had dancing instruction while Darcy was ensconced in the library with their father, learning how to balance account books.

Bridget was not an excellent dancer, but she seemed to be having more fun than anyone else. She was genuinely smiling, laughing at whatever Rupert was saying, and her cheeks were pink in a way that someone would have deemed pleasant or even fetching if someone were in the habit of using such words.

Even Darcy couldn't stifle certain thoughts that occurred to him. He was a red-blooded man with a pulse, and so of course he wondered if she would be so unabashedly enthusiastic in bed. If that blush weren't confined to her cheeks, but lower . . . His gaze had dropped, taking in the creamy expanse of skin and the swell of her breasts.

Then he schooled his features into one of his do-not-disturb expressions. God forbid anyone have an inkling of the mad thoughts in his brain.

A few days later, Rupert availed himself of Darcy's company while he was at his desk, drafting a new bill for Parliament.

"Have I mentioned lately how glad I am that you're my brother?"

Darcy didn't bother looking up. "Yes, just last week when you wanted funds."

"You are very clever. Sharp. Smart. Charitable. God-fearing. Kind to women and children."

Darcy set down his pen and glanced at his younger brother. If it wasn't a trick of the light, he seemed pale, drawn. There were shadows under his eyes, as if he hadn't slept. Something was troubling him. More debts, probably.

"How much, Rupert?"

"Just, oh, a thousand pounds."

Then he rambled on about "putting it in perspective" and did Darcy know that some other idiot had lost his own late mother's beloved sapphire engagement ring in a wager, and another bloke with a half-empty brain box managed to lose his sister's dowry in a literal pissing contest.

Whereas Rupert had merely lost a small amount of money during an unlucky card game. It happened to the best from time to time. Darcy resisted pointing out that "from time to time" was now a regularly scheduled occurrence.

Darcy hadn't forgotten that the last time they

had this conversation, he said it was the last time he'd provide the money.

"There are other ways of obtaining funds," Darcy pointed out.

"Is this where you lecture me on marriage?"

"Well, I don't think the army or clergy will pay enough to cover your debts," Darcy said dryly. It went without saying that actually working in a profession was out of the question. "You should marry."

"Would you believe me if I said I'd been considering it?"

And for a moment, Darcy was stunned. Speechless. His carefree, sworn-bachelor little brother beating him to the altar.

"No."

"Well, I have," Rupert said.

"Have you been considering it abstractly, or with regards to a particular woman?"

"Lady Bridget."

"No."

Darcy's response was swift, immediate, and certain. No. His brother could not marry her. Not at all. Not in this lifetime. No. The force of this no took him by surprise, locked his breath in his lungs, made his heart stumble from its steady rhythm.

He hoped, prayed, and begged God that Rupert thought it was because Darcy was a horrible snob and refused to welcome Americans into their family . . . even though it was an eminently sensible match. She was the sister to a duke; her dowry was probably so large even Rupert couldn't gamble it away. And yet . . . no.

Something inside Darcy rebelled at the notion. No one could know the truth: that Darcy was struck with the mad urge to possess her. To have her himself.

Chapter 5

Lady Bridget Wright?
Mrs. Rupert Wright?
The Right Honorable Mrs. Wright?

Well, this will finally teach me the proper forms
of address! Here I am, wishing to write my hoped-
for married name and I have no idea what to write.

LADY BRIDGET'S DIARY

Lady Bridget was in love. Head over heels, stars in her eyes, shout it from the rooftops LOVE. Her heart raced whenever she saw him. The butterflies in her belly stifled her appetite. (Finally seeing results from reducing diet, hurrah!) Sleeping was impossible; when she closed her eyes, there he was in her mind's eye, and her heart started to beat in triple time.

It was impossible not to love Rupert Wright. He was so handsome. Was it the dimple in his left cheek when he smiled? Was it the long, dark lashes framing his warm brown eyes? His nose was noble. His jaw was strong. His dark brown hair, the color of chestnuts, tumbled into his eyes in the most alluring way. She dreamt of gently brushing his hair aside as they gazed into each other's eyes and then he would lean in and kiss her with his sensuous mouth . . . They had yet to kiss, but she dreamt of it often. Too often.

An opportunity for a kiss presented itself during yet another ball. It was another ball at which she trailed along after Lady Francesca, Miss Mulberry, and Miss Montague, and tried to get noticed by all the suitors who crowded around them, and tried not to wince at all the cutting remarks the girls made about everyone else.

When she spied Rupert—he had given her leave to use his Christian name, an indication of intimacy that thrilled her to no end—alone on the terrace, she didn't think twice about joining him. As she stepped closer she noticed that he was alone, brooding, and thus looking remarkably like his brother at that moment.

"Hello, Rupert." She tentatively approached.

"Bridget, hello." He offered a half smile. She took that as an invitation to join him.

"You seem down. What is troubling you?" She wanted to rest her hand on his arm in an affectionate yet suggestive way. It would have been forward. Did she dare?

"It's nothing." He smiled at her halfheartedly.

"It's obviously not nothing. You look like your brother, all dark and broody," she said to make him laugh. It worked.

"I suppose I can confide in my friend," he said, smiling down at her. "You know, Bridget, I do feel like I could be myself around you."

"Yes," she said breathlessly. They were friends, weren't they? Now she wanted to be more.

"It's my brother."

Of course it is, Bridget thought.

"Hmm," she murmured noncommittally, because Josephine said True Ladies never spoke ill of others (which someone clearly never told Lady Francesca).

Rupert sighed and frowned and said, "I need funds and he will not give them to me."

"Why ever not? Certainly he can afford it, and you are his brother." She knew, with bone-deep certainty, that her own brother would do anything for her, or Amelia or Claire.

"Something about taking responsibility for my own actions. And that it's about time that I stay out of trouble. I feel that he is punishing me because I am not like him."

"Don't be like him," she whispered. Rupert was the one person she'd met in London with whom she could just be herself. She couldn't stand if he became distant and disapproving, like Darcy.

"I could not be like him even if I tried. It's hard enough for Darcy to be as he is." Bridget didn't quite understand that, but decided not to press. "He wasn't always like this, you know," Rupert continued. "He used to be as mischievous and fun-loving as the rest of us. But now he feels it is his duty to teach me responsibility. Which may help me in the long term, I grant you, but not presently. In fact, presently, I am doomed."

Try as she might, she could not imagine Darcy as a mischievous young boy, or a young man who raised hell and caused trouble like all the others. It boggled the mind.

"What do you need the funds for?"

Rupert stared off into the distance for a long moment. Her unease grew; he was in trouble. Real trouble. She wanted to save him.

"I cannot say. But there are threats if I do not pay."

"Is it gaming debts?" Of course it was; what else could it be? She continued on, vaguely aware that he didn't confirm. "How much do you need? I'm sure James can lend us the money."

Rupert's head snapped up to look at her, shocked at the offer.

"I could never accept it."

"Please." She dared to place her hand on his. "How much?"

After a momentary pause he said, "A thousand pounds."

"A thousand pounds!" She gasped. "How much is that, really? I still think of everything in dollars."

"A family of four could live on it in a respectable fashion for a year."

"Ah. I see. That must have been quite a game." For a moment, Rupert looked confused. "The gaming debts," she explained.

"Right."

His hand was still under hers. Touching hers. It occurred to her that for once she could be the one to save someone from certain disaster. Her heart leapt at the opportunity.

"I'll ask James about the money, Rupert."

He clasped her hand, lacing his fingers through hers, and gazed into her eyes. At this moment, there was nothing, nothing she wouldn't do for him.

"I would never ask you to do that."

"I know," she said lightly. "But I want to."

Because I love you. The words were there, quivering on the tip of her tongue, ready to take the leap into the world, if she would only just let them out.

"I cannot ever tell you what this means to me, Bridget."

Rupert lifted her hand to his mouth and pressed a kiss on the back of her hand. Then her palm. And then her wrist.

And then, tragically, he let go.

Things I dislike about Lord Darcy
He does not dance. Once cannot trust a man who does not dance.

He is the sort of man who leaves young ladies standing alone in the middle of a ballroom. Most ungentlemanly.

He refuses to aid his brother in his Hour of Need.

LADY BRIDGET'S DIARY

The clock struck midnight when Bridget slipped out of bed, donned her robe, lit a candle, and headed toward the kitchens. It was a long, slightly terrifying journey in a house this massive. But it was worth it, because when she arrived she found James. And cake.

She stood in the doorway and peered into the dimly lit room.

"Your Grace, if I may have an audience?"

She dropped into a little curtsy.

James looked up from where he sat at the large table, with a generous slice of rum cake before him. He eyed her warily.

"Where is my sister and what have you done with her?"

"Whatever do you mean?" As if she didn't know perfectly well.

"Since when do you address me formally? And speak like the duchess?"

She flounced over to him. And the cake.

"I'm trying to conduct myself as befitting our station. One of us must. You are useful to practice on, being a lofty duke and all."

"Oh, shut up," he said, in the affectionate way that only a brother could. He mussed her hair as

she came close, which made her scowl. To everyone else she was practically a spinster, but he still
treated her like a child.

"Well, this is quite ducal of you, illicitly stealing into the kitchens to devour cake." Lord above,
but she was hungry, and that rum cake was calling her name.

"I hope you're not expecting me to share,"
James said, evilly.

"Oh please, Your Grace, I beg of you."

"You know I hate being called that."

"Oh, I do. You may be a fancy duke, but you
are not above some sisterly teasing."

He muttered something to the effect of "Glad
to hear it."

She served herself a generous slice and took
a bite. She closed her eyes, the better to savor it.

"What brings you down to the kitchens at this
hour?"

"Would you believe me if I said just cake?"

"Yes."

"I'm not sure I care for the meaning of that."

"I hope you're not above a little brotherly teasing now that you are a lady."

"Oh, I'm not above it," she said. And then,
grinning, added, "But it'll cost you."

"How much?"

Bridget's heart started to pound. This was the
perfect moment to ask him.

"A thousand pounds?"

"You are not joking."

"No."

"Are you in trouble?"

Her brother's blue eyes were full of concern and she was lucky, because she knew he would do anything for her. He looked, she thought with a pang, just like their father, who would always say, "My little Bridget, what are we going to do with you?" before lifting her into his arms and whirling her around.

She hesitated, because for a moment she was struck with an overwhelming feeling of home-sickness for her parents, and their boisterous house at Duncraven farm, where everything was comfortable and familiar.

But she remembered Rupert, and her love for him. This was her life now.

"It's for Mr. Wright," she explained, because she didn't want James to worry about her. "He has gaming debts."

"Can't his own brother help him out?"

"He says Darcy will not. I'm not surprised really. He is such a cold and unfeeling man."

"I wasn't aware you were so well acquainted with him," James said, insinuating that she was. As if he had, oh, noticed Darcy staring at her or her staring at Darcy.

"I'm not."

She wasn't. She just knew that he was the sort of man to leave a young lady standing alone in the midst of a ballroom and the sort of man to refuse to help his own brother.

"But you vehemently dislike him."

"We're not talking about Lord Darcy."

"Of course. We are discussing Mr. Rupert Wright, the man of your dreams and fondest yearnings of your heart."

"It sounds ridiculous when you say it like that."

"Don't lose your sense of humor, Bridge. You don't want to end up like Darcy."

"Horrors," she said flatly. Then stuffed her mouth with more cake.

"Are you sure he needs the money for gaming debts? Because I would hate to lend him money that he squanders on gifts for his mistress or because he got another woman in trouble, when you are so obviously in love with him."

"He would never do such a thing." She was certain of him. He was good, and kind, and would never take advantage. He was probably just a poor card player. Because he was so nice.

They fell silent for a moment, enjoying each other's company and the informality of eating cake in the kitchens at midnight. She could almost pretend that they were back home in Duncraven and none of this ducal business had ever happened. Almost.

"You know, Bridget, you have one hell of a dowry."

"Josephine has mentioned something to that effect."

"The man who marries you will get twenty thousand pounds."

"Twenty thousand!" Bridget turned to her

brother with wide eyes. "No wonder Josephine is always warning us about fortune hunters."

"I'm just saying there's another way for Rupert to get the money he needs. If his heart were in the right place."

Chapter 6

Here's another curious rule: at a ball, women are not supposed to promenade around the ballroom, unaccompanied. And here's another ridiculous rule: a lady might refuse a dance but then she is not to accept any other invitations for the rest of the evening.

LADY BRIDGET'S DIARY

*I*t was another evening and another ball. Another day spent paying calls, practicing the pianoforte, learning more phrases in French (*J'ai faim, je suis fatigue, je* wish to stay in bed and read fashion periodicals). Hours were spent preparing—hair was curled and styled, dresses pressed, corsets tightened, cheeks pinched.

They had arrived, along with three hundred of England's finest, and crushed into this ballroom. The scale of the events still impressed her. The ballrooms were large, the chandeliers enormous, the gowns gorgeous.

And then there was Bridget, a horse breeder's daughter, trying her best to fit in.

Amelia had manufactured some excuse about needing a moment in the ladies' retiring room, though she was far more likely to be found snooping about the house; the family had yet to attend an event without Amelia causing some incident or minor scandal. Claire had discovered something to amuse her at balls: she spent most the evening in the card room, divesting drunk, idiot lords and ladies of their fortunes. Bridget was torn between pride and distress because it made her sister—and the family—an object of gossip.

The duchess was engaged in a private tête-à-tête with one Lady Esterhazy, her close personal friend and fellow terrifying matron.

Which left Bridget. With Miss Mulberry and Miss Montague. They were the only girls with whom she had become friendly in London. Lady Francesca was dancing with a young handsome lord; how she managed to dance only with them was of particular interest to Bridget, as she, far too often, ended up with invitations she was forbidden to refuse from the old, slightly infirm, or lethally dull men of the ton. Although Rupert had penciled his name on her dance card for the fifth waltz, and thus her entire existence was now counting the minutes until it was time for him to sweep her into his arms and whisk her around the ballroom.

In the meantime, she lingered on the perimeter of the ballroom with her friends.

"Do you think that Lady Francesca actually fancies any of her suitors?" Bridget wondered.

"Oh no," Miss Mulberry said. "They are just for amusement. Everyone is expecting Darcy to propose to her."

"Darcy?"

"You know, the one who always looks like he's perishing of boredom?"

"I know who he is," Bridget said darkly.

"It's the funniest thing," Miss Mulberry continued. "She was concerned you might be a rival for his afflictions."

"You mean affections," Bridget corrected. She was not interested in his afflictions or affections.

"That sounds so romantic," Miss Montague sighed dreamily. "Rival for his afflictions."

"That is absurd," Bridget said flatly.

"That's what I said!" Miss Montague exclaimed. "I said it was absolutely ridiculous that he should fancy you!"

This was of no consolation to Bridget.

"Don't tell her we told you," Miss Mulberry said.

"I won't." But she had to wonder: if Lady Francesca saw her as a rival for Darcy's affections, why then befriend her?

It was another night and another ball. Darcy was actually enjoying the evening, having had interesting conversations with his friend the Duke of Hamilton and Brandon about parliamentary concerns; and he spoke to the Duke of Ashbrooke about the man's new invention. Earlier in the evening, he had spoken with Lady Francesca on the terrace—listened to her gossip, mainly—and then made his excuses when he saw her friends, the vapid Misses Mulberry and Montague, heading their way. And Lady Bridget, trailing behind.

Darcy was about to call for his carriage when Rupert found him. His brother seemed rushed and worried, not at all his usual self.

"Darcy, I need you to do me a favor," Rupert said impatiently, grabbing on to Darcy's arm.

"Let me guess," Darcy said dryly. "More funds?"

For a second, his brother looked wounded. No, he looked truly hurt that Darcy would say such a thing. He immediately regretted the flippant comment and felt guilty to have thought so little of his brother.

"No, actually. I have taken care of that," Rupert said, straightening up to his full height. "I need you to waltz with Lady Bridget."

Oh bloody hell. He'd been looking forward to returning home, perhaps having a brandy in his study before retiring. And now he was to go back into the din of the ballroom and dance. With Lady Bridget.

"You know that I—"

"I know, I know, you don't dance," Rupert said dismissively, and no small amount of annoyance in his voice. "We all know that Lord Darcy does not dance, and he certainly does not do so with one of the Americans. But I promised her and now I have to leave. Something has come up."

"Is everything all right?" Rupert was definitely not himself tonight; something was obviously wrong.

"It's Frederick. He's been hurt. There was a fight." His brother was clearly anxious to rush off to his old friend.

"Is there anything I can do?" Darcy asked.

"Yes. Dance with Lady Bridget."

And with that Rupert rushed off.

Darcy found himself doing the unthinkable: entering a ballroom with the intention of seeking out Lady Bridget. He had, in fact, made it a point to do exactly the opposite because the woman did things to him and to his state of equilibrium that he did not care for.

But Rupert had asked him a favor. Feeling guilty for that offhanded comment about the money, and wanting to help his brother in what was clearly a distressing situation, Darcy had found himself agreeing. Well, he hadn't exactly had an opportunity to disagree, what with Rupert running off like that.

Thus here he was, standing before her.

"Good evening, Lady Bridget," he said, because it was polite and he was nothing if not polite.

"Good evening, Lord Darcy," she said graciously. She did not draw out the *ooo*'s. No, she spoke like the duchess was succeeding in her attempts to turn her into a proper young *English* lady. "I don't suppose you have seen Rupert."

She called him Rupert. Not Mr. Wright. This suggested an intimacy between them that Darcy didn't care for.

"I have. He had to depart unexpectedly. He sends his regrets."

Lady Bridget heaved a sigh, which he mainly noted due to the dramatic rise and fall of her breasts. Of course he looked, briefly. He might be a gentleman, but he wasn't dead. He definitely wasn't dead, owing to the pulse-pounding way his body reacted to her.

Then she gazed down at the dance card dangling from her wrist.

"He owes you a waltz."

"He doesn't *owe* me anything. But he did promise and I have been looking forward to it."

The words he uttered next were not spoken lightly. He told himself it was his duty as a gentleman not to leave her idling like a wallflower; he ought to ask her to waltz. If anyone asked, and they would, he would explain that he was simply standing in for his notoriously distracted brother.

He didn't want to dance—he hated dancing. But even he had a hard time denying the desire to touch her, and he had been presented with the perfect opportunity to do so, without it meaning anything.

"Would you like to dance?"

"Of course I'd like to, but my dance partner is missing."

He exhaled shortly, frustrated. She misunderstood him. He ground out the words, "Would you like to dance with me?"

"It's not that I wish to dance for the exercise or because I am bored standing on the sidelines," she explained, while scanning the room for her desired dance partner. "It's just that I wish to dance with Rupert."

"Right."

Darcy gritted his jaw. He had just been rejected. By Lady Bridget, of the American Cavendishes. The only thing more mortifying was that he had, for a brief, shining moment, looked forward to the prospect of holding her with something like anticipation. This was exactly why feelings of all sorts were to be ruthlessly ignored.

And he had been rejected in favor of Rupert, who was off doing God knew what with God only knew whom.

Maddening, that.

"But it's very good and honorable of you to offer to stand up in his stead." She smiled sweetly at him and patted his arm, as if he were a small child. It was so bloody *ladylike* of her, and that saddened him. They were changing her, from an exuberant creature into one who was polished and refined, and who lauded honorable behavior. It was the same thing they'd done to him. "You are such a gentleman, Lord Darcy."

Except right now, he didn't want to be a gentleman. In fact, if he dared to examine the state of his emotions, he would find that what he wanted was to pull her against him, claim her mouth for a deep kiss, sink his hands into her hair. He wanted to thoroughly and utterly ravish her until she would say, breathlessly, *Rupert who?*

Of course that was completely unacceptable and exactly why he made a point of avoiding her or at the very least avoiding anything that wasn't a reasoned and rational thought.

And then he spoke in haste, words spoken from a place of hurt and words he regretted the second he gave voice to them.

"I would think that even you are aware that young ladies are not supposed to refuse a gentleman's offer to dance."

Her eyes flashed with anger. He might as well have said, *Or you would know that if you weren't raised on a horse farm.*

Her cheeks reddened considerably.

"I am very well aware, thank you," she said so sharply, he almost felt as if he'd been stabbed. "As I am also aware that a lady must honor what is written on her dance card. So you see, I am in an impossible position due to your stupid rules."

"They are not my rules."

She gave him an utterly disparaging look.

"The only thing keeping me from storming off is that ladies are not supposed to stroll around the ballroom unaccompanied," she said. "Actually, no. The only thing keeping me from storming off is that you might then have even more reason to chastise me."

"I didn't mean—"

And then the unimaginable happened. She turned away from him, steadfastly refusing to look in his direction. He, Lord Darcy, received the cut direct from Lady Bridget, of the American Cavendishes.

Chapter 7

Kisses from Rupert: 0
Moments for possible kisses with minimal risk
of discovery: 4
Hours spent wondering why he hasn't: embar-
rassing

LADY BRIDGET'S DIARY

Lady Millicent Winterbourne's garden party
was not to be missed by "her dearest nephews,"
even though, to Darcy's knowledge, they were
not in fact blood relations. She had been quite
good friends with their dearly departed mother,
and apparently that was sufficient basis to claim
them as her own family . . . with all the obliga-
tions and nagging that entailed.

She bustled over to the brothers upon their arrival.

"There you are, Darcy. I knew you wouldn't
refuse me. Hello, Rupert, I don't mind if you

cause a scandal or are caught kissing behind a hedge." She patted his cheek affectionately.

"Good afternoon, Lady Winterbourne."

"Don't Lady Winterbourne me, Darcy. I held you on my lap when you were just born. Call me auntie."

He was a grown man and as such would lose his bollocks if he called anyone auntie.

"Aunt Winterbourne," he offered as a compromise.

"Auntie Millie," she countered.

"Lady Millicent," he offered as a compromise.

"Lord, but your father wrecked you." She sighed.

There was only one possible response to that.

"The weather is very fine today," he said stiffly.

"Makes me wish I could take off this jacket and jump in the lake," Rupert added. To be honest, Darcy had half a mind to do the same thing. The sun was actually shining, which meant he felt exceedingly warm under this fitted, dark wool jacket. Between that and the length of starch wrapped around his neck, he felt like he was being strangled.

"As I said, I do not mind if you cause a scandal, so long as it's at my party."

"Hostessing is as competitive as ever, I see," Darcy remarked.

"You have no idea," she said dramatically. "Look, there is the Duchess of Durham with her new charges. I thank God they are in attendance."

Do not look. Do not look.

He looked. His gaze strayed immediately to Lady Bridget. Like every other unmarried lady, she was all done up in a bonnet and gloves and a white dress with frills, and ruffles and bits of lace.

And she was beaming at Rupert.

"I was hoping to see them today," Rupert said brightly.

"I as well," Lady Winterbourne replied. "While the ton has not quite accepted them yet, a party is considered a failure if they do not attend. What else will we talk about?"

"New initiatives in Parliament, the plight of war widows and orphans, new advances in steam technology."

"You're too funny, Darcy." She laughed. "No, at parties one is to talk of scandals and love matches and judge each other's dresses. And the Americans. What do you think of them?"

"I do not." It was a hideous lie.

Lady Bridget intruded upon his thoughts with an alarming frequency. And if that weren't bad enough, she made him feel things.

Things one would categorize as lust. A lust that would never be satisfied because he was Lord Darcy, one of the most esteemed peers of England, and while she might be sister to a duke, there was no denying her unconventional upbringing. She was not his type.

Which was neither here nor there, given how things were progressing between her and Rupert and the hints he dropped about marrying her.

"Well I quite like them," Rupert declared. "Particularly Lady Bridget."

Case. In. Point.

"You know, the duchess is keen to marry them off," Lady Winterbourne remarked with pointed looks and all the subtlety of an invading army. "She is afraid they will abandon the dukedom and return to the colonies if they do not. God forbid anything should happen to the new duke. The next in line is that horrid Mr. Collins."

"I cannot imagine what relevance this has to us."

"Don't be deliberately obtuse, Darcy," Lady Winterbourne said. "It doesn't suit you."

"It so happens that one of us is considering taking a wife," Rupert said. Even Darcy couldn't conceal his shock that he would say such a thing to such a known gossip as their hostess. He might as well have printed an announcement in *The London Weekly*: "Wealthy bachelor not completely adverse to matrimony. Queue up here." Even if he was considering marriage, why the devil would he announce it and make things impossible for himself?

Darcy's obvious shock made it abundantly clear which brother was considering a wife. And Lady Winterbourne's smile made it abundantly clear what would happen with such information.

Bridget might have steered Rupert here, behind the hedges. He might not have made it difficult for her to do so.

Her heart beat swiftly, flutteringly, like hummingbird wings. Her gaze searched his for a sign of his true feelings and his intentions. She prayed that they matched hers.

He might be about to kiss her. Dear Lord, she wanted to be kissed. And loved. And by this *nice* man.

Rupert gazed down at her, lips parted. She closed her eyes, waiting to feel the brush of his lips against hers. Her life might become perfect in three . . . two . . . one . . .

"Nice to get a bit of a respite from the party," he remarked. She opened her eyes to see him standing a foot away, clasping his hands behind his back and rocking on his heels.

Or not.

Nevertheless, she agreed with him. "It is. I've become so accustomed to everyone watching me to see what disaster will befall me next. You know, I am still known as the girl who fell."

"I think of you as the girl who has a unique manner of appreciating artwork," Rupert corrected. "Never mind those old bats."

And that was why she loved him.

That was why she wanted to marry him.

And she knew for a fact that he had told Lady Winterbourne that he was thinking of marrying, because she told the duchess, who looked the other way when Bridget and Rupert began strolling in the direction of the hedges.

"Well, it is nice to get away from everyone's prying eyes," she remarked, hoping to get him to acknowledge that they were alone. Out of sight.

"Indeed." He seemed pensive.

"I feel that everyone is always watching and waiting for me to make another misstep."

"Society is a challenge. Even for those of us born and raised for it."

"You can't possibly have trouble with society. Everyone adores you."

"Aye. But I have seen how unforgiving they can be," he said thoughtfully. This was another side of Rupert, one she hadn't often seen and suspected that he didn't often reveal. "Which is why it is so wonderful to have true friends."

There was no mistaking his meaning by the way he gazed at her, smiled at her. He thought her a true friend. But what about *more*?

Bridget stood there, experiencing a thousand agonies. Here she was, alone with a handsome rake—the newspapers all said he was—and he was making a declaration of friendship. Which was wonderful, and she cherished it and thought him the only true friend she'd made in England (Lady Francesca certainly didn't count).

But never mind that. Her heart had skipped a beat. And then fell.

Rupert turned to her. He gazed into her eyes and murmured her name. "Bridget."

Her heart starting beating again, and then it started beating faster and faster.

But then Rupert paused at the sound of footsteps approaching. She turned, furious, to see who could possibly dare to interrupt this moment. Possibly the greatest moment in all of her three and twenty years. The Moment in which the man she loved was about to propose marriage or kiss her or both.

The intruder revealed himself.

Her eyes narrowed. "Darcy."

> Things I dislike about Dreadful Darcy
>
> *He ruins private interludes in which a lady might be kissed for the first time by the man she loves who mentioned publicly that he was considering marriage. This is unforgivable. UNFORGIVABLE.*
>
> LADY BRIDGET'S DIARY

Darcy had only wanted a moment of solitude. Just a moment away from the idle chatter and gossip. Just a moment to think about what the devil Rupert was about these days. The ever increasing debts, rushing away from a ball, the declaration of his intention to wed. Just a moment to find his equilibrium again.

He never meant to intrude on what was obviously a private moment between his brother and Lady Bridget.

Her eyes narrowed when she saw him. "Darcy."

There was no small amount of venom in her voice.

He cleared his throat.

"I hope I'm not interrupting something," Darcy

said, glancing from Bridget to Rupert. It was obvious he had.

"Not at all," Rupert replied hastily. "I was just . . . I'm quite parched. Are you quite parched, Bridget? I shall go fetch us lemonades."

Darcy watched his brother retreat. Rupert was acting odd—in this moment, and for the past few days—and it was a mystery why. This presented a feeling of something like hurt or dismay because they were close. They weren't just brothers, they were the only members left in their family (distant, possibly fictional, relationship to Lady Winterbourne notwithstanding). And they were friends.

He would have to talk to him later, for Rupert fled.

And with that Darcy found himself alone with Lady Bridget. She was either crestfallen, heartbroken, or furious, or some terrifying combination. He'd never made a study of identifying emotions, especially those of women; after all, he made it a point to stifle his.

"Oh, look," she remarked, interrupting his silence. "We are without a chaperone. I shall go find one and return approximately never."

"Lady Bridget." He hadn't meant to say anything. But then she whirled around to face him, all the flounces and lace of her dress fluttering in swift movement. She glared up at him fiercely.

All thoughts fled. Except one: *I'm sorry. For whatever I've done.*

"I owe you an apology."

He would apologize for interrupting her private moment with Rupert. Not that he was sorry to interrupt a proposal, if that's what had been about to happen.

But then she surprised him.

"Just one?"

"I don't take your meaning."

"I'm wondering what, exactly, you wish to apologize for. Do you owe me an apology for being exceedingly rude when we first met? For leaving me standing alone in the middle of a ballroom at my very first London ball where I knew no one?"

He felt the color draining from his face. That *had* been rude of him. But she had been so . . . shocking.

"Or would you like to apologize for saying that I am not pretty enough or well-mannered enough for you?"

And now he paled, certainly. He remembered saying the words, making a deliberate effort to sound bored as he uttered them. Because no one could know that he had found her so . . . arousing. He hadn't realized she had overheard.

"Or do you mean to apologize for chastising me when I refused your obligatory offer to dance? We both know it was just a favor for Rupert. I couldn't possibly have hurt your *feelings*."

It took all the self-control he possessed to not look around for someone to save him, to fight the desire to loosen his cravat, to stifle the urge to flee. Because Lady Bridget, enraged, was something else entirely.

His heart started to pound.

He wanted to kiss her, but she obviously wanted to slap him.

"All are lapses in honorable behavior and I apologize for them." He hoped that would appease her.

"I'm curious, Lord Darcy. Are you sorry that you weren't a perfect gentleman or are you actually sorry that your behavior might have made a perfectly lovely girl feel badly about herself and her family?" She paused and added, "And by the way, I am the perfectly lovely girl."

She said this in such a fierce whisper that he couldn't help but wonder if the words were meant for *her* more than for him. Because why could she possibly care what he thought of her?

He felt a pang of . . . something resembling a feeling . . . that she felt the need to tell him that.

"On all accounts, I owe you an apology."

"Yes. Yes you do."

A moment of silence stretched between them. He was mesmerized by all the emotions he could detect in her eyes—anger, curiosity, annoyance, determination—when he was sure she saw nothing in his.

"I am waiting for an apology. I was given to understand that it was rude to keep a lady waiting."

"Usually, one simply says that one is owed, they don't actually . . ." His voice trailed off. It was the way of things. Peers of the realm never actually apologized for things. But Lady Bridget didn't care about that, did she? He promised her an apology and then failed to deliver, digging himself a deeper hole.

Ah, now he could see fury in her eyes and the reddening of her cheeks. He was at once terrified and entranced by her display of emotion. As a result, he didn't say anything.

"Excuse me," she said grandly. She gave him the briefest nod before turning on her heel and stalking off.

He deserved that.

He suspected that there was a good chance she was fighting a grin as she stalked away, and the thought brought the faintest smile to his lips, and a very troubling thought to his brain. Why was he already thinking like he *knew* her?

"Lady Bridget—wait. Please." She stopped and turned around, curiosity getting the better of her, no doubt. "I was rude when we first met. Your unusual behavior caught me off guard."

"Are you saying this is somehow my fault?"

"Not at all."

"We do not have a chaperone," she said in an overdramatic stage whisper. "We should not be speaking."

She stalked off again.

Oh dear God. He would have to chase her. Through crowds. Crowds full of gossips. He never chased women.

He caught up with her in just a few strides.

"You don't want to ask for a chaperone," he said, falling in step beside her. "Because I will have to request it—it would be too forward for a lady to ask. Then people will talk. They will say that I am interested in you. That we are interested in each other. Then, at every opportunity, we will be thrust together—all under the watchful eye of the biggest gossips in England. Is that what you wish?"

"Perish the thought."

"I have no doubt that you wish to be free of me. Which is why I beg you to accept my apology now. And we shall go our separate ways. I am sorry that I was an arse."

He needed his conscience clear. He needed to make things right before Rupert proposed. The last thing he needed was Lady Bridget glaring at him over Christmas dinner for the next fifty years.

"Very well, I accept. Good day, Dreadful Darcy."

"What was that?" He caught her wrist.

She looked down at the unexpected sight of his hand clasped around her wrist. He did as well. Then he felt a surge of heat—embarrassment? desire? confusion?—and let go.

"Oh, just a little name I have for you in my diary," she said meekly.

"Your diary. You write about me in your diary."

This struck terror into his heart. And something else, too, that he couldn't or wouldn't identify.

"Indeed," she said, mustering her courage. "I

have an ongoing list of all the dreadful things about you."

Of course she did. He could see it now: Bridget, bent over her desk at night, writing furiously of her hatred of him. The lone candle would lend a soft glow to her skin, revealing her cheeks red with anger as she detailed her loathing for him. Perhaps her wrapper would fall open, revealing . . .

Bloody hell.

"Such as?" He spoke sharply, more angry with this absurd direction of his thoughts than at her.

"Shouldn't we be speaking of the weather? Or gossiping about mutual acquaintances?"

"No."

"It's very sad that you won't help your brother."

"What the devil are you talking about?"

"You wouldn't help him with his debts."

"Did he tell you that?"

"Obviously. Who else would I have heard it from?"

So Rupert had confided in her—to an extent. He wondered if she had given him the funds. It hadn't escaped his notice that Rupert had been despondent one day and back to his cheerful self the next. He had obviously come up with the money. But how? Darcy began to get an idea.

The answer was staring him in the face. Lady Bridget, to the rescue.

Perhaps things were more serious between her and Rupert than he thought. This was a good thing, was it not? His brother should marry, though Darcy wished he would marry someone a bit more . . . English. Or perhaps a bit less prone to inciting unwanted lustful thoughts in him.

He wondered what else she knew. Darcy had made some inquiries, discreetly of course, and learned that Rupert didn't have any significant debts, but perhaps they had been paid off quietly. He had no stupid wagers in the betting books at White's. Whom, then, did he owe the money to? And why?

"Thank you for helping my brother," he said. "But it is not your place."

"Someone has to do it, especially if *you* will not. It's one thing if you're so high and mighty as to look down at me for slipping and falling or forgetting the proper way to address a marquis. I can't fault you for sharing the same stupid, judgmental sentiments as the rest of the ton. But refusing to help your own brother is honestly the worst thing I have ever heard."

Her eyes flashed accusingly. He found himself unable to breathe.

Apparently Rupert had *not* told her of all the money Darcy had given him over the years for other debts. Apparently he had not told her of all the punishments Darcy had endured on behalf of his mischievous little brother—their father would never hurt his *heir* too badly. But his spare . . . well, he could spare him. And Darcy didn't mind, not one bit, because in Rupert he had one person who would treat him like a boy, or a man, or a human. Not an heir, or an earl.

He lived to protect his brother, and her accusations that he was failing hit like a fist to his gut. But she didn't know the half of it and she never would. There was no reason for her to be privy to their private family matters. There was no reason he had to prove himself to *her*.

"It seems you are determined to think ill of me, and given the facts you have, I cannot blame you for it. I shall now endeavor to stay out of your way."

Someone thought it would be a splendid idea to have row boat races on the lake. By some revolting stroke of ill fortune, Darcy found himself in a boat with Lady Bridget, who was looking longingly at the boat just beside theirs, bearing Rupert and her sister Lady Amelia.

She seemed vexed to be with him. Well, he didn't wish to be here either.

The only saving grace was that rowing provided an excuse to remove his confining jacket. Darcy dug the oars into the water and pushed off. Rupert did as well, keeping his rowboat right alongside.

"Mr. Wright, is something the matter with your brother?" Lady Amelia asked loud enough for him to hear.

"With Darcy? No, he's just the brooding sort," Rupert answered with a laugh. "I haven't seen him crack a smile since Christmas morning in 1808."

"I am not 'the brooding sort.' I am merely thinking of other things with which I could occupy my time instead of this frivolous activity."

For example: He could be balancing account books. Or sticking a hot poker in his eye.

"Why did you even attend?" Lady Amelia asked.

"Aunt Winterbourne," the brothers said flatly, in unison, which made the sisters laugh.

"Ah, now I understand, Mr. Darcy."

"It's Loooord Darcy, Amelia," her sister corrected. "And he is a stickler for propriety and won't let you forget it."

She leveled him with another sharp glance from her blue eyes.

"I humbly beg your pardon, Your Grace."

"The proper form of address for him is *my lord*," Lady Bridget corrected. He heard the waver in her voice betraying that she wasn't quite sure.

"It's actually Lord Dreadful Darcy," he said. She glared at him murderously.

"Oh, have you been reading her diary, too?" Lady Amelia asked with a laugh. Lady Bridget turned red.

And then, because his temper still hadn't quite cooled, he said, "Tell me again how important family is to you, Lady Bridget?"

"I shall. In a few days' time when I think of a devastatingly cutting remark," she said sharply. Then she turned away from him, nose in the air, determined to ignore him even when they were in a bloody rowboat together.

He dipped his oars in the water and thrust,

launching the boat forward. Rupert matched his pace.

Tension welled up inside him. The starch in his shirt and cravat suddenly seemed excessive. He would have to speak to his valet about it later. Everything was altogether too damn confining. But that was being a gentleman.

"She walks in beauty, like the night," Rupert declared grandly. Of course he had to recite poetry while rowing.

"Of cloudless climes and starry skies," Amelia added. The pair of them were trouble.

"And all that's best of dark and bright Meets in her aspect and her eyes." After Rupert's line, Amelia clamored to her feet, standing in the unsteady rowboat, and recited the next line:

"Thus mellow'd to that tender light Which heaven to gaudy day denies."

"Amelia, sit down! You are causing a scene," Bridget hissed. She glanced at him. He could see that she was embarrassed by her sister's behavior. And Lady Amelia was oblivious to it.

"Exactly! No, we are acting a scene. It is a slight difference. One is outrageous, the other is artistic."

"Both are going to get you in trouble. You're going to get all of us in trouble! This will be in the papers . . ."

Bridget closed her eyes and groaned. In that moment, he empathized with her: trying to do the right thing, with an exuberant younger sibling determined to cause a scandal anyway.

"My dear sister, when did you start to sound like Loooord Darcy? What happened to the girl who wrote and performed plays with me when we were young?"

Bridget reddened once more. He didn't think it was just the sunlight. "I do *not* sound like Lord Darcy," she said through gritted teeth.

"*One shade the more, one ray the less, Had half impair'd the nameless grace,*" Rupert carried on, beaming. Then, grinning, he said, "You take the next line, Lady Bridget!"

Oh God, Darcy saw her soften a little. Even more when Rupert smiled at her. He wanted to roll his eyes. But gentlemen did not roll their eyes.

"Oh very well," Bridget muttered. She rose to stand as well, while the boat rocked precariously. "*Which waves in every raven tress Or softly lightens o'er her face, Where thoughts serenely sweet express How pure, how dear their dwelling-place.*"

"You're rocking the boat," Darcy pointed out. Indeed, it was swaying side to side, as she was unsteady on her feet.

"Let's go faster!" Rupert shouted. "Race you, Darcy!"

"It's 'Race you, Loooord Darcy,'" Amelia corrected, still standing, still wobbly on her feet.

It was just the excuse he needed to thrust the oars in the water and pull with all his strength. Aye, he would race his little brother all the way back to shore so he could get out of this damn *situation* of lovesick girls and grown men spouting poetry, of brothers with secrets, and of a woman who had the perfect knack for bringing out the worst in him.

He didn't quite see how it happened; there was a collision between their two boats and then there was a splash as they were all launched into the water.

Darcy did not rush to the surface. Under water it was dark, quiet, and cool. There was no hot sun beating down on him, no conversation to annoy him, no Lady Bridget to at once tempt him and infuriate him. He lingered under the water as long as he could stand it, taking advantage of the much needed respite. There was only so much a man could take before he broke.

When his lungs felt like bursting, he broke the surface of the water. He saw Rupert and Amelia a few steps ahead, laughing. A crowd had gathered on the shore to watch the spectacle. And nearby, a creature was thrashing about in the water.

Darcy reached over, wrapped his arm around her waist, and hauled her up. She gasped when she broke the surface, and took in big, heaving gulps of air.

Funny, as he also found himself unable to breathe.

He gazed down at her, past the shock and fury in her eyes, straight down her dress. Her wet dress. Her wet white dress that clung to her every curve the way she currently clung to him. God, her breasts were amazing. Full, luscious, more than a handful. He could see the stiff peak of her nipples through the dress (thank you, Lord, for cold water), and could just faintly detect the dusky pink centers, and for one maddening second when he took leave of his wits, Darcy considered taking one in his mouth, teasing her until she moaned his name.

"What are you doing?" she demanded, as if she wasn't the one clinging to him for dear life, holding on to fistfuls of his wet shirt.

"I'm saving you from drowning. You're welcome."

"I wasn't drowning. I can swim."

"Then you are the worst swimmer I have ever seen."

"Hasn't anyone ever told you that if you don't have anything nice to say, don't say anything at all?"

"No."

He did not like this. He did not like this.

Certain parts of him liked this very much. Too much. Would dream about this later too much. Would take himself in hand tonight—though he could stand to do so now—just thinking about her too much. He didn't want her to know that, so he took a few steps through the water, holding her, until they reached a place where she could likely stand.

He let go and stepped away. Something in him

howled at the loss of her warmth, of just the feeling of her body pressed against his, of the feeling of holding her in his arms. Darcy stood very still, and willed the howling to cease.

Lord Darcy, when soaking wet, was something else entirely. Lord Darcy, when holding her firmly against his hard chest with just one arm, left her breathless. She hoped he thought those gasps were because of water in her lungs or something like that, anything but the truth: Darcy, when wet and holding her, took her breath away.

The water was freezing, so she ought to be cold.

She followed his gaze down, to where her nipples had hardened, visible through the wet fabric of her dress. She ought to be outraged to have a man so blatantly look at her breasts with such intensity.

She ought to do a lot of things she didn't do.

Something tightened in her belly, and a marvelous heat pulsed through her.

She wasn't cold. Not in the slightest.

Lord Darcy, when soaking wet, didn't look so lordly at all. With his hair wet and tousled he almost looked boyishly handsome. Bridget watched, transfixed, as a water drop slid down his cheek. She had the mad urge to lick it off. What would he do if she dared?

Before she had the chance, they were bickering and then he pushed through the water until it was shallow enough for her to stand. Then he thrust her aside as if she were too hot to the touch.

But it was too late. She had seen the way he looked at her. And she had discovered how it made her feel. And it was not what she expected at all.

Chapter 8

> *Times I have thought about Darcy in his wet shirt: 27*
> *Times I have felt something resembling lust when I think about Darcy in his wet shirt: 27*
> *Times I have written* Rupert and Bridget *in my diary since Lady Winterbourne's garden party: 0*
> *I am dreadfully confused.*
>
> LADY BRIDGET'S DIARY

*T*wo days after the garden party, the outrageous behavior of the Cavendish sisters was still being discussed in the papers and in drawing rooms all over town. This time they had done the unthinkable: they had dragged the unimpeachable Darcy and his universally beloved brother down with them.

Bridget had been hoping to lie low until the scandal died down. But the duchess, as usual, had other ideas.

"Your friend Lady Francesca has called and left her card," the duchess said while she and the sisters took tea in the drawing room on a rainy afternoon. "We owe her a return visit."

"Oh, I'm sure we'll see her at a ball or soiree or garden party," Bridget said. "If we're ever invited to one of those again."

"Certainly not if there is a body of water nearby," Claire said.

"Etiquette requires that we call upon her," the duchess instructed. "Besides, are you not friendly with her? I'm sure she is merely concerned with your health after that ill-advised spill in the lake."

The duchess had not been happy about that spill in the lake. She'd been more unhappy than either Bridget or Amelia, who had to sit in wet dresses for the long carriage ride home.

She also made it sound like Francesca and Bridget were actually friends. But Bridget wasn't so sure. They might have gone for ices at Gunther's and coordinated their ensembles to Almack's, but she suspected Francesca was more concerned with discerning Bridget's intentions toward Darcy.

I am, yet again, a subject of gossip. My name has been linked with Darcy's in all of the newspapers. The duchess said it could be worse, but I cannot fathom how.

LADY BRIDGET'S DIARY

It was a truth universally acknowledged that the ton liked to gossip, particularly if the subject contained a lord, a lady, and some hint of scandal. So much the better if it also included a man who never provided fodder for gossip, a lady who was already an object of interest, a dash of impropriety, elements of seduction, hints of a love triangle, and something too outrageous to be believed. The sight of Darcy and Bridget, clinging to each other in a lake at a garden party, satisfied all requirements.

Darcy sought to avoid the gossips—and indeed, any mention of that event—at White's. He was unsuccessful.

"You probably ought to call on Francesca," Fox had told him, dropping into the chair beside him. "She's distraught about you and Lady Bridget."

You and Lady Bridget, clinging to each other like star-crossed lovers. Whilst soaking wet.

"There is no me and Lady Bridget."

"Well, tell that to everyone in London who thinks there is. Including my sister."

What was left unsaid: *who is expecting a proposal from you, oh, any day now.*

"Well, then I suppose I shall pay a visit to your sister."

"Thank you. There's nothing worse than a sulking female about the house. Not that you'd know. But I suppose you will know soon enough."

Most men would probably be livid if their good friend had such an understanding with their sister. But in this instance, it was different. Darcy was a good man with honorable intentions. Francesca and he were well suited. There were no revolting displays of love and affection. Fox, though not known for his deep thinking, recognized how convenient it would be to have his friend as his family. And so, the months and years passed with this understanding that no one was in a particular rush to formalize. Legally. Until now. Darcy risked losing one his best friends if he didn't.

Darcy promptly went to call upon Lady Francesca. He had but a moment alone with her and her terrifying chaperone, Lady Wych Cross, before the Cavendishes arrived. Francesca smiled like all her plans were falling into place.

"I am so glad you have come," she said, strolling toward her guests, arms out to greet them. "Look, Darcy is here as well."

If he'd been paying attention to his intended, he would have seen how closely she watched him to gauge his reaction. As it was, he was arrested by the sight of Lady Bridget. She looked every inch the lady in her *dry* clothes. But it was too late. He had seen what he had seen. And now he could not stop envisioning her like that . . . in less . . . more wet . . .

The group settled into the polite but barbed conversation that passed as female friendship, and he was glad to have a reputation for scowling and speaking little. His thoughts and attentions kept drifting to Lady Bridget. He didn't understand why, and he very badly wanted to so he could put a stop to it.

In the midst of the conversation, Lady Claire excused herself to visit the ladies' retiring room, which he suspected was more a ploy to escape the conversation. Very clever; he wished he'd thought of such a thing. He was about to remember a vitally urgent appointment, but then Lady Francesca gave him reason to stay.

"Lady Bridget, I was so worried you had caught a terrible illness after falling into the lake," Lady Francesca said.

"Right as rain," Lady Bridget quipped.

"Speaking of rain, I so detest this weather! I long to stretch my legs. Lady Bridget, would you care to take a stroll about the room with me?"

There was, of course, only one answer to that; very few refused Lady Francesca. Bridget stood; the ladies linked arms and proceeded to stroll about the room at a glacial pace.

"I want to hear all about your beaux," Lady Francesca said just loud enough for the rest of them to hear.

"Where to begin?" Bridget remarked dryly.

"A girl might have lots of beaux, but only one matters."

Lady Francesca gazed at him. Darcy understood that was meant to be a subtle comment about her. And him. But it wasn't very subtle at all. And he wasn't very interested.

There was the matter of Lady Bridget perplexing him. Fascinating him. Drawing his eye and making him think unwanted thoughts and feel unwanted feelings.

"'Tis a pity the weather prevents a stroll outside," Lady Amelia said from her perch on the settee, next to the duchess. "It seems quite inane to walk in slow circles around the drawing room."

"Oh no. It is so much better to walk inside," Lady Francesca exclaimed. "It is all the better to gossip about the gentlemen of our mutual acquaintance," she drawled, eyeing Darcy. Again, with subtlety. The duchess harrumphed.

But it was Darcy who elucidated upon Lady Francesca's motives.

"Is that really your motive, Lady Francesca? I thought it was because when one is strolling about the room, it is all the better to show one's figure to an advantage."

It was so clear in the way she arched her back, thrust her bosom forward, and preened. She didn't know that it was Bridget's figure that had gotten him up and kept him up at night. It was those full breasts, the lush curves . . .

"Comparing our figures, are you? Whatever are you about, Darcy?" Francesca laughed again.

Bridget reddened and stumbled, tripping over the edge of the carpet. He winced because he realized now how that would sound to her. *Good*, he tried to tell himself. Make her hate him. This mad desire would pass, she would marry his brother, he would marry Francesca, and they would all live happily ever after. But it did not feel good. In fact, he felt remorse. But not enough to declare that in a competition of figures, Lady Bridget's was the one that made the blood rush from his brain. The consequences of saying that . . .

"After all that exercise I find myself parched," Bridget said, making a beeline for the settee.

"I as well," Lady Francesca said, gracefully lowering herself into a chair.

"Tea?" Lady Amelia offered her.

"Please."

Lady Amelia poured gracefully; the duchess beamed. And then, as she was handing Lady Francesca the delicate cup and saucer, there was an accident. Or rather, an "accident."

"Oh my goodness! How horrid of me!" Lady Amelia exclaimed after spilling tea all over the hostess.

Lady Francesca leapt up, eyes flashing, a dark stain spreading across her skirts.

"What a clumsy girl you are!" Lady Wych Cross bellowed to Amelia.

"How clumsy of you, Lady Francesca, to spill tea on yourself like that," the duchess murmured.

Darcy didn't miss the glance between the sisters or the gleefully devilish smirks they exchanged. That was no accident. That was family.

Chapter 9

Breakfast: toast, dry
Luncheon: broth and more dry toast
Tea: yes, but no sugar. Ugh.
Supper: minuscule portions.
Desserts: none!
Times I have thought about Lady Francesca's humiliating scheme to compare our figures: 187

LADY BRIDGET'S DIARY

*A*t breakfast the next morning, Bridget nibbled on toast, wondering why she bothered eating at all. Her reducing diet had been a moderate success—if one did not count all her midnight forays to the kitchen to assuage her starvation. She eyed the heap of food on her brother's plate. Men never had the slightest concern about their figures.

Amelia, who was always the first down to breakfast, was on her second serving and as slender as ever. It just wasn't fair.

The only thing keeping her from lunging at the sideboard and helping herself to enough food to feed an army was the memory of calling hours yesterday. Particularly when Lady Francesca insisted on displaying how slender she was and how slender Bridget wasn't. In front of Lord Darcy. How mortifying.

"Tonight we shall dine at home as a family, as we will have a very important guest with us," the duchess announced from her place at the head of the table.

"Don't keep us in suspense, Josie," James drawled from the other end.

She scowled, as she always did when they addressed her as Josie. But she had at least stopped correcting them.

"It is your heir, Your Grace."

"My heir?" James was alarmed. Bridget giggled as James paled.

"Your cousin, Mr. Peter Collins. It's very important that you meet him and perhaps take him under your wing." The duchess took a sip of her tea and said, very pointedly, "Just in case something should happen to you."

"Is my life in danger?" James inquired. "Did this duke business suddenly become life threatening and thus, interesting?"

"I most certainly hope not," the duchess said

passionately. And when Bridget met Mr. Collins, she knew exactly why.

Upon meeting Mr. Collins that evening Bridget realized quite clearly that any wishes for James's continued good health might have had as much to do with affection for him as with despair at the prospect of Mr. Collins inheriting Durham.

"It is such a great pleasure to meet my esteemed cousins who have journeyed from such a faraway land," he declared.

"Are we cousins?" Amelia inquired.

"Actually, I consulted *Debrett's,*" Bridget said, and the duchess beamed. "And we are more like second cousins."

"Then I use the term affectionately," Mr. Collins said grandly.

"I think it's fortunate that you are all not so closely related," Josephine said. "A match between you, Mr. Collins, and one of the sisters is quite possible."

Josephine promptly received horrified glances from her nieces. Collins was short, portly, and hardly the stuff of any girl's dreams.

"Perhaps if he were the last man on earth," Amelia whispered.

"Not even then," Claire murmured.

"Shh, you don't want him to hear you," James said quietly.

"Or do we?" Bridget murmured.

But Mr. Collins obviously appraised each of

the sisters in turn. Bridget found it revolting
having his eyes—pale, watery eyes—appraise
her, and it put into perspective the way Darcy's
dark gaze made her feel, whether he was scowling at her from across a ballroom or staring at
her breasts in her wet dress.

"A splendid prospect," Mr. Collins said.

Claire paled and Amelia burst out laughing.
Bridget cursed Darcy for interrupting her would-
be proposal from Rupert.

"We would want to keep the dukedom in the
family," the duchess said in response to the girls'
looks.

"I'm still here," James drawled from his spot at
the end of the table.

James clenched his jaw. Josephine smiled like
a queen.

"I see what you did there," Bridget whispered.

"Mmm." Josephine murmured, refusing to
confirm, deny, or engage in a private conversation at the dinner table.

"I say, is this the good silver or the everyday
silver?" Mr. Collins inquired, selecting a fork
and holding it up to the light of the chandelier.

"Only the best for the duke and his heir," Josephine replied. She gave the tight smile Bridget
was coming to recognize as The One Where I
Am Too Ladylike to Point Out How Ghastly Your
Behavior Is.

"Lady Bridget, I understand you are on a regimen of self-improvement," Mr. Collins said.

"Why and how have you come to understand that?" Bridget asked. Surely this could not be proper dinner table conversation.

"I spoke with Lady Amelia about all of your lessons."

"Ah. Did Lady Amelia tell you her fondest wish is to live simply as a vicar's wife?" Bridget inquired, in spite of her sister's glare.

"She did not," Mr. Collins said. "I think it's so important for a lady to strive to better herself and to become accomplished in the ladylike arts."

"And which ones do you think are most important?" Bridget asked. "Needlework? The pianoforte? Simpering?"

"Smiling demurely at idiotic comments?" Claire asked innocently.

"Well, a woman's duty is to support a man in all things and be a respite at home for a gentleman made weary from his dealings with the greater world," Mr. Collins replied.

"How fortunate for you," Claire said. "And gentlemen everywhere."

"Indeed. It's only fitting, as men are the stronger and more intelligent sex."

"Is that so?" Claire inquired coolly. Claire, who was certainly more intelligent than at least half the men they met.

Mr. Collins then carried on the conversation for the rest of the meal entirely by himself. He elucidated, at length, upon what he believed were the most important of the feminine arts: tending to one's husband, bearing children, maintaining a good reputation, and singing sweetly whilst playing the harp after supper.

If that was all a woman could aspire to with marriage, then Bridget began to wonder . . . was it really worth suffering through a reducing diet for? Or biting her tongue or cultivating friendships with influential but despicable ladies? Spinsterhood began to sound appealing. She could have a cottage by the sea and eat cake for breakfast.

As he rambled on about the Perfect Lady, Bridget pushed food around on her plate, took small sips of wine, and wondered why she bothered. Why was she trying to shrink herself, anyway? She had no desire to impress Mr. Collins or men like him. She did not want to starve herself or restrain her speech, learn to play the harp or keep her spine straight all the time just so an arse like Mr. Collins might think favorably of her. It wasn't just Mr. Collins. It was the whole haute ton. She'd been trying and trying to earn their favor but she never stopped to wonder *why*.

Was it because she wished to marry well? Did she want their stamp of approval so badly?

She realized, with some alarm, that the one she really wanted to impress was Lord Darcy. Not the likes of Lord Darcy, as she had been supposing all along, but the man himself. He was the one she saw in her mind's eye, judging her.

The man who didn't wish to speak to her because they hadn't been introduced. The man who did not dance but then reprimanded her for refusing his grudging invitation. The man who told her to remember her reputation. The man whose dark eyes had looked at her, really looked at her, that day in the lake. And in that one moment, she hadn't felt wanting . . . she had felt wanted.

I daresay we have made the acquaintance of someone worse than Dreadful Darcy. In fact, he's not so dreadful at all in comparison to Mr. Collins.

LADY BRIDGET'S DIARY

Later that night, the Cavendish sisters found their way to Claire's bedchamber one by one. They had not planned on it, not even in hushed whispers or secret signals. It was simply understood that the events of the evening needed to be discussed and that the place to do it was in Claire's bed.

"Well, that was ghastly," Claire said, falling back against the pillows.

"Though in its own way, it was sort of amusing," Amelia said, pulling the covers up around her.

"Which part was so funny, Amelia? When he questioned whether women needed to learn how to read or when he droned on and on and on about his patroness at the vicarage?" Claire asked.

"Just . . . all of it," Amelia said, waving her hand. "He's a ridiculous man."

"You have a twisted sense of humor," Bridget replied.

"But you have to love me anyway." Amelia grinned. "Because we are *family*."

The obvious reply to that was to hit her in the face with a pillow, which made Amelia laugh. There was a time and place to be a true lady, and it was not when little sisters were being vexing.

"Why did you have to mention my improving regimen?" Bridget demanded.

"What does it matter?" Amelia shrugged. Then, with a sly glance, she added, "Unless you are trying to impress Mr. Collins?"

"Obviously not." Bridget made a face of disgust. "He is the worst gentleman we have met thus far."

"Worse than Looord Darcy?" Claire teased. Bridget did not want to think about him now. Or, oddly, discuss him with her sisters. So the obvious reply to that was to hit her in the face with a pillow, which made Claire laugh. There was a time and place to be true lady and it was not when one's older sister was being vexing.

"*Sisters*," Bridget lamented, looking heavenward, much in the way James had done at least thrice a day for as long as she could remember.

"If anyone is to lament about sisters, it is I," James said, having just joined the group. He pulled up a chair next to the bed, sat down, and stretched out his legs.

"We thought you might be having drinks in the library with your heir," Claire said. James just grinned.

"There was a pressing estate matter that required my immediate attention," he said, and they all knew there was no such thing. "And then I had to deliver a stern lecture to my sisters about . . . something."

"Well, do go on. We are all here." Bridget gave him an attentive smile.

"I am sorry you all had to endure that man," James said, pulling a face. He was genuinely sorry.

"It's not your fault, James," Bridget said softly.

"But it is. The duchess is trying to impress upon me how much I am needed here. And how I am able to be duke," he said, with a pause, revealing that he'd doubted it. "I have refused to recognize it. Mr. Collins was a way to show me that I could do it, that I must do it."

The sisters fell silent. Bridget knew that the only way Mr. Collins would inherit was if James *died*. Even if he boarded the next ship to America, there was no relinquishing the title. But there was the not-small matter of him deciding to accept all the responsibility and trying to succeed at it.

"And she is trying to make our other suitors seem more . . . suitable," Claire said thoughtfully. "So that we marry, and stay here."

"And keep me here," James said, glancing up at them.

"She is so devious," Bridget murmured.

"Is it wrong that I am quite in awe of her?" Amelia asked.

"Lord help us all," Claire muttered. And then she tossed a pillow at her.

Chapter 10

*If only Rupert would propose! I have no idea
why he hasn't. He always seeks me out for a dance
(or two!) and we have the best time together. I
swear he was about to kiss me at the garden party,
if Dreadful Darcy hadn't interrupted.*

LADY BRIDGET'S DIARY

The following evening, while Lady Bridget
was wearing pink and trailing after Lady Francesca, Miss Mulberry, and Miss Montague at
Almack's, Darcy was at a far more exclusive
haunt: White's, an aristocratic men's haven
from women, society, and anything that wasn't
friends, a game of cards, and an endless supply
of food, drink, and cigars. Cravats were loos-
ened and inevitably lost, jackets hung sloppily
on the backs of chairs, no valets present to despair over the state of their attire.

The group that evening included Darcy and

Rupert, who probably shouldn't be joining the game of cards given his recent propensity for racking up gaming debts, as well as Mr. Alistair Finlay-Jones, their longtime friend, who had recently and unexpectedly returned from a six-year tour of the Continent.

"Ah, so this is where the party is," Fox said as he strolled in, late, and pulled out a chair and collapsed into it. "I was at Almack's earlier, dying of boredom. And sobriety."

"Were you expecting otherwise?" Darcy inquired.

"Touché. I had promised Francesca I would escort her." He turned to Darcy. "I noticed you weren't there."

"I had an urgent matter to attend to," he murmured. The urgent matter was playing cards, having a stiff drink, and doing his best to forget about matters of Parliament, estate management, and certain American women. Or rather, a woman.

"Still drying off from your spill in the lake?" Fox asked.

"What did I miss?" Alistair asked.

"You won't believe it," Rupert said, and he proceeded to explain. There was little detail given to the rowboats, the race, and the collision, and far too much information regarding the aftermath.

"Fancied a swim, did you?" Alistair quipped.

"If that's what we're calling it these days," Rupert replied.

"I overheard Fran and her friends gossiping

about it," Fox said. Only an older brother could get away with calling the Lady Francesca something as plain as Fran. "They were going on and on about Darcy here, in his wet shirt. Giggling like schoolgirls. It was horrifying."

"It has been said by some that Lady Bridget swooned right into Darcy's waiting arms," Rupert said, laughing. Darcy merely lifted one brow. Should his brother, who had essentially declared his intentions to wed her, be laughing about this? Or did that just prove how ludicrous it was that Lady Bridget should swoon. Over him.

"She wasn't swooning. She was thrashing about in the water, attempting to swim." Darcy did his best to sound bored.

"And then you clutched her to your chest . . ." Fox said dramatically, mockingly.

"And she gazed into your eyes . . ." Rupert added.

"I couldn't very well let her drown," Darcy said.

Alistair was laughing heartily. "Let me guess. She swooned in your arms once you rescued her from an untimely demise."

"I daresay she swooned," Rupert said. "I was there."

"And they say ladies aren't much troubled by sexual feeling of any kind," Fox remarked.

"My regards to the women in your life if you believe that," Darcy replied.

"Sod off," Fox retorted, and took a long swig of his drink. Matters with women were not going well in his life at the moment and everyone knew it.

"My, how the mighty have fallen," Alistair murmured, glancing at his friends. "I go away for a mere six years . . . and come back to find Fox here in a snit over women and Darcy gallantly rescuing young women at garden parties."

"I don't know about you gents, but I came here to win all your money at cards and drink obscene amounts of brandy. I have no intention of gossiping like schoolgirls," Darcy said. And with that they began to play in earnest. A pot of money on the table grew then shrank as they changed hands over the course of the evening. An ancient waiter ensured their glasses were never empty. But even amidst the smoky air and alcohol haze and intense focus on the cards in his hands, something did not escape Darcy's notice: Rupert, of the ongoing and ever increasing gaming debts, kept winning.

It was long after midnight when the gents stumbled out of the club onto St. James's Street, where Darcy's carriage was waiting.

"Would you like a ride?" he offered to Alistair.

"No thanks, it's a nice evening. I think I'll walk."

Shrugging, Darcy climbed into the carriage, and Rupert joined him.

"That evening was much more amusing than if we'd gone to another ball," Rupert said, leaning back against the squabs and closing his eyes.

"Especially for you," Darcy said, thinking now of all the rounds of cards. "You played well and have a fat purse from your winnings."

At first he hadn't given much thought to it, but at some point in the evening when he'd drunk enough to stop thinking about stupid business matters or Bridget's breasts, he noted his brother was winning. A lot.

It was curious, that.

"My lucky night," Rupert quipped.

"No, you played well. It seems that luck had little to do with it," Darcy said, straightening in his seat. He had been drinking, but not so much that his brain had stopped working. And it was working now, putting two and two together.

"Well, I've had some practice."

"I wonder, Rupert, about all your gaming debts over the past year. Given how well you played to-night."

"I told you, it is just luck." Rupert spoke sharply, revealingly, because he hadn't had the lessons and practice in modulating his tone and stripping all and any emotion from his voice that Darcy had.

"Are you sure it's not something else?"

"Of course not. It is nothing."

It was probably something. But there was only one thing to say.

"You can always confide in me."

They rode the rest of the way in silence. A tense silence. But one that Darcy simply waited out because he had years of practice in waiting out silences. The trick was to just breathe and give in to it and to know that the other person was probably suffering through it more.

Upon their return home, Danvers was present to take their hats and gloves and to present a letter to Rupert. "An urgent letter."

"Thank you, Danvers, that will be all for the evening."

Darcy watched his brother closely. Rupert's face fell upon seeing the handwriting. Then he paled when he read the contents.

"Rupert."

"It is nothing."

It was obviously something. Letters that arrived in the dead of the night were never *nothing*. Letters that made his normally happy and carefree brother become as shuttered as . . . him . . . were not nothing.

"Join me for a drink," Darcy said, even though they had had enough to drink that evening.

"I'm tired. I think I shall retire."

"Join me for a drink." He repeated himself in his I-am-the-earl-do-as-I-say voice.

"Don't get all high and mighty with me now, Darcy. I'm not in the mood."

But they stalked into the library and Darcy closed the door behind them. A fire still burned in the grate and from it, Darcy lit a few candles so they could see.

"I want to help you. But I cannot do so if you won't confide in me."

Rupert laughed bitterly. "Help me? Not even *you* can help me. Not with *this*."

He shook the paper in Darcy's face, and Darcy was sorely tempted to wrench it away and wrestle the truth out of him.

"So it is something."

"Aye, it's something. Two thousand pounds of something." Rupert crumpled the sheet of paper in his fist.

"More gaming debts?"

There was a long silence. A silence so long and so dark that even Darcy grew anxious. This wasn't just something, it was *something*. It took all of Darcy's self-control to stay still and not, say, cross the room and throttle his brother until he spoke the truth.

"More like blackmail," Rupert said. Finally. Darcy exhaled. Blackmail he could handle. He asked the next logical question.

"Why are you being blackmailed?"

Rupert swallowed hard. He leaned against the mantel. And then he spoke, softly.

"Something that would ruin this family and see me hanged."

Darcy wracked his brain for something Rupert might have done. But Rupert was not prone to trouble; not serious trouble, anyway. He kept decent company, he played cards well, he wasn't a liar or a cheat. Perhaps there was an accident that he was somehow involved in?

"Have you hurt someone?"

"Quite the opposite," Rupert said, his voice

hoarse, head down. And after a long, excruciating silence, he said quietly, "All I have done is love someone."

Love someone? That didn't make sense. He thought first of Bridget—but he couldn't imagine a blackmailable offense there. Perhaps there was another woman and an irate husband? A mistress deceiving her protector? Whom did Rupert love, anyway? He had never mentioned any one woman's name. He seemed fond of Bridget, but these "gaming debts" had been coming in long before she arrived on the scene.

Whom, then, did Rupert love? And why was he being blackmailed over it?

It was another long, aching moment before Rupert lifted his head. And when their eyes met, Darcy knew that Rupert didn't fear the blackmailer as much as he feared his own brother. But *why*?

It was another long, aching moment before he understood.

When they were young, perhaps thirteen or fourteen or so, Rupert's best friend was one of the stable boys. Their father discovered this and thrashed his younger son within an inch of life. *No son of mine*, he had roared. Darcy had assumed it was because of the social disparity between them. The late earl was a horrible snob.

But perhaps it hadn't been snobbery at all.

Darcy thought back over the years at Eton, then Oxford . . . Rupert had flirted with girls, but never spoke of anyone in particular. He had earned a reputation as a rake and did nothing to dissuade people of it. Meanwhile, he was always with his close friend, Frederick Croft.

Darcy thought of the night Rupert had rushed to be by his side, and all the stories that began "Frederick and I . . ." Slowly the puzzle pieces fit together, revealing a picture Darcy had never even considered.

Rupert loved someone he shouldn't. Rupert's love was a crime.

It *was* a crime. It was on the books, the law of the land. It went against the teachings in the Bible, the sermons in church, and the natural order of things. Darcy believed in order.

He paused, considering all these things. It was a long pause. An endless, agonizing pause. But the simple fact was that he loved his brother more.

His heart broke for Rupert. To keep this secret he had to suppress his natural desires and inclinations. He had to flirt with women, dance with young ladies, and constantly maintain the charade of perfect gentleman, the devil-may-care second son.

He must be exhausted. And frustrated. And Darcy understood.

Rupert was more like him than he realized.

"Why didn't you say something?" Darcy asked softly.

"This is not something one says. I have been paying hundreds and thousands of pounds to make sure this person doesn't say something. I have been putting it about that I'm interested in a wife so that in the event that this person does say something, it is unbelievable. I have even considered taking a wife, but I cannot drag her into this."

Darcy sucked in his breath. Then he let it go.

"But why did you not tell me? I am your brother."

"You are my perfect brother. You are a paragon of gentlemanly virtues. You were trained by our father to think only of the estate, the legacy, our reputations. Your first instinct is always the right, proper thing. How could you do anything but turn me out and cut me off? If news of this gets out, I will ruin this family's reputation and legacy. You have to put the estate and the family name first. I will have to go. I will go."

Rupert was right about one thing; Darcy's first instinct was always to do the right, proper thing. This moment was no exception.

"You are my brother. I will protect you. And I will not turn you out."

He meant every word.

Though the light was dim, he thought he saw Rupert's chin tremble.

He managed to elicit a promise that Rupert would tell him everything in the morning and they would take care of this once and for all.

But in the morning, Rupert was gone.

Chapter 11

Had a horrible fight with Amelia last night after she caused a hugely embarrassing scene at Almack's.

LADY BRIDGET'S DIARY

The less said about the previous evening, the better. The family spent an exceedingly tedious evening at Almack's. Amelia then caused a scandal—one that was perhaps worse than anything Bridget had done thus far. What followed was quite a row between the two sisters. It only ended when Bridget stalked off and slammed the door to her room and when Amelia calmed down after a dose of laudanum was snuck into her water.

As a result, everyone, even the duchess, had slept in. But eventually, they all made their way to the dining room for breakfast.

Josephine was seated in her usual spot at the

head of the table, sipping from her elegant china teacup. Everything about her was elegant, at all hours of the day.

But the way she surveyed the breakfast table was more like a general observing his troops before battle. Her trusty lieutenant, Miss Green, beside her.

Cavendish family versus the haute ton. The score was dismal.

"Where is Amelia?" Josephine asked. "That girl is late for everything except for breakfast."

"She's probably sleeping off the laudanum or out exploring," James said with a shrug.

"Duke, you seem remarkably unconcerned that your sister is missing in a foreign city," Miss Green said softly.

"Foreign? It is apparently home now," he said, with a pointed look to the duchess. "And we don't know that she is missing."

"Frankly, I'm inclined to pity anyone who crosses her," Bridget replied. Her sister was probably still abed, exhausted from all the drama of the previous evening.

The duchess turned to a maid, "Do go inquire on Lady Amelia's whereabouts." Then, fixing her attentions to the rest of the siblings she said, "Now, shall we go over our plans for the day?"

Bridget and her siblings exchanged glances. They were particularly directed at James, who shared their sentiments.

"Just out of curiosity, dear duchess, what are the chances that the day's activities include, say, lazing around with books or playing parlor games, whiling away the hours in the stables or going out for a ride?"

Miss Green smiled. "This may come as a shock to you, but Her Grace doesn't care for parlor games."

"And there is still so much you all need to know. Claire, last night you refused a dance with Lord Banbury. A lady should not decline a dance with a gentleman unless her dance card is full."

It went without saying that her dance card was not full. Not even close.

"He is a moron."

"But he is a rich moron."

"I thought we were rich."

"But one can always be richer," Josephine said. "And Bridget, you went in to supper before your turn."

"I know, but I was starving."

"Ladies do not have appetites."

"Josephine." James's voice was a warning. In the best of circumstances, they had little patience for all the formality and rules of the aristocracy. But this morning, after a late and trying night, they had none. "We know we possess one of the oldest and most prestigious titles in England. We know have a sacred duty to live up to its legacy and reputation, increase its wealth, and pass it on to our heirs."

"Ah, so you have been listening, Duke. Perhaps you are more than just a pretty face."

Miss Green choked on her tea.

"With all due respect, our father left it all behind and never looked back. And that is the example that we were raised with. We never expected this. I never expected this."

"Nevertheless, here we are, and we haven't much time," Josephine said briskly.

"We have all the time in the world. We're here, aren't we?" James's question hung in the air. "But that is not enough, is it?"

Bridget noticed the duchess's grip on her teacup was firm; her knuckles were paling. Would it shatter in her grasp? What a statement that would make.

It was not enough to simply be here, to live in the house and ride about in the carriage with the ducal crest in gold on the doors. They had to become Durham—live it, breathe it, own it—and to do so they had to leave behind America, the life they led there, and even, Bridget mused, the people they were there.

Her brother wasn't born to be a duke; he was most comfortable out in the stables, raising and training horses.

Her sisters were too impulsive and exuberant (Amelia) or too intelligent (Claire) for the haute ton's taste.

And as for Bridget herself . . . she wanted so badly to measure up and belong. But she also wanted to eat a proper meal, to tease Darcy and laugh loudly, to live instead of attempting to walk with a particular air, or learn every possible form of address for every possible person she might meet, or master the steps of every obscure country dance she might be called upon to know. She wanted to be without trying so hard.

"Well, this is a serious topic so early in the morning," Miss Green chimed in. "Shall we discuss the weather instead?"

But first, the maid returned. "Lady Amelia is not in her bedchamber, Your Grace."

"Well, where is she?" Josephine demanded.

"I'm afraid I don't know," the poor maid answered, trembling.

"Search the house for her," the duchess ordered. The maid didn't move. "And why are you not the slightest bit alarmed that your sister is missing?"

"She runs off all the time. She eventually returns," Bridget said. At home, it had not been a problem, for they had a large property for Amelia to explore.

"Yes, she gets hungry, or the weather becomes unpleasant, or she simply has to tell someone, particularly us, of her adventures," James added. "I suppose you think it's terrible that I indulged her in such unladylike behavior."

"Your Grace . . ." The poor maid was trying to gain attention.

"London is a dangerous city for unaccompanied young ladies," the duchess said.

"I hope you haven't said that to Amelia." James groaned.

"Of course I have. She needed to be warned."

"And that was your first mistake," Claire said with a sigh. She'd had years of acting a surrogate mother to their wayward younger sister.

"Your Grace . . ." The poor maid was still trying to gain attention.

"What are the chances she's just in the attic or the kitchens?" Miss Green asked. "I have found her exploring the house on a few occasions."

"I'd put my money on the Tower of London or a gaming hell," Claire said.

"Your Grace! Her bed was not slept in!" the maid cried out.

> *Missing sisters: 1*
> *Scandals looming: at least 1, possibly several*
> *Hours spent tense in the drawing room: 4*
> *Pots of tea drunk: 4*
> *Times the duchess cared that I took extra sugar:*
> *0, as far as I could discern*
>
> LADY BRIDGET'S DIARY

A few hours later, there was no denying the truth: Amelia was gone. One of the upstairs housemaids could not be found either, and everyone desperately hoped that they were at least together. James and a few servants had gone out to discreetly obtain any intelligence about her whereabouts.

One by one they returned. No one had seen a proper lady and her housemaid dashing about the neighborhood between the hours of midnight and morning. Or at least, that's what they gathered. It was hard to ask questions about a subject one desperately wanted to keep secret.

While the servants were send out to make discreet inquiries, James, the duchess, Miss Green, Claire, Amelia, and Bridget gathered in the drawing room to plot their next steps and strategy. The air was thick with tension. The tea was strong. Nerves were beginning to fray.

Even Bridget and Claire, who had been firm in their belief that Amelia had gone off on one of her adventures, started to worry. And James—their poor brother looked like he'd aged a decade in a day.

A ferocious debate as to their strategy for locating the wayward Cavendish sister ensued.

James paced back and forth across the carpets. He pushed his fingers through his hair, frustrated.

"If we enlist the assistance of the Bow Street Runners—"

The duchess cut him off.

"Then we risk the ton finding out that she has been missing overnight."

"I'm more concerned that she's *alive*," James said witheringly.

"And I'm concerned that she has a life to live when she returns," Josephine replied. "She will be ruined if the merest whisper of this gets out."

Bridget knew that this inactivity was killing him. That he wanted to be out of the house searching for his wayward sister and not stuck in the drawing room with a bunch of ladies and their endless pots of tea and worries about reputations. She felt a bit useless herself.

In the midst of it all, Pendleton, the butler, stepped in to announce a caller.

"Lord Darcy requests an audience."

Bridget choked on the sip of tea she had just taken. A very sweet cup of tea; with the duchess so distracted, she took the liberty of adding extra sugar.

What was *he* doing *here* now?

"We are not at home to callers this morning, Pendleton."

But the butler returned but a moment later.

"He says he wishes to see Lady Bridget for just a moment regarding an urgent matter."

"Well, that is unexpected," Bridget murmured. Her heart started beating rapidly.

She met in him the smaller receiving room on the other side of the foyer.

"Lady Bridget."

"Lord Darcy."

They were alone, quite alone. Bridget eyed him, noting that he was, alas, in dry clothes. Perfectly tailored dry clothes that hugged his broad shoulders and clung tightly to his muscled legs.

He cleared his throat. She had been caught staring.

"Pardon the intrusion. I was wondering if you had seen my brother today."

"I have not. Why do you ask?"

"He seems to be missing."

Bridget paled.

"What is it?"

"Come with me."

They were halfway across the foyer before she realized that she had taken his hand and pulled him along—a stuffy peer of the realm—as if he were a horse on a lead. It was another second or two before she realized that he hadn't protested her informality or attempted to withdraw his hand from hers. After that, it was only an instant before she became aware of the warmth from his hand stealing through her.

It was funny what could happen in the time it took to cross the foyer.

> *Amelia and . . . Rupert? My heart breaks at the betrayal.*
>
> LADY BRIDGET'S DIARY

"I hope I am not intruding," Darcy said when he was shown into the drawing room. By *shown* he meant dragged into the room against his will, in a most informal manner. The downfall of civilization was imminent. "But I inquired with Lady Bridget regarding my brother, who seems to be missing. It appears this information is relevant to you?"

"Do come in, Darcy," the duchess said wearily. "Perhaps you can help."

Darcy lifted one brow.

"It's a delicate family matter," Josephine said, at the same time James said, "It's a bloody disaster."

"You have my word that I will protect your confidence. I would be grateful to be of assistance."

"I suppose you can be trusted," the duchess said, eyeing Darcy. Then to no one in particular she said, "His mother and I were close. But the less said about your father, the better," the duchess said. Now *that* aroused Bridget's curiosity and begged for more questions. She hadn't even considered that Darcy had parents; he seemed like he was born fully formed, a perfect gentleman who emerged from a rock or the head of Athena. "But nevertheless, Darcy, we have a situation on our hands. Lady Amelia has taken leave of us."

"Of her own free will or do we suspect something more dire?"

"Knowing Amelia, she's just run off for a bit of adventure," Bridget replied. "She has a habit of it."

"But that doesn't mean something bad hasn't happened to her," James said gravely. He swore softly under his breath. Ever since their parents had died, he'd been the one responsible for them all. And they hadn't always made it easy on him, but this was the worst.

"There wasn't a ransom note," Claire added. "One doesn't kidnap an heiress without leaving a ransom note. Unless one is utterly insane."

"Thank you, Claire, for suggesting that a madman has kidnapped our sister," James said dryly.

"Thus we are searching for one runaway heiress in a city of nearly a million people without the slightest clue where she could be," Darcy summarized. "It so happens that my brother is also missing."

"An interesting turn of events," Josephine mused. "Would you care for tea?"

"Or something stronger? I could use something stronger," James muttered.

"No thank you. In a few short hours I'm sure we will celebrate Lady Amelia's safe return with a bottle of your best brandy."

"Right," James said. "In the meantime, the duchess and I are at odds as to how to ensure her safe return."

Claire explained the two positions.

"You are both right," Darcy said. "It is impossible for us to find her by ourselves. But if word of this becomes public, Lady Amelia will be ruined. And she may not be the only one."

Darcy's gaze landed on her for just a second.

Bridget knew she was *not* supposed to feel a thrill at the word "ruined." It was just so dramatic, so mysterious, so final. One was fine and then one day one was ruined and never quite knew why. It usually had something to do with being alone with a man. People were always left to imagine the worst. She did not wish this for herself or her sisters, of course.

But still, the word gave her a little thrill.

"We'll also look pretty damn suspicious if all of us split up and go searching for her," James said.

"We shall perhaps go search for her in turns, and someone should wait here in the event that she returns on her own," Darcy replied. "Duke, Lady Claire why don't you go for a stroll and see what you can learn about Lady Amelia . . . or my brother. You'll also want to send some footmen out in plainclothes to seek information. If she does not return this morning, we'll enlist a few Runners for the afternoon."

And just like that, Lord Darcy ended the standoff between the duchess and the duke. He had calmly defused the tension in the room. It was impressive, that.

Or had he? There was a knot in Bridget's stomach now. Because Darcy was here and now he was deeply embroiled in their private family drama, which would hardly improve his already low opinion of their family.

"Lady Bridget, why don't you and Lord Darcy visit Hyde Park. Perhaps you'll see your sister," Josephine suggested. "Perhaps you'll even find her with Mr. Wright."

Bridget frowned at the duchess. What a bloody terrible idea. If she and Darcy were seen taking a pleasant stroll in the park, it would only attract undue attention and more gossip, especially after all the nonsense about clinging to each other in the lake. Honestly.

Or so she desperately believed. But the thought of being alone with Darcy made her feel anxious and strange. He was not one for conversation, she had learned, and she so hated silences.

Most of the time she found him insufferable, except for when his clothes were wet and she could gaze wantonly at his body. She doubted that would happen today. Alas.

"I'm sure we wouldn't wish to trouble Lord Darcy anymore," Bridget said, opting for the more polite response. "I'm certain he wishes to search for his brother instead."

"It is no trouble," he said evenly, his gaze resting on her alone. "I mean to spend the day making inquiries about Rupert. We can look for Lady Amelia as well."

"But won't it look suspicious? Won't I be ruined if I am alone with a man?"

"I think we can all agree that it would be much better if the gossip were about you and someone as proper as Darcy here, rather than the truth," Josephine said. She punctuated it with a look at her as if Bridget were batty to refuse to take this opportunity. In fact, the duchess looked as if she was glad of this opportunity to foist one of her unmarried girls on the company of an eligible bachelor.

"We'll take my curricle, which shall allow us to cover more ground than on foot," he said.

"It is acceptable for you to be out together if you are in an open carriage and not gone for very long," Josephine said. "It will simply appear to be a social excursion. In fact, it shall probably provide an excellent distraction for the ton."

Chapter 12

It seems that I shall be spending the day with Dreadful Darcy, roaming the city in search of my wayward sister. Horrors. But no worse than French lessons.

LADY BRIDGET'S DIARY

*O*nce they were both ensconced in the curricle, Darcy cracked the whip and they were off. It went without saying that searching for missing siblings in the company of Lady Bridget Cavendish was not how Darcy had intended to spend his day. He was an important man, a busy man, and he had matters of vital importance requiring his attention.

But after Rupert confessed what he had confessed, everything had changed. Parliamentary matters could wait. An issue regarding a drainage ditch on their Lincolnshire estate could wait. He needed only to find his brother so they could find the blackmailer and ensure Rupert's secret was safe.

Nothing else mattered.

Which was why he was in an open carriage with none other than Lady Bridget Cavendish of the American Cavendishes, fueling rumors that there was some romance between them. It was better that the ton speak of them, rather than Rupert. Or Amelia.

It was only logical.

And yet, Lady Bridget had brought a book. They were supposed to be searching all the faces in the crowds or at the very least, giving the appearance of a suitor calling upon a lady. He hated what it suggested about his company and her interest in him that she had brought a book.

He hated that he hated that.

There was no reason for him to care in the slightest what Lady Bridget, the girl who fell, thought of him.

"Well, I tried, Lord Darcy," she said, heaving a sigh. "My apologies that you are now embroiled in my family's affair and stuck spending hours with me when surely you have more lordly matters to attend to."

"Lordly matters?"

"Yes, such as stomping around your various properties, issuing orders to servants, answering extremely important correspondence with very important Persons of Quality, and generally putting on airs."

"Is that what you think I do all day?"

"You and every other lord I've met since I have arrived."

"Let me assure you that I am able to spare a few hours from my important work of strolling around my properties and answering my correspondence to search for missing siblings. After all, it has been impressed upon me that nothing is more important than family."

He glanced at her, to see how she took his reference to their earlier conversation when she dared to do what no one else in the haute ton would do: chastise his behavior.

"I am glad you have your priorities in order," she replied. "Where do you think Rupert has gone off to?"

"He is not with his . . . friend," Darcy said. He'd gone to call on Frederick Croft but Croft was not at home. Not that Darcy could say that to her. "I thought he might have spoken with you."

She was quiet for a long moment, while they traveled the length of Curzon Street. Out of the corner of his eye, he saw her tapping her fingers on the book—that book—in a nervous manner. Something was vexing her.

"Do you think they are together?" she asked, finally.

Ah. Of course. She was nervous that her sister had run off with the man she fancied herself in love with.

"I have no idea. But it would be for the best if she were with him."

"How could you say that?" she asked angrily.

"Because I am thinking rationally. It is vastly preferable that she be in the company of Rupert, who will respect and protect her, rather than some nefarious creature who would use her in the worst ways imaginable."

"Well, when you phrase it like that . . ."

"Furthermore, if it were discovered or suggested that they were together, they could marry to avert scandal."

It was the truth. It was logic. It was reason. And it was, according to Lady Bridget, a personal affront.

"How could she do that to me?" There was no denying the anguish in her voice.

He didn't know how to reply. Especially not when confronted with the depths of her emotions. He thought she fancied Rupert because Rupert was charming, but glancing at her now, he realized she seemed actually heartbroken at the thought of him with another woman. Worst of all, he knew what he knew about Rupert and couldn't say his brother wasn't interested in any woman.

Darcy, being either diplomatic or cowardly, changed the subject.

"What are you reading?"

"It is Amelia's guidebook to London," she replied, and he felt vastly relieved. "I found it while snooping through her room because I am the sort of person who will snoop through someone's rooms. You probably disapprove."

"In this instance, I think it's a laudable activity,"

he said, noting an expression of slight surprise on her face. "In other circumstances, less so."

"We shall never suit, Darcy. For I would snoop through all your things while you were at Parliament or your club or wherever you go to be lordly all day."

"You wouldn't find anything of interest."

She leaned in and peered up at him. "Oh, Darcy, you don't have any deep, dark secrets?"

He glanced down at her. At her breasts. At the wicked smile on her lips and the spark in her eye. His deep, dark secret was how much he fantasized about tasting those lips, caressing those breasts . . .

"If I had any secrets, I wouldn't be so foolish as to leave them about where any snoop could find them," he said stiffly.

"You would make an excellent spy."

"Yes, in all my free time," he remarked dryly, and she laughed.

"I suppose one could trust you not to snoop through their private belongings. Why, I bet I could leave my diary lying around and you wouldn't read it."

Ah, again with that diary of hers. He would rather read parliamentary reports on taxation and agricultural treatises on the latest technological advances in drainage ditches than the intimate ramblings of a young woman. She probably had pages with nothing but *Rupert and Bridget* written on them. And he knew she had a list of things she disliked about him, the Dreadful Darcy. No, he did not need to read all that.

"You could be assured that I would respect your privacy," he said. "Anyway, are there any indications in that book of where your sister might have gone?"

"She has circled a few things, including Hyde Park, so we might as well carry on with our original plan. Besides, she is a country girl at heart and loves nature more than cities. I bet she misses it."

"There are people who prey on country girls who are innocent to the ways of the city," he said grimly.

"She is not innocent to the ways of the city, but do tell me all the dangers a young lady faces in London. I'm imagining packs of roving marauders with murderous intent. Don't the words 'murderous intent' just send shivers up and down your spine?"

"No. Men do not get shivers," he informed her. "On their spine or otherwise."

"Oh."

She seemed deflated. Was it the lack of marauders with murderous intent or the fact that men did not feel ridiculous shivers and thrills? Probably both.

"There are pickpockets," he said, indulging her in listing the dangers that might befall a maiden and trying to, oh, amuse her.

"This dress—most dresses—do not have

pockets," Bridget pointed out. "It ruins the line of the gown."

"To think I have lived my whole life without knowing that," he said dryly. "They might snatch your reticule, then. It's easy enough and happens often. There are also men who have little regard for a woman's virtue."

She grinned. Oh bloody hell, he thought, mentally kicking himself. He had to introduce that line of conversation.

"Yes, young ladies are warned from an early age to protect our virtue. It is apparently in constant peril and we must protect it at all costs. We are under strict orders to avoid finding ourselves alone with a man. And yet . . ." Her voice trailed off. He glanced over and caught her gazing at him. God, he felt something like a shiver. She dropped her voice to a deliberately dramatic low tone. "Here we are. Alone."

"You needn't fear for your virtue now. We are in an open carriage."

Even if they were married one wouldn't act intimately in an open carriage. Public displays of affection or emotion were high on the list of things that were Not Done.

"And if we were in a closed carriage? Alone?"

If they were alone in a closed carriage he would find himself in a torturous internal battle, wanting to kiss her senseless and touch her everywhere until she begged for him to take her.

"Obviously, as a gentleman, I would treat you with the utmost respect," he said. But his voice was a bit rough. He coughed and added, "And this is not an appropriate topic of conversation."

She sighed. Disappointed. Chastised? Didn't she realize that he couldn't, just physically could not, say such thoughts aloud? He was English, for God's sake.

"Well then we mustn't speak of it. Let's consider other dangers. What about being kidnapped and held for ransom?" Bridget's voice was actually breathless when she asked.

"It's a possibility."

"Well, I would pity whoever took Amelia," she declared.

"You don't really mean that, do you?"

"Not really. I am beginning to get nervous. Amelia has always embarked on 'explorations.' Once she even spent the afternoon at the circus with the lion tamer. Thank God we found her before they set off for their next destination. But she's never been away this long, or overnight."

"Are you going to cry?"

"No." She sniffed. Then she smiled. "Perhaps. Only to distress you."

Darcy drove the carriage through the park, where they joined the throngs of carriages and riders on Rotten Row. In her opinion, this was one of the more ridiculous habits of the haute ton. Whoever thought that it was a capital idea to cause a buildup of traffic for amusement? If one wanted to go that slowly, one might as well walk.

She hoped Darcy was keeping an eye out for

Amelia and Rupert because she was too distracted by the carriages full of lords and ladies who were out only to spy on one another and gossip endlessly. He nodded at some acquaintances as they passed, but she was all too aware of the stares and whispers and the shocking sight of an esteemed earl with one of the Americans. Especially her, the girl who fell first in the ballroom and then into the lake. She watched as they all glanced at her, then Darcy, and then turned to whisper at each other.

I can see you talking about me, she wanted to shout. But perfect ladies did not shout things out at random. She didn't need Josephine to tell her that.

Perhaps it was even a good thing that she was seen with the stuffy old Darcy. As if his company implicitly endorsed her and would provide some of the approval that had eluded her and her family. They would need all the help they could get if there were rumors about Amelia, roaming the streets of London without a chaperone.

Because it was polite and proper, she and Darcy chatted amiably with many of his acquaintances that they encountered. But the conversations were simply about the weather or other inanities; there were no clues about Amelia or Rupert.

Lady Tunbridge, a buxom, forthright woman of middle age, was the only person who had something interesting to say. Bridget had made her acquaintance at her first London ball, which Lady Tunbridge had hosted.

"Hello, Lord Darcy and . . . Lady Bridget." She did not conceal her surprise. "What brings you to the park together?"

"We thought it would be lovely to spend some time out of doors," Darcy replied. Just then, at that exact moment, there was a rumble of thunder. As if God was punishing them for the lie.

"Indeed." Lady Tunbridge looked from one to the other, as if she suspected that something suspicious was underfoot. Which it was. Which Bridget could not say. Which made her want to say it.

"I had gone to visit with the new duke over the matter of a shared border property line," Darcy said. She was quite sure that he was lying. The notion of Darcy *lying* was oddly thrilling. "I stayed for tea and then in the course of conversation over tea, Lady Bridget and I agreed that it might be nice to visit the park." There was another rumble of thunder. "Before the rain."

Lady Tunbridge appeared skeptical, even though Bridget thought Darcy was doing an admirable job with this fictitious story. This, oddly, raised her opinion of him. Perhaps he wasn't such a stuck-up, self-righteous man after all. Who knew such a common vice as lying could make a man more attractive?

"In America, it is far less rainy and unpredictable," she volunteered. "Here, it is so rare for it not to be raining, one must venture forth when one can."

She and Darcy were allied in a lie against Lady

Tunbridge and they had a secret to keep from the whole world. How intimate. It was thrilling enough to give her a shiver down her spine (*she* got shivers). This was a far, far better way to spend the day than practicing her penmanship or helping with preparations for the ball.

"And how are your sisters, Lady Bridget?"

"Why do you ask?"

Darcy coughed.

"Because it is the sort of benign question one asks when making polite conversation with an acquaintance on the street," Lady Tunbridge answered sharply. "Good Lord, what do they teach you in America? I daresay I have no wish to know."

"My sisters are *very* well, thank you."

"And Darcy, your brother . . ." She sighed, and both Darcy and Bridget straightened with interest. "I suppose you've heard the latest."

Beside her, Darcy tensed. She felt the muscles in his arm and leg go positively rigid and she was sure he was clenching his jaw . . . and yet somehow managing to speak.

"I have not."

"Well," Lady Tunbridge huffed. "I don't know if I can even say."

"And I'm sure I do not wish to know," he said stiffly.

"I wish to know," Bridget said, and everyone ignored her.

"Suit yourself, Lord Darcy. But you will find soon enough what your brother has been up to—and who he has been with."

It didn't seem possible, but Bridget felt the moment Darcy became positively stiff. And yet, by all outer appearances, he seemed exactly the same as always. She only knew this because they were sitting side by side and very close in this carriage. So close they were touching. When had that happened? She realized that, although he might always appear so calm, cool, and collected, perhaps he was not. Perhaps he got as flummoxed as the rest of them and only hid it better. Perhaps, if he lied so adeptly, he wasn't so perfect after all. The notion that he had feelings and flaws was surprisingly . . . intriguing.

"A good day to you both." Lady Tunbridge nodded firmly. "Lady Bridget, I look forward to the ball you're hosting with your sisters."

"What is this ball Lady Tunbridge mentioned?" Darcy asked as the carriage rolled away.

"Oh, just a little soiree we are planning for five hundred of our closest friends. And by friends I mean people we are desperately trying to impress."

"I think I recall seeing the invitation."

"You ought to attend, though it might be a disaster, in spite of all our best efforts. The duchess says planning and hosting a ball is an important skill every lady must possess. Thus, we are learning to plan and host a ball."

The duchess was right. A man of his position, especially given his political ambitions, required a wife who could be an asset socially. She would have to cultivate the right relationships, impress the right people, behave so impeccably that nothing bad could be said about her or, by extension, him. Lady Francesca fit the bill perfectly, which was why he had every intention of proposing to her.

This was why, even if he did lust after Lady Bridget, he could never act upon it. He could never propose to her. She and her family were regularly gossiped about for all the wrong reasons, and it was likely to become worse if this business with Amelia got out.

"This is, of course, in addition to our daily regimen of acquiring all the other essential qualities of a True Lady," she continued.

"And how does an aspiring true lady spend her day?"

Honestly, he wasn't entirely interested. But he found her chatter not altogether unpleasant—she did have a lovely voice—while he concentrated on driving the carriage and scanning the faces of everyone they passed, hoping to see Rupert or Amelia or both. He also noted the ever darkening clouds and low rumbles of thunder in the distance. A rainstorm was imminent.

"Well, for example, I must practice my pianoforte and singing for an hour each morning, in the event that we are called upon to perform at a musicale. This happens to coincide with the duchess's constitutional walk. I do not think that is a coincidence. After that, but before luncheon, we memorize pages of *Debrett's*. Did you know your great-grandfather was related to the Marquis of Wyndham? You and Lady Francesca are practically related."

"I did not," he said. "And we are not."

"You're welcome for the family history lesson. After that, my sisters and I are supposed to learn French, which is a hopeless and pointless prospect. The lessons are only livened up by our efforts to persuade our tutor to teach us grossly indelicate language, which he refuses to do. In the afternoon, we have dancing lessons because one must not only waltz, but know the steps to at least a dozen strange and intricate country dances. Through it all, I'm bloody starving."

Darcy had really heard only the last thing she said, and he responded to that.

"Why don't you eat something?" Darcy asked.

"Have you tried to fit into ladies' dresses these days?"

"I cannot say that I have," he said dryly.

"Then you would know why one must be in a constant state of starvation."

Darcy sensed that he had broached a sensitive subject and was all the more sure of it when he saw her shoulders shaking. Oh bloody hell, had he made her *cry*?

"I apologize if . . ." He paused, looking over at her. "Are you *laughing*?"

And with that she burst out laughing. And then he just knew what caused her such amusement.

"You're imagining me in a dress, aren't you?" he asked grimly.

"Perhaps," she said, still laughing. "You look rather fetching. I think a dark blue silk would suit you tremendously. It would go well with your complexion."

Darcy just stared at her. The things that went on in her head . . . And the things that came out of her mouth. It was always so unexpected. He found it oddly intriguing and even arousing.

"People don't tease you very much, do they?" she said.

"No," he said flatly. No one dared risk insulting him, an esteemed earl and valued member of Parliament. He knew he didn't exactly encourage such informality either. And then he added, "Rupert does, occasionally."

Lady Bridget surprised him once more. She placed her hand on his arm and said, "I think, Looord Darcy, that you might *need* me."

It was then that he took a wrong turn.

Chapter 13

We have not yet had a lesson on what to do if one finds oneself alone with a gentleman. We have only been instructed to avoid it at all costs.

LADY BRIDGET'S DIARY

Lady Bridget didn't say anything and neither did he. A silence ensued. A long, tortuous silence in which he became acutely aware of their surroundings: the birds in the trees, the wind rustling through the leaves, the distant rumble of thunder. He noticed the way her leg was pressed against his, the way her entire body, in fact, was pressed against his. It was because the curricle was small, he told himself, knowing better deep down.

Darcy also noticed that the sky was darkening and they had definitely taken a wrong turn. The wide fields and broad avenues full of people had given way to quiet paths through the forest.

"It seems that we might have taken a wrong turn," Bridget said. "But then again, I can't imagine that Looord Darcy would ever take a wrong turn."

"I know exactly where we are." He did; they were in Hyde Park. In the remote corner where, as Bridget might say, Danger Might Befall Them. But the dangers he had in mind had nothing to do with gangs of marauders with murderous intent. No, he feared being alone with her, and his desire for her, away from the watchful eye of the public.

There, he admitted it. He desired her. Wanted to lay her down and have his way with her.

"I don't suppose this is all part of an elaborate plot to abscond with me?"

"Do I strike you as the sort of man who absconds with gently bred young ladies?"

"No," she said glumly. As if she wanted him to abscond with her. He slowly exhaled.

"Rain seems imminent. We should turn back soon," he said, wondering if she detected the reluctance in his voice. If she did, would it even matter? Darcy reminded himself that she was in love with his brother. Who would never love her.

"Do you think we'll make it home before the storm?"

"Doubtful. I heard of a gazebo in this area where we might wait out the storm."

"I wonder if Amelia has returned. Perhaps she'll be there when we get back. Then I shall curl up with a pot of tea and a shawl and listen to her adventures." Bridget paused. "Gah, that makes me sound like an aged spinster."

He cracked a smile at that.

"Are you cold? Would you like my jacket?"

"I shall be fine, thank you."

"Suit yourself. I am only being chivalrous."

"That's the thing about chivalry. For a second you think it's about you and then you realize it's just how a gentleman treats all women. Which is a very good thing—manners, respect, not absconding with females against their will, etc., etc. But a woman wants to feel special, I suppose. Like she's the only one."

"I had never thought of it that way. It's how I was raised to behave. It's like breathing." He declined to mention that it was beaten into him by his tutors, his father, and the headmasters at Eton.

"Your instinct is to always be chivalrous?"

Not when you look at me like that. Not when you lean into me so close that I can breathe you in.

"Yes."

She just gave him a wicked smile that suggested she knew he was lying.

"Well, my instinct is not to be chivalrous or ladylike or well behaved at all," she said. He thought that she shouldn't say such things. Especially not when they were alone like this. "You may have noticed, but I regularly find myself doing the wrong thing. Why, I forget the correct forms of address, or when it's my turn to go in to supper, or all the steps to the quadrille, and I don't always walk with a certain air."

"I imagine the duchess is trying to remedy all that."

And it was a pity. Because a perfect lady would be simpering instead of treating him to wicked grins. A perfect lady would have spoken only of the weather. And a perfect lady would never tease him and call him Looord Darcy.

"She is. But that's not why I'm trying." He didn't say anything, afraid of what was coming next. "It was what you said at my first ball."

His throat tightened. He'd said something awful. But he could not explain to her that she had surprised him, aroused him, sent his world spinning off its axis. That he could not let anyone, least of all, Lady Francesca, suspect as much.

But now he bore some responsibility for a lively, engaging, and interesting young woman trying to shrink herself to fit into a little perfect box. So stuck-up gents like him and the rest of the haute ton would approve or, at the very least, have less to gossip about.

"Lady Bridget, I do apologize . . ."

"You already apologized."

"But then it was merely to mollify you. Now I know you better and I am sorry if you are trying to change yourself because of some stupid, idle chatter."

Spoken by a man who lusts after you and is afraid to acknowledge it. Because what will people say?

"Now that, Lord Darcy, is an apology."

They exchanged smiles. Nervous but kind smiles.

"Now I suppose I owe you an apology," she confessed. "I am sorry that I have called you Dreadful Darcy in my diary."

"You have wounded me terribly, but I'm certain I shall survive," he deadpanned. She laughed. He delighted in the sound.

And storm clouds loomed ahead.

It was about to rain. The air was thick with the possibility of it, the promise of it. Low rumbles of thunder foreshadowed the looming storm.

For the first time since Amelia left, Bridget started to fear for her sister. There had been no sign of her on the streets of Mayfair or in the park. No one they had spoken to provided even a hint of clue. And now their search would be hindered by the weather.

They had traveled far from the populated areas of the park into some remote corner. If Bridget hadn't been with Lord Darcy, Earl of Chivalry and Protector of Virtue, she might have been nervous to be here alone with a man.

But she was safe with him. Of course she was. She glanced over at the man beside her. He was tall, dark, strong, and inscrutable. Until a few hours earlier, he'd been a stranger at best. More often she considered him her nemesis, for he embodied everything about England and the haute ton that made her feel worthless. But the man she'd been with today was harder to hate. He was almost becoming . . . human.

"This will probably be a quick storm. We'll

seek shelter in the gazebo," he said, gesturing toward the structure looming ahead. It was built in a classical style and impossible to discern if it was new or a hundred years old. "You go ahead while I cover the carriage," he said. Then he jumped down and went around to help her alight.

She placed her hand in his.

Her gaze locked with his.

There was a rumble of thunder.

Neither of them hurried.

"And Lady Bridget—take my jacket. I insist."

He shrugged out of the gray wool coat and draped it around her shoulders. As he did, his fingers brushed against her skin. He might not feel shivers of desire and pleasure but she certainly did in that moment.

She dashed for the cover of the gazebo and glanced over her shoulder at him; he stood there, just in his white shirt and waistcoat, watching her with his dark eyes.

There was a strange fluttering in her stomach. She clung to his coat with one hand, wrapping it around her, and inhaled deeply. It carried his scent—like expensive wool, expensive soap, and something indescribably masculine. It affected her strangely, making her want to envelop herself in the jacket . . . or his arms.

There was another rumble of thunder, then an unholy crack of lightning, and the heavens exploded with a deluge of plump raindrops just as she reached shelter. She turned to watch Darcy as he rushed to cover the carriage, becoming soaked in the process.

When he was finished he walked toward her at a slow, steady pace; he didn't rush, not even in the downpour, as if he were impervious to the rain. So she had ample time to notice his long strides, and the way the wet breeches clung to his very muscular legs. Ladies weren't supposed to notice such things, probably, but she couldn't tear her gaze away—except to take note of the broad expanse of his chest, plain as day underneath his wet shirt. White linen was plastered against his arms, revealing the significant curve of his biceps and the broad outline of his shoulders.

His hair, usually brushed back, fell into his eyes, rakishly.

She had seen this before . . . that day at the garden party, more particularly during that unforgettable moment when she clung to him in the lake. But this was different because they were alone.

This was different because at some point during the day, she had been wounded by Rupert and the possibility that he'd run off with her sister. More to the point, she had ceased to loathe Darcy. Little by little, as the moments passed, he had lost some of his reserve. And now the look he gave her was raw, wanting.

Her breath caught in her throat.

It made her nervous. In an attempt to defuse the moment she gave a little laugh and said, "You look almost like Rupert with your hair like that. A bit more rakish, a bit more dashing."

His eyes flashed. Had she angered him? How could that have angered him? He took a step toward her.

"I'm nothing like Rupert," he said in a low voice.

"I know," she said in a whisper.

He took another step closer. His chest was inches from hers. She had to tilt her head back to look up at him. She had to, for his gaze had locked with hers, mesmerizing her, and she could not look away.

"You don't know," he said in a fierce whisper. Her heart began to pound, hard. *"You don't know."*

He placed one finger under her chin, tilting her face, her mouth, up to him. "Rupert will never do this."

And then he kissed her.

His mouth was firm on hers; yielding was the only option. There was no question of teasing or resisting. Because he was right: she didn't know *anything.* The world as she knew it had tipped upside down, spun around, all her truths were now in question.

Because Darcy was kissing her.

Never had she imagined that she would kiss him and that he would kiss like this. A toe-curling, knees-weakening, breathtaking kiss as the rain fell around them. All these feelings were new and wonderful and brought on by *Darcy.*

She placed her palm on his chest as if to stop

him. Or brace herself. His shirt was wet under her palm and she could feel his heart pounding. Oh God, he was feeling this as intensely as she. And that took her breath away.

And still, he kissed her. His mouth firm on hers, urging her to yield and open to him. And she did. Oh, she did.

There was thunder. There was lightning. And there was Darcy. Kissing her.

The world spun around her, whirling out of control, so she did the only sensible thing: she clung to him and kissed him back with a fervor that surprised her because this desire was intense and he was awakening it within her with every second of this kiss.

Good God, he had kissed her.

It was inevitable, he supposed. A man could take only so much of her wicked smiles and the feeling of her curvy little body, warm up against his. A man could take only so many quick glances at a woman's breasts before he needed to feel them.

She kept going on and on about Rupert, who would never desire her the way Darcy did, at this moment. He was consumed with it, possessed by it.

And he just broke.

Apparently there were only so many feelings and desires he could shove into a small ball, bury in the pit of his stomach, and ignore. He had reached his limit.

So he kissed her. And he took his time about it, too. No longer fighting his desires, he just gave in and enjoyed his downfall.

But sense and reason, rude little bastards, intruded.

She is a lady.

You are an unfeeling gentleman of honor. Get a bloody mistress, not a proper virgin.

Darcy broke away, suddenly, and she stumbled into his chest. He caught her and held her there and kissed her again.

Her hands slid up to his neck, fingers twining in his hair, then she clasped his jaw in her small hands. He needed to feel her, feel her skin, and so he clasped her face in his hands and then, like a fool, he moved lower until he felt her breast beneath his palm. He groaned softly, because to touch her was better than he imagined, because his cock was unbelievably hard and he wanted to explode with desire for this woman, and because they were kissing and they shouldn't be.

He actually started to entertain thoughts of taking her on the stone floor of the gazebo. In public.

What kind of Englishman was he? What kind of peer of the realm behaved so scandalously?

So much for his infamous self-control. What had he been thinking? One did not kiss gently bred ladies, especially if they were sisters to a duke and especially if the lady in question fancied his brother.

He hadn't been thinking. Correction: He was

thinking . . . about her breasts under his palm, and desperately wanting to close the small distance between them. And nothing else.

He stopped. He had to.

Darcy opened his mouth to say, *I beg your pardon*, or something to that effect. But the words never crossed his lips. He wasn't sorry.

He wasn't sorry *at all*.

And then he smiled. A roguish smile even. For a moment there, he had cast off *Lord Darcy* and all its attendant responsibilities and was just a man, kissing a pretty girl in a rainstorm. For a second he felt like . . . lightning or something powerful, and uncontainable. And he felt . . . light.

"You . . ." Bridget said, breathlessly. *He had left her breathless. Good.*

"Yes."

". . . just kissed me?" *He had addled her wits. Good.*

"You did not imagine it," he confirmed. His heart was still pounding.

"And it was. . . ."

He lifted one brow.

". . . not what I expected."

"Lady Bridget—"

"You cannot call me *lady* at a time like this," she cried.

And then Lord Darcy returned, bringing back common sense. He straightened, and he was sure his expression sobered.

"You are still a lady, even though I took a liberty."

"It wasn't a liberty! It was a devastatingly romantic kiss in a rainstorm. When Amelia reads about it in my diary she will accuse me of making it up, it's so perfect. And you cannot go back to being all proper and stuffy after *that*."

"Very well, Bridget." *Devastatingly romantic and perfect kiss. Well done, man.*

"Lord Darcy."

"Now, Bridget you can't be all proper and stuffy after *that*."

She quirked a smile. "Are you teasing me?"

"It seems so. I am as shocked as you."

"We kissed and I don't even know your Christian name."

"Colin Fitzwilliam Wright, Lord Darcy." And then he bowed. And she laughed. And he wanted to kiss her again. Her hair was a wreck and her lips were swollen from his kiss. And he was sorry to note that the rain had lessened to a misty drizzle and this moment was coming to a close.

"We ought to go," he said reluctantly. "I fear the wrath of the duchess. And we do not want anyone to suspect anything untoward."

"No, we wouldn't want that, now would we?" Bridget replied. He didn't miss the sharpness in her voice. He had clearly said the wrong thing and ruined the moment. He told himself it was for the best.

Chapter 14

HE KISSED ME.
Darcy. Kissed. Me.
LADY BRIDGET'S DIARY

*A*fter seeing Lady Bridget home, and learning that Lady Amelia was still at large, Darcy returned to his own residence, having matters to attend to there. Matters such as pouring a large glass of brandy and trying to make sense of the fact that he had kissed Bridget. And liked it. More than liked it.

Out of habit, he looked up at the portrait of his father. He left that glaring, scowling portrait as a reminder to always do his duty toward the estate and the family name. Nothing like a father's anger and disappointment to keep a son in line.

But if his father only knew that his younger son didn't care for women and that his distinguished heir had done something so common as to nearly ravish a woman in a park, he would probably drop dead from an apoplexy all over again.

Darcy couldn't say he regretted it, though. And that was the problem he was contemplating when Rupert returned.

He strolled in, poured himself a brandy as well, and took a seat.

"Where have you been?" Darcy asked. His voice was calm and measured and somehow did not reveal the turmoil within. Or so he hoped.

"Out," Rupert said flatly.

"I figured that much."

"I just walked through London . . . getting lost . . . thinking . . . Trying to find a way to solve this problem," Rupert said. He sighed.

"You know I will help you."

"I know. But you always solve everyone's problems. And I should start taking care of my own. And I think I know a way out. It was my original plan and I think it's the best."

"What is it?"

"I should marry. If the blackmailer does reveal the truth, I shall at least have the sort of cover that makes the story implausible."

"An excellent plan. And I suppose a wife's dowry will also give you funds to pay that blackmailer."

"The thought crossed my mind," Rupert said, his mouth in a grim line. He clearly did not like this plan, but he was clearly resigned to it.

"Who did you have in mind to be the lucky

woman?" No, he couldn't keep the note of sarcasm out of his voice. But Rupert didn't seem to detect it.

"Lady Bridget."

But of course. Darcy's heart stopped, paused really, for just a moment. Of course his brother was plotting a marriage of convenience with the woman he'd just lost all self-control with. And liked it. That was the worst part. Holidays were going to be torture if Rupert married her.

"Well?"

"Does it matter what I think?"

"Of course it does! You're my brother. And I know you were concerned about welcoming Americans to the family. I believe you did echo the popular sentiment that their presence here marked the downfall of civilization."

"Why Lady Bridget then?"

Because of the way she kisses. Because of the way she feels. Because of the way she teases and laughs and makes me feel human again.

"She and I get along. I do quite like her and I think she fancies me."

"It is a sound plan," Darcy said, his voice only a little bit strangled. He drained the last of his brandy, immediately refilled his glass, and changed the subject.

"I don't suppose you saw Lady Amelia while you were out?"

"American Amelia? No, why do you ask?"

"It is nothing."

"It is not nothing for you to inquire about

the Americans whom you so loathe," Rupert pointed out.

But Darcy was now growing even more concerned. It was one thing when Lady Amelia might have been gallivanting around with Rupert, and he realized he had convinced himself that they were together. It would have been bad, but not disastrous.

But now the hour was growing late and Lady Amelia was at large, presumably without a protector.

"A gently bred lady is lost in the city of London, presumably alone. I have spent the whole day searching for her. And for you."

"I honestly do not know anything. I didn't see her," Rupert said. "How is Lady Bridget handling it?"

"She is fine. We spent a few hours looking for you both."

"Did you now?" Rupert asked, that familiar, teasing glint in his eye. "You. And Lady Bridget. Alone. How was it?"

Wonderful. Horrible. Full of angst, lust, and . . . fun. Yes, that was the word he was looking for. Even when she was driving him mad with her curious notions of chivalry or ridiculous image of him in a dress, he had . . . fun. And it was wrong to feel thusly when beloved family members were in trouble. And when there were estate matters to attend to and he hadn't yet solved all the problems in the world. It was wrong, all of it.

"It was fine."

"She doesn't like you, I'm afraid," Rupert said. "Did you know she calls you Dreadful Darcy in her diary?"

"Yes, actually."

"You don't find that funny?"

"I'm not known for my sense of humor."

"Anyone would find it funny. Unless . . ." Rupert's eyes widened. "Unless it hurts your feelings. Because you like her."

"Don't be ridiculous."

Rupert just grinned. As if he didn't have massive, life-ruining problems to deal with. Darcy was glad to see his brother have a reason to smile. But he was vastly relieved when Danvers, the butler, interrupted.

"My Lord, this was left in the carriage."

It was Amelia's London guidebook, presented on a silver tray. He took one look at it and knew how he would spend the rest of the day and evening and it would not be discussing his feelings regarding Lady Bridget with anyone, least of all Rupert. Who planned to marry her.

I daresay everyone is gossiping about the inconceivable sight of Darcy and myself out for a pleasant outing in the park today. As long as they are not gossiping about Amelia. Who has still not returned!

To say we are worried about her is a vast understatement of epic proportions.

LADY BRIDGET'S DIARY

In a drawing room across town, Lady Francesca closed the drawing room door and turned to her guests.

Miss Mulberry and Miss Montague were pouring tea and eating cakes and chattering away as if they had no idea of the gravity of the situation. No idea that her world was collapsing.

"I have a dire situation," Lady Francesca said, taking a seat and commanding the attention of her guests, er, friends. They immediately gave her their attention.

"Were you ruined?" Miss Mulberry asked breathlessly.

"Don't be silly. I would never allow that to happen," she scoffed at her friend's stupid idea. Unless it wasn't a stupid idea at all, and she *made* it happen. Being caught in a compromising position was the swiftest way to the altar, especially when caught with a man as upstanding and honorable as Darcy. She tucked the idea away in the back of her mind.

"Is it your hair?" Miss Montague asked, concerned.

"What's wrong with my hair?" Francesca's hand flew up to gently touch the elegant coiffure her maid had done. It was a new style, the very latest from the French magazines.

"Nothing," both girls chimed quickly.

Francesca scowled, then remembered how that caused wrinkles, and immediately composed herself.

"It's Darcy."

"Oh, did he propose?"

Dear Lord, please save her from her silly little friends.

"Would that really be a dire situation?" She ground her teeth. "It is Darcy. And he has *not* proposed. And he seems to have taken a liking to . . . *Lady Bridget*."

Both girls made appropriate faces of shock, horror, and disapproval.

"First he asked her to waltz."

"You waltz with people all the time," Miss Montague pointed out.

"Yes, but Darcy doesn't."

"Oh, right."

"Then he took her to Rotten Row where anyone—no, *everyone*—would see them."

Both girls ooohed appropriately. Then Miss Mulberry said, "Wait, what does this mean?"

"It means we have to do something drastic to make him forget any ridiculous ideas or *feelings* he might have for Lady Bridget. And then I must get him to propose."

"How are we going to do that?"

"I don't know," Lady Francesca admitted. "But when I do have an idea, I vow I will act swiftly."

Chapter 15

Returned sisters: 1
Relieved family members: 4
Explanations of where she has been: 0
Times spent reliving kiss with Darcy: 247
                    LADY BRIDGET'S DIARY

There were five ladies gathered in the blue drawing room. Claire sat on a chair, reading some mathematical paper whilst sipping tea. Amelia lay on the settee, staring glumly at the ceiling and tormenting them all with her silence. Bridget wrote in her diary. Miss Green embroidered, and the duchess pored over the gossip columns in at least six different newspapers to determine whether Amelia's escape had been reported.

"*The Morning Post* reported on your absence at the ball, Amelia," Josephine said, frowning, holding a copy of the paper. They had to abruptly cancel their appearance at a ball last night, due to Amelia's absence. They put it about that she had been gravely ill, in her bed, at home. "And *The London Weekly* is hinting at an exposé," Josephine said. "I shudder to think what their gossip columnist has dug up. She is ruthless."

"No one saw me," Amelia said.

"That you know of," Josephine said, leveling a stare over the pages of *The London Weekly*.

"And I didn't do anything scandalous," Amelia added.

"Were you out of doors without a chaperone?" Josephine asked, blinking frequently, and they all knew where this was leading.

A staring contest and battle of wills ensued between the duchess and Amelia. It was of more interest than Claire's mathematical paper or the recording of Bridget's first real kiss.

"Who do you think will blink first?" Bridget whispered.

"I'm betting on Amelia," Claire whispered back.

"I don't know. Josephine has spent decades staring people down," Bridget whispered.

In the end, it was Amelia who broke. She blinked away a tear or two and turned back to staring at the ceiling. A different Amelia had returned last night: one who was more reserved, more poised, more centered. She had cut her hair. There was an air of something wistful about her.

They were all dying to know where she had been—and with whom, because no one believed that she'd just been on her own—but not a word crossed her lips.

"Claire, what are you reading that has your cheeks positively pink?" the duchess asked.

"Nothing. Just an article from a mathematical journal."

"Really?" Bridget peered over her shoulder. "Oh. It really is about mathematics. But you have been reading for quite some time and yet you are only on the second page."

Bridget eyed her sister. Was she woolgathering? Were her daydreams making her blush?

"It is very challenging material," Claire replied. The duchess just sighed. It was the weary sigh of a woman who had to find husbands for three unconventional and unpolished girls, one of whom was reading a paper on advanced mathematics. For pleasure. "If you are looking for something more interesting, why don't you ask Bridget what she is writing about in her diary?"

"Her cheeks are also pink," Amelia noted. "What did you do yesterday, Bridget?"

"I spent the whole afternoon traipsing around London searching for you."

"In the company of Lord Darcy," Claire added, with a smug smile.

"Dreadful Loooord Darcy," Amelia said.

"You know his reputation. You can imagine how tedious the day was. We went to Hyde Park before being caught in a thunderstorm. Then we returned. Nothing remotely interesting occurred."

This of course was a hideous lie. The most momentous thing had occurred. Darcy had become . . . human. He had become more than a man with a disapproving stare, hurtful words, or the embodiment of propriety. But really, really—and this was what was making her cheeks turn pink—what happened was that she had become aware of him as a man. A tall, dark, and brooding man with pounding heart and a hard chest, who murmured devastating things and kissed her.

Her. Bridget Cavendish, the girl who fell.

This paragon of virtue and English gentlemanliness had desired her. Even though she wasn't sure whether a marchioness or a viscountess would go in to dinner first, and she didn't know all the steps to the quadrille, and she had to look up the proper form of address for an earl when writing a letter. Not that she wrote letters to earls. But that was beside the point.

For one shimmering, sparkling, raining moment, Darcy desired her.

And yet she was in love with his brother. Why, just three pages earlier in her diary, she had written:

Mrs. Rupert Wright
Mrs. Rupert Wright
Mrs. Rupert Wright
Mrs. Rupert Wright

But she had not heard from Rupert—or Darcy, for that matter, since yesterday. Amelia refused to say whom she had spent the day with, so

Bridget couldn't help but wonder if her sister had been with the man Bridget was in love with.

Or loved?

Verb tenses. Not trifling things. So very significant.

She wondered what Darcy thought of the events of yesterday. Or rather, the kiss. Their kiss. Who cared in the slightest what he thought of anything other than their devastatingly romantic kiss? She knew, deep in her bones, that a man like Darcy did not kiss a woman like her lightly.

Was he horrified by his sudden lack of self-restraint?

Did he care for her, or had she just vexed him into kissing her?

Was the kiss a momentary lapse of good judgment?

Did he regret behaving like a dashing rogue and kissing her until her knees were weak?

Did he think less of her because she did not refuse him?

And now she might have ruined everything because she was quite certain that a True Lady would not allow liberties with a gentleman to whom she was not wed or betrothed, and they ought not act so wantonly in public. Or at all.

And then there was the matter of her feelings. Complicated, utterly uncertain, completely confused feelings.

Bridget flipped through the previous pages of her diary, words jumping out at her: "crashing bore," "he's the worst," "Rupert makes my pulse quicken," "dreadful, dull, Darcy." And then in more recent pages, with the ink still fresh: "*HE KISSED ME.*"

A kiss complicated everything. She no longer knew how to think of Darcy or Rupert in her head . . . or in her heart, to be honest.

And she would have to live with all these questions and confusion because she couldn't possibly call on him herself, and who knew when he might deign to call upon her?

The butler Pendleton opened the door. "Lord Darcy is here. Are you at home?"

Of course he would have such perfect timing.

The five ladies glanced around the drawing room—which was strewn with Miss Green's embroidery things, a thick stack of newssheets, and some pillows on the floor. Claire was slouching in the chair. Amelia was lounging— languishing—on the settee with her ankles exposed. Bridget's hair was a mess, having hastily been pinned up, but then again it always was. A tea tray was on the table, but one that had been devastated by five parched and famished ladies.

They all glanced at one another, panic wild in their eyes.

"We shall need a moment, Pendleton," the duchess said, utterly poised in spite of the mess. "Send a maid for this tray and please bring round a fresh one."

The embroidery was shoved in a basket, which was shoved behind a turquoise upholstered chair. Amelia sat up like a lady with a stack of books on

her head, Claire put her things away and Bridget
shoved her diary under a seat cushion.

Then she pinched her cheeks.

"They're already pink, Bridget," Claire said
with a smirk.

"Is it because of Loooord Darcy?" Amelia
asked, drawing out the *oooo*'s just to vex her.

"Do shut up, Amelia."

"Language, Lady Bridget," the duchess ad-
monished.

Bridget heaved a sigh, the long-suffering sigh
of the sibling who got caught even though the
other provoked it.

Then all the ladies stood and turned their attention to the door.

And there he was.

Loooord Darcy.

Tall, proud, perfect. He paused in the doorway. Was that a flash of panic in his eyes when
faced with the prospect of three unruly sisters,
the fearsome duchess, and her faithful companion? Five women, five sets of eyes all on him.
Waiting. Expecting.

Bridget suddenly found it difficult to breathe.
Their parting had been formal and inconclusive
and surrounded by people, so there hadn't been
any secret message exchanged via whispered
words or pleading gazes and the like. He was as
inscrutable as ever and gave her no clue as to his
innermost thoughts and feelings.

They all sat down. Darcy, of course, took a seat
on the chair with Bridget's diary tucked under

the cushion, which caused Amelia to giggle, Bridget to kick her in the ankle, and the duchess to glare at them both.

"Good day, Lord Darcy," Claire asked. "To what do we owe the pleasure?"

Now Bridget's heart was racing. Would he say that he was calling to see her? Would he ask for a moment alone? Would he apologize for the kiss or would he propose? If so, what would she say? She was still half in love with Rupert, probably.

"I have come to see how Lady Amelia is faring," he replied. "I am glad you have returned safely."

None of the above. That was the worst.

"I am quite well, thank you," Amelia answered. But she wasn't quite well. She seemed wistful.

"I am glad to hear it."

"We are so grateful that you accompanied Bridget on the search yesterday," Claire said.

"It was my pleasure," he murmured, his eyes locked with Bridget's. The intensity of the look between them left little doubt in her mind that he was thinking of the kiss and speaking of the kiss. She felt warm and she felt an ache of longing for more. Was she blushing? Dear God, she hoped not.

She bit her lip, wanting to ask approximately 724 questions. Her every heartbeat was a question.

Ba-bump, what does this mean?
Ba-bump, will it happen again?

Ba-bump, what are you thinking, you madly inscrutable man?

Ba-bump, why do I even care in the slightest?

"I do hope we can be assured of your discretion," Josephine drawled.

Darcy glanced at her, then to Bridget.

"Of course. It would be a pity for a lady's prospects to be tarnished because of unfounded rumors."

Bridget felt a prickling sensation along her skin. She had the peculiar feeling he wasn't speaking just of Lady Amelia's great adventure, but of their mad kiss in the rain. He must only care about her prospects if he wasn't going to propose—which was fine, she supposed, as she had no intention of marrying him just because he once kissed her.

But still.

She found herself feeling dismayed.

"You're a good man, Darcy. Now how is that scoundrel of a brother of yours?"

"As much a scoundrel as ever, in spite of my efforts to keep him from the falling over the brink into disaster and ruin."

"He is fortunate to have your support," Josephine said. "But what he really needs is a wife."

"He is thinking of marrying, finally," Darcy said, his eyes locked on hers.

"Bridget has taken a liking to him," Claire said, smirking.

Oh, that was the wrong thing to say. Or was it? There was no measurable difference in his expression. There was no indication that he gave one whit that the woman he had passionately and illicitly kissed in a rainstorm actually preferred his brother.

There wasn't even the slightest shift in tone when he said, "I have noticed."

She couldn't quite hold his gaze now. Instead she looked pleadingly at the duchess, who flashed her the briefest and smallest of smiles before turning to their guest.

"What of your prospects, Darcy? Have you proposed to Lady Francesca yet?"

Bridget tried to take a page from his book and adopt what she hoped was an inscrutable expression. Darcy and Lady Francesca were perfect together: they knew all the rules of society and had no trouble obeying them. But she wondered what Francesca would think of Darcy visiting with her misfit family. How would Francesca feel if she knew her intended was kissing another woman . . . a girl like her. She probably wouldn't like it at all.

"Pardon me if I will refrain from gossiping about my personal affairs," he said diplomatically, which only fanned the flames of Bridget's curiosity.

"I ask only because I have three girls to get married off," the duchess said, as if it were the cruelest hardship imaginable.

"I will never marry," Amelia said dramatically.

"What happened yesterday?" Claire asked.

"Nothing," Amelia declared. "Everything."

Well, that summed it up quite nicely, Bridget thought.

> Things I dislike about Dreadful Darcy
>
> *I can never tell what the man is thinking. This is especially vexing after our passionate kiss. But then again, I don't even know what I am thinking! Why, I'm still in love with Rupert . . . right?*
>
> *Rupert, who might have spent the whole day gallivanting and doing God knows what with my sister.*
>
> LADY BRIDGET'S DIARY

Darcy had taken his leave of the ladies when he encountered the duke in the foyer. He'd just been out for a long horseback ride and invited Darcy to join him for a drink.

They settled into the library, a masculine space with chairs of the proper size, unlike the delicate twigs and pillows called chairs in the drawing room. The late duke had left an excellent whiskey and they enjoyed it now.

"I came to see how yesterday's situation resolved," Darcy began.

"Amelia returned on her own last night," Durham answered. "She's fine. Cut her hair."

"I hadn't noticed."

"I hadn't either. But all the women did and there was a fit of hysterics about it. Which is something I happen to be used to. It's why I have aged beyond my years." The duke took a sip of his drink and closed his eyes. "You don't have sisters, do you?"

"Just one brother."

"Thank God that you don't have sisters," the duke said, though Darcy had the distinct impression he adored his. "They are a plague upon a man's sanity."

"I can imagine," Darcy murmured, thinking of how Lady Bridget was a plague upon his sanity and self-restraint.

"One minute they are begging you to take them to England so they can wear pretty dresses and be called lady and be fancy. And once you bring them halfway around the world, one of them runs away and all of them want to go back to America."

Lady Bridget wanted to leave England? It made sense; she had struggled to fit in, thanks to people like him who had resented their difference because it made him examine his own behavior. Darcy sipped his drink and refused to consider why he felt something that might be labeled alarm at the prospect of her leaving.

"What does it matter what they want?"

"Spoken by a man who does not have sisters," the duke said, laughing. The dukedom might be an awesome responsibility, but he imagined it paled in contrast to shepherding three beautiful, unruly sisters through life.

"I see that you care greatly for them."

"I'd do anything for them." He sighed. "And that's the problem."

Darcy understood perfectly. Too perfectly.

He thought of his own brother, and the delicate and dangerous situation he found himself in. Blackmail for unnatural acts was no laughing matter, and it wasn't something that could be swept aside easily, like trifling gaming debts or arriving drunk to Almack's.

They *would* stop the blackmailer. And they would have to stop any rumors. A wife was the perfect cover. Especially a wife like Lady Bridget, whom Rupert did care for and who adored him.

Never mind that Darcy was stricken with the urge to say no and slam his fist down when he thought about it. He had kissed her and it had done something to him; it had unlocked the box where he ruthlessly shoved anything like feelings, and now they threatened to burst out, spill over, and wreak havoc on his life.

And he could not imagine a greater torture than seeing her as his brother's wife. His brother, who would probably never kiss her the way Darcy had done.

But he wouldn't stop the match either.

From their earliest days, Darcy always looked out for his younger brother. It had always been his role to explain away the problems, or take the punishment for his little brother, or help him in whatever scrapes he got into as a young man. That bond and those roles had only strengthened as the years passed. Rupert was his only family.

That would not change now.

"I hope your brother is not as much trouble as my three sisters," Durham said. He had no idea.

"Not for lack of trying," Darcy said dryly. "How are you settling in?"

"I think you're the only person to ask me that who is interested in a truthful answer. This duke business is something else. Complaints from tenants I've never met, repairs needed on estates I've never been to, absurd social rules that I need to know, the pressure to wed—and not for pleasure but for business. Much more complicated than horses."

Darcy had learned to be adept at all facets of being a titled gentleman. His father had spent hours, days, months, years, lecturing him on the duties of managing their vast estates, dragging him along to tenant visits and, upon occasion, using beatings to make sure the information stuck.

Darcy learned how to stifle his own feelings, to mask his expression, and to put duty to the estate above all else, particularly any personal desire.

It was only in this moment that he realized that Durham probably had no one to show him how to be Durham, other than the duchess, which only made things worse.

"Do you have an estate manager?"

"Crowley or some fellow. And the duchess, of course."

Both men drank, because the duchess was the

kind of terrifying matron who drove a man to drink. It was either that or admit to being afraid.

"I am happy to be of assistance if you require it. We can always meet at White's for a drink as well."

"I've heard of White's. Apparently I am a member."

"No women allowed," Darcy said, allowing himself a grin.

"Just what I need," the duke said, grinning. "I shall see you there."

Chapter 16

According to the duchess, a True Lady is one who knows how to plan and host a ball for five hundred people. I asked Rupert if that was something he looked for in a wife and he just laughed and said he loved parties.

LADY BRIDGET'S DIARY

The Cavendish family had spent hours, days, weeks planning their first ball. According to the duchess, it was vitally important that all the sisters become accomplished hostesses so that they might be an asset to the husbands they might one day (soon, please Lord, soon) acquire. Claire couldn't care less about any of it, though she was helpful with any sums, such as how many bottles of champagne to order if they invited six hundred people and most of them agreed to attend.

Amelia's contributions consisted of absurd suggestions for entertainments: Gypsy fortune-tellers in the ladies' retiring room or tightrope walkers from Astley's Amphitheatre.

But Bridget devoted herself to the planning of everything, from the guest list (Rupert's was the first name she wrote down), to the menus ("Do you think that is a bit much?" the duchess inquired upon seeing her three-page list. "You made me write it before lunch," Bridget explained.). She might not have been able to successfully adhere to her reducing diet, or master French, or sing on key, but being a hostess seemed like a ladylike task that she could do.

She and her sisters had no help from their brother. James, being a useless male, just said yes to whatever was asked.

"Would you rather serve ratafia or punch?" Bridget asked.

"Yes."

"Your Grace, do you think we should have silver or gold as part of the color scheme?" the duchess asked, looking down her nose at him.

"Yes, Your Grace," he murmured, without looking up from the sporting pages of the newssheet.

"Your Grace, it is vitally important that we throw a ball," Josephine said, revealing her irritation. It was, she informed them, a crucial part of their ongoing campaign to woo high society. Apparently it was not enough to possess an old and prestigious title, or pots of money. One needed a pristine reputation and the favor of the movers and shakers in the haute ton.

Just in case, say, they needed to weather a scandal.

Which, thanks to Amelia, they did.

Their ball marked their first appearance after they abruptly canceled their attendance at a soiree due to Amelia's adventure. They had blamed it on a sudden and dire illness. And now it was all anyone wished to discuss.

An hour after the ball began, it became clear that while everyone accepted the excuse, no one believed it.

Bridget never thought she'd long to discuss the weather, but after a certain point, she was desperate to discuss anything other than her sister's "precious health." No one complimented the décor, or the menu, or the orchestra, or any of the little details she had so carefully attended to. It was maddening.

The conversations invariably followed the same pattern.

"Lady Amelia, we are so glad to see you have recovered from your sudden illness," someone would say.

"Your very sudden, very mysterious illness," someone else would say with a sly wink and a knowing smile. "From which you have made a most dramatic recovery."

"I am not quite myself again," Amelia replied, and it was the truth. But no one in the family knew why or where she had been. Or what had changed her. For once, Amelia wasn't talking, and Claire and Bridget had spent a good hour devising schemes to make her talk, to no avail.

"You must have been terribly worried for your sister," someone would invariably say.

"You cannot imagine how much," Bridget would answer. And then her thoughts would stray to the day she had spent searching for her sister, which somehow involved passionately kissing Lord Darcy.

And then she would think about that kiss . . .

And then she would wonder what it all meant.

Did she dare just ask him?

Perhaps, if he deigned to arrive. Both Darcy and Rupert had agreed to attend, but had yet to make an appearance. She was on tenterhooks waiting for them, and their friendly, familiar faces.

In fact, there were very few familiar or friendly faces in the crowd.

"Duchess, have you invited all of our enemies?" Claire inquired after Lord Fox and Lady Francesca made their entrance.

"'Enemies' is such a strong word, dear." But she smiled in that sharp and knowing way of hers.

"Keep your friends close and your enemies closer," Bridget quipped.

"Precisely. If you are to stay here, you need to win these people over. Simply being Durham is not enough," Josephine said. And then turning to the next guest, she greeted him warmly. "Ah, Mr. Collins! We are so pleased to have you join us this evening. The ladies cannot express how delighted they are that you could join us."

Indeed, they could not.

"I look forward to dancing with all my cousins. We hardly get such delights as this at the vicarage and I shall be sure to enjoy it."

The ladies were less than enthralled with the prospect.

A few hours later, Bridget found herself lingering along the perimeter of the ballroom, in an endless round of polite chatter with her guests and striving to avoid Mr. Collins. Earlier, he had penciled his name on her dance card (bad) and pinched her cheek (worse) and said he thought women were too slender these days and he was glad she bucked fashion (the very worst).

She sought out her sisters. Claire was speaking with Lord Fox (!), Amelia was being introduced to a gentleman Bridget didn't recognize (?), James had disappeared, and Rupert was nowhere to be found, which Bridget found troubling. He had promised he would attend and claim two dances. Here she was, her dance card glaringly empty, save for a few obligatory dances with unappealing prospects. Ahem, Mr. Collins. She had learned the hard way that ladies did not refuse gentlemen's invitations to dance.

But there was Darcy threading his way through the crowd, with his eyes set upon her. Her heart started to pound, hard and slow in her chest. He was something else entirely in his evening clothes—he was even more Darcy-ish, if such a thing was possible. Everything was black and white and starched and fitted and perfect.

It was hard to believe this man had been overcome with passion for her. She couldn't imagine him overcome with passion for anything and yet . . . She pressed her fingers to her lips, remembering. She almost wanted it to happen again, just so she could be sure. Or did she need it to happen again because she just *needed* to feel that wanted again?

Darcy stood before her, gazing down intensely with those dark eyes of his. Making all thought, rational and otherwise, flee.

"Good evening, Lady Bridget."

How had she never noticed how low his voice was? How had she not noticed the way it made her tremble slightly?

"Good evening, Lord Darcy."

Was that the faintest hint of a smile? Rupert laughed so easily, but his brother . . . his expressions might as well have been carved in granite. That faint upturn of his lips was some sort of triumph. She felt elated.

"How are you enjoying this evening?" she asked, ever the polite hostess.

"Very well. You and your sisters have done an excellent job planning this affair."

Bridget leaned in close to confide in him and caught the scent of his jacket, which reminded her of the time she had worn his coat . . . and then for a moment she forgot what to say. "It was mostly the duchess and myself. Claire couldn't be bothered, and if Amelia had her way, there would be a tightrope strung up between the chandeliers."

"I actually would have liked to see that," he remarked, glancing up to the ceiling.

"I as well, though the duchess nearly had an apoplexy when Amelia made the suggestion."

"I don't suppose your sister has revealed anything about her day spent abed whilst gravely ill from a malady from which she has miraculously recovered?"

She smiled. She and Darcy shared a secret. Two secrets. Whoever thought she would share secrets with a man like him? It made her feel so connected to him.

"She has not breathed a word. It is highly unusual for her."

And then Darcy said something that surprised her. In fact, he leaned in close to whisper in her ear.

"She was not with Rupert," he said softly. And suddenly the air between them changed. If it had been charged before, it was positively electric now. She didn't know what to make of this feeling. She didn't know what to say.

She just knew that her heart leapt because Amelia had not been with Rupert, which meant that perhaps she still had a chance with him.

But then why did she feel a bolt of lust when Darcy approached?

"Oh, I didn't know," she replied. "Will he be here tonight?"

"He said he would be late."

She had been counting on Rupert to be here especially because she was nervous to be hosting her first ball. He made her laugh and feel at ease. He was her friend. She wrote *Rupert and Bridget* in her diary an embarrassing number of times and fancied marrying him.

But he had never kissed her. Not once, not even a little, and not at all the way Darcy had done, with all the fierceness of long-restrained passions finally bursting free.

Passions that seemed to have been gathered and restrained.

She couldn't make sense of this man, or her feelings for him.

And then he surprised her again.

Darcy ought to be used to this feeling of war within him: there was the desire to do one thing, cold rationality demanding he do another. Rupert wished to wed her. And Darcy wished to bed her.

Rupert had gone out and said he would arrive at the ball late. Darcy forced himself not to be the first guest in attendance, forced himself not to make a beeline for Bridget, forced himself again and again to stop thinking about her.

Her lips. Her sighs.

Her everything.

No.

He should have avoided the ball this evening, but that seemed wrong. For one thing, showing his support for the family after befriending the duke and nearly ravishing Bridget was the least he could do. But the truth was he wanted to see Bridget. And he wanted to test himself.

Could he be near her and not want her?

He ought to start thinking of her as Rupert's, not his. Never his.

But here he was, standing before her, full of wanting.

He had complimented the hostess, they had spoken briefly of mutual acquaintances, and now he was free to make his excuses and go find a strong drink and high-stakes game of cards.

But he didn't want to leave her. Not yet. Not because he had seen her standing along the perimeter of the ballroom alone, watching everyone else have a marvelous time at her party.

Because, if he were being honest, Darcy wanted to feel her in his arms again, and there was only one socially acceptable way to do that.

"Would you care to dance, Lady Bridget?"

She appeared shocked. Rightly so.

"But you do not dance."

So this was what it felt like to have a knife wound to the heart. God, and this was the second time he had asked her to dance. And the second time she refused. No wonder he made a habit of avoiding dancing entirely.

"Right."

"But it is the proper thing to ask me," she remarked, smiling. "And of course you always do the proper thing."

"Indeed."

He was vastly relieved that she should interpret it that way, was he not? She still knew nothing of his tortured feelings, still thought him a right proper stick-in-the-mud. And he would still, possibly, get to dance with her and hold her in his arms.

This was perfect, was it not?

"I would hate to tempt you into behaving improperly," she said softly, smiling wickedly, and it did things to him. Then she added softly, "Again."

Tempt me. He experienced a perverse desire to have a monumental test of his self-control and personal resolve.

"My self-control is legendary," he told her. And himself.

"Is it?" She gave him a knowing smile that spoke of what had happened between them in the gazebo in the rain that afternoon . . . Proper English gentlemen didn't do such things, and they certainly didn't talk about it if they did.

"Well, possibly merely mythical," he said quietly, so only she could hear. A blush stole across her cheeks.

"Shall we?"

He swept her into his arms. Darcy gently clasped her gloved hand and placed his other hand on the small of her back. Memories flooded his brain, such as how she felt flush against him. The pressure of his palm must have been too much; he was out of practice. She was right; he did not dance. She stumbled a little, nearly into him. Her gaze flew up to his.

"My apologies."

"It's all right," she said softly.

The orchestra launched into a song, and they began to move in time to the music. Mostly. It was easy enough for a gentleman to lead a waltz; the steps were simple, but it was damn hard to navigate around all the other dancers when one was driven to distraction by his dancing partner, who was, admittedly, not an excellent dancer herself.

They were a disaster together.

Her eyes were so very blue.

That he was fixated on the blueness of her eyes was just one reason they were a disaster together. They had a few near-miss collisions with other couples on the dance floor. In effort to avoid them, she stepped on his feet. Her skirts tangled around their legs. They stumbled slightly. Her breasts brushed against his chest and she laughed nervously.

He wanted to die. Not only was this a mockery of dancing, the entire ton was watching this self-inflicted torture. All because he wanted to bed her. Bury himself inside her. Lose himself in her. Feel everything until he exploded from the intensity to it. Then, perhaps, he could return to his calm, orderly, unfeeling existence.

But he could not. That would require marriage. That would interfere with his plans, with Rupert's plans.

And this waltz was doing *nothing* to diminish his desire for her—quite the contrary, in fact. And it was doing everything to torture and embarrass him, so much so that marrying Lady Bridget seemed like a more reasonable way to hold her.

"You are quiet," he said. For once her every thought wasn't tumbling out of her plump mouth, and it wasn't obvious what thoughts were jumbling through her head. It was those very qualities that had at first repelled him and now he missed them desperately. Missed her.

"I am too busy feeling."

"What are you, ahem, uh, feeling?"

"Like I should have practiced waltzing more. But then perhaps not. Is it horribly wanton that I enjoy stumbling against you?"

"Yes," he rasped.

"Do you disapprove, Lord Darcy?"

Tempting minx. She was deliberately torturing him, he was certain of it. When he spoke, his voice was rough, "I am in no position to judge."

Rather than satiate his desire to hold her, he only wanted her more.

Bloody hell.

"I'm certain Lady Francesca is an excellent dancer," Bridget remarked. He followed her gaze and saw the lady in question standing near the windows overlooking the terrace. Lady Francesca was poised, as always. But something was different now, and he saw the anger in her eyes.

Slowly he became aware of other curious stares and glances. Of course. Lord Darcy did not dance, and everyone knew this, just as they knew the Earth was round, Sunday was the Lord's day, and spring followed winter.

But hundreds of them had all borne witness to this violation of natural law. Not only had Lord Darcy danced, but he had done so with one of the Americans.

Something was happening. Bridget had no clue what it was. But there was *something* between her and Darcy. She wanted to puzzle out what it was, what made her heart beat faster, what made her feel a jolt of longing, and whether it, whatever it was, meant she should write *Lady Bridget Darcy* (or whatever the proper form of address would be) in her diary instead of *Mrs. Rupert Wright*.

And then they were interrupted. By Mr. Collins. "Ahem."

Darcy and Bridget stopped suddenly at the interruption, tumbling into each other. She crashed against his chest. His hard, firm, hot chest. His big, strong arms wrapped around her and did not let go immediately. She wasn't sorry.

In fact, she thought about feigning a swoon.

Instead, she turned to face the small little man who had interrupted her *something* with Lord Darcy.

"Oh, Mr. Collins. Hello."

"I do believe this is my dance, Lady Bridget." She strongly considered murdering him. In front of five hundred witnesses.

Mr. Collins looked pointedly at the dance card

dangling from her wrist. It was his dance. And she had been all too eager to dance with Darcy instead. For obvious reasons that anyone with a modicum of brain function would understand.

Bridget glanced up at Darcy. His expression was priceless. It seemed that it wasn't every day that he was interrupted thusly, especially by a man so, so, so far beneath him socially.

"It says so, right there on Lady Bridget's card," Mr. Collins insisted. Turning to Darcy, he said, "We are cousins, you know."

"I did not know. In fact, I do not think I have made your acquaintance."

Oh good Lord, she would have to perform introductions. Josephine had spoken to them about this; in fact, it was one of those lessons that Bridget had skipped. She had pleaded a megrim halfway through and retired to her room to read fashion periodicals in bed.

Was she supposed to present the lower-ranking person to the higher-ranking one? Or was it the other way around? If she got this wrong, she would reveal herself to be as socially inept as Mr. Collins, perish the thought.

Oh, and Josephine had also said to include a little bit of information about the person when performing the introductions. Her mind went blank, except for the most inappropriate things.

"Lord Darcy, may I present my brother's heir, Mr. Collins," she managed to say. *He is a plague and a nuisance and I haven't any clue why he was invited*. No, no, mustn't say that. Instead she said, "He is visiting from his vicarage in, ah, um, a shire."

Was that a quirk of Darcy's lip? Was he finding this amusing?

"Berkshire, actually," Mr. Collins corrected. "But we cannot expect women, with their diminutive brains, to have more than a passing knowledge of geography."

He elbowed Darcy as if they were chums. Darcy looked down at him as if he had been poked with a stick dipped in horse dung.

"Mr. Collins, this is Lord Darcy," Bridget said. *His kisses leave a girl breathless. Oh Lord, she could NOT say that aloud. But what to say about him?* "He is a very gentlemanly, uh, gentleman."

Oh Lord, she was making a cake of herself. Her cheeks felt hot, which meant they were probably a violent shade of pink. Mr. Collins, being obtuse, wouldn't notice. But Darcy would. She couldn't imagine what he would think.

"I shall leave you to your dance," Darcy said politely.

"Thank you for the dance, Lord Darcy." Bridget curtsied, rather elegantly, given how cross and out of sorts she felt.

He nodded. And walked away. And Bridget was left with Mr. Collins.

Oh bloody hell, she wanted to mutter. But she did not, because a True Lady did not use such language. Not even in moments like these.

* * *

Darcy turned and walked away. A small part of him was actually relieved for the interruption. Something was happening between Lady Bridget and him and . . . it could not.

He had to think of Rupert.

He had to think of the expectations of a man of his station and position. And the intentions he'd indicated toward another woman already.

Lady Francesca.

He took a second to ensure that anything he might be feeling was smothered and stuffed into a box deep inside. Then, his expression inscrutable, he made his way to face Lady Francesca. She did not look pleased. They'd known each other for an age, and he'd never seen her like this. If he didn't know better, he'd suspect that she was angry with him. Was she jealous of "one of those provincial Americans," as she called them? It seemed preposterous.

"I thought it only polite to waltz with the hostess," he replied to the accusation in her eyes.

"Will you waltz with all four of the hostesses, the duchess included?" Lady Francesca inquired. "That I would like to see." She threw back her head and laughed.

He heard not the amusement but the bitterness. And it reminded him of his father, laughing at him for making mistakes. That laugh took him back . . . back . . . though he stood in this ballroom as a man of three and thirty, he felt like a thirteen-year-old boy, chastised. Nothing was more effective at putting him in his place than mocking laughter—not beatings, not even nights without supper.

It went without saying it was not a point in his life he was keen to revisit. It occurred to him that if he married her, he would hear that laugh again and again, for the rest of his life. The prospect made his throat feel tight, as if his valet had tied his cravat too tightly.

But if he did not care to hear that laugh, if he was not going to wed Lady Francesca . . . Darcy's heart started to pound as he followed that thought to its logical (illogical?) conclusion: he would be free to marry Lady Bridget.

That was, if he were to steal her from his brother, who needed her.

He spied her through the crowds. She was dancing again, and smiling, and laughing. This time she was dancing with Rupert.

Chapter 17

Last night I waltzed with Darcy, who does not dance. Of course he was probably being polite. He is nothing if not polite. It certainly couldn't signify something else, could it?

LADY BRIDGET'S DIARY

The ball was not quite the smashing success that the duchess had hoped for. Oh, it had been so well attended that the ballroom was at capacity. The guests had nothing but compliments for their hostesses. But the papers the next day did not report on any of that. After all, news of a successful ball paled in comparison to even a hint of scandal.

"*The London Weekly* is reporting that Amelia was seen quaffing an excess of champagne," Josephine said with a frown at Amelia, who, this morning, most certainly did appear to have consumed an inordinate amount the night before.

Her complexion was wan and she was not her usual animated self. "When she wasn't quaffing champagne," the duchess read, "she was seen shooting daggers with her eyes at Mr. Alistair Finlay-Jones, the vaguely disreputable heir to Baron Wrotham."

"I don't know what you are talking about," Amelia muttered. "One cannot shoot daggers with their eyes."

"It's not I that am talking about it, but rather *The London Weekly* and thus the entire town. My only consolation is that they are not speaking about your mysterious illness."

"The Morning Post is," Claire said, peering up from a different newssheet. "The Man About Town says that Lady Amelia appears to have made a remarkable recovery from her grave and sudden illness." Then she read from the column. "In fact, the lady looked as if she had a spent a day out of doors rather than a day on her deathbed."

"If only they could see you now," Bridget teased. "You look incredibly ill."

Amelia halfheartedly swatted at her.

"Sisters," James groaned. He, too, seemed to have consumed an inordinate amount of spirits the previous evening. "What did I ever do to deserve three sisters?"

"Oh, you are not off the hook. Your Grace," Claire said, smiling devilishly. James scowled; he hated when his sisters addressed him formally. "His Grace crushed the hopes of many a young maiden by waltzing twice with Miss Meredith

Green, companion to the duchess, while eligible young ladies languished on the sidelines."

"I wanted Miss Green to have a pleasant evening," James said.

Miss Green blushed at the attention and focused on her sewing.

"That is very admirable and I share your sentiment. But might I remind you that you have one job, Duke," Josephine said sharply. "In fact, all of you have one task. To marry and marry well."

"Well, perhaps Lady Bridget might do us proud," Claire said. Then she continued reading from the paper. "Lady Bridget was seen waltzing with Lord Darcy. It would be an excellent match for her, and. . . . oh."

"What does it say?"

Claire closed the sheet quickly. "Nothing."

"You are such a liar, Claire. What is it?"

"It says it would be an excellent match for you and a surprising choice for him," Claire said softly.

"She is the sister to a duke. It wouldn't be surprising at all," Josephine replied.

"Does it say why?" Bridget asked, even though she suspected she would regret it.

"It just says that it would be surprising if one of England's most refined gentlemen wed the girl who fell," Claire said with an apologetic smile.

"My thoughts exactly," she said brightly, though it was an effort to do so.

She could not shake her reputation, even with the "friendship" of Lady Francesca, the attentions of Lord Darcy, and attendance at countless balls where she committed hardly any improprieties. Still, she was known as the girl who fell and considered an unsuitable match for someone as perfect as Darcy. She tried to tell herself it didn't matter, anyway. Rupert had mentioned marriage again last evening and she dared to hope he would ask her soon.

Never mind that she had kissed his brother. And liked it.

"If we'd had the tightrope walker, they wouldn't report on any of this," Amelia said.

Any further conversation was brought to the halt by the arrival of Mr. Collins, who wished to visit the family before returning to whichever shire he came from.

In particular, he wished to visit with Bridget.

Why she was singled out for his attentions, she knew not. Claire and Amelia could not flee the drawing room fast enough. Even Josephine moved at a brisk pace across the Aubusson carpets.

The doors were scarcely closed behind them—and closed *all the way*—when Mr. Collins made the purpose of his visit clear. He clasped her hands, dropped to one knee, and bowed his head.

"I have come to generously bestow my protection upon you and your sisters."

Bridget gaped. Even though ladies did not gape.

"I beg your pardon?"

"You all must marry," Collins explained patiently, as if he were speaking to a young child or feebleminded adult. "But there are rumors about your sister Amelia and her mysterious illness. Scandal is so unbecoming in a lady. And your eldest sister is quite the bluestocking, which I think is a deplorable quality in a woman of quality. Don't you agree?"

"No."

"Which leaves you, Lady Bridget."

"Me."

"You must marry. And you cannot do better than I, the heir to Durham."

That left her speechless. She glanced around the room, searching for something that would enable her to bash some sense into the man.

"Our marriage will repair your sisters' reputations," he continued, oblivious to anything but his own delusions. "And you shall be known as Mrs. Collins instead of the girl who fell."

Ah, so he read the papers, too.

"Do you really think that is what I am looking for in a marriage?" Bridget asked incredulously. She'd always imagined marrying for love, like her parents. And she didn't think she was mad for considering love, friendship, and respect as a sound basis for marriage. She certainly wouldn't commit herself to an idiot for a lifetime just to avoid being known as the girl who fell. In fact, she was now sorry she had ever even complained about it.

"I have a fine house," Mr. Collins continued,

as if she had not spoken. "My position is secure and should only improve with the demise of your brother."

Bridget choked. "I'm actually fond of my brother."

"I know every woman fancies being a duchess," Mr. Collins intoned.

"Actually, I do not care about being a duchess. Not in the slightest. Especially not if it means losing my brother."

Titles and whatnot were vastly overrated. She now knew this from firsthand, personal experience. Her brother's title had not made them any happier.

But Mr. Collins didn't seem to hear her, or register that females spoke and possessed opinions. She watched in horror as he stood, closed his eyes, and leaned forward.

"Let us kiss to seal our engagement."

He puckered his lips. Waiting.

She pinched him on the arm, hard, even though ladies probably should not pinch gentlemen callers, and he opened his eyes in shock.

"Mr. Collins, I have agreed to nothing!"

"Shall I woo you? I can tell you about the annuity an elderly aunt has provided me, and the pin money I will be able to set aside for you . . ."

"Mr. Collins, I will *not* marry you."

". . . It isn't much by London standards, but you'll find things are far more reasonably priced in the village. It's a lovely little town . . ."

This was unbearable. It had to stop. There was

only one thing to do. Channeling Darcy, she declared in her most I-am-Lord-Darcy voice, "Cease talking at once, Mr. Collins."

He stopped. She was surprised. Behold, the power of Darcy, she thought, not without a surge of pride. She wished to tell Rupert—he would find it so amusing. No, she wished to tell Darcy. But that would have to wait.

Now that she *finally* had Mr. Collins's attention, she proceeded to crush his hopes and dreams as delicately as possible.

"Thank you for your proposal. I am flattered. But I will not marry you." She thought about adding, *I would rather be pecked to death by pigeons a thousand times than be your wife*, but it seemed a bit much.

She had shocked him. She knew this because his mouth flapped open and closed a few times. Then he stumbled over his words and her heart broke a little for him, but not nearly enough to reconsider.

"Very well, Lady Bridget. If that is your choice . . . I suppose I must accept. Even though it is a foolish and regrettable decision. But ladies never were blessed with sense or reason."

She somehow managed to stifle the urge to kick him in the shins. Why, she was becoming more like Darcy by the minute. She ought to tell him.

"Good day, Mr. Collins," she said firmly, still using her Darcy voice.

He opened the door and a group of ladies—

including her sisters, Miss Green, a downstairs maid, and the duchess herself—straightened up and tried vainly to appear as if they hadn't been shamelessly eavesdropping.

The butler had to hand over a bottle of champagne to a footman in order to hand Mr. Collins his hat and cane. It was deuced awkward. But finally her not-future-husband had stepped out of the house and hopefully out of her life forever.

"Don't bother to open the champagne, Pendleton," the duchess said with a disapproving frown. "It is clear we have nothing to celebrate."

"Did you honestly think that we would?" Bridget asked her incredulously.

"You must marry. You must all marry!" For once, the duchess actually raised her voice.

"I do not think we are opposed to marriage," James said evenly.

"We are just opposed to pledging our troth to cork-brained men with nothing to recommend them," Bridget said.

"Well, if you continue to flaunt society, you may only have the likes of Mr. Collins to choose from!" the duchess cried. "And he is not the worst possible person. At least the dukedom would stay in the family. You would be provided for. What if your brother dies and you are all unwed? How will you support yourselves? Who will marry you then, when you have no reputations because you have flaunted the rules at every turn and when you have no dowries because everything has gone to Mr. Collins?"

"James won't die," Amelia protested.

"People die, Amelia. Look at our parents," Claire said softly.

"Yes, but people love, too. Look at our parents," Bridget said. "Don't we all want that?"

Everyone, from the duchess to the butler, fell silent. Thoughtful. Amelia bit her lip. Claire exhaled deeply.

"We want what our mother and father had, Josephine. Love," James said quietly. "The kind of love you throw a dukedom away for."

Chapter 18

Sometimes I do not know which affects me more: Rupert's charm or the dark and intense way that Darcy looks at me. It reminds me of the moment before our kiss—which has not been repeated, alas. Alas?

LADY BRIDGET'S DIARY

If Bridget had any doubts about Rupert's feelings or intentions for her—and she did, given that he had been scarce and distracted of late—this evening assuaged them. And if she had any ideas about the goings-on of Lord Darcy's heart or mind, this evening brought no clarity.

She and her siblings had only just arrived when Rupert sought her out. He looked so handsome in his evening clothes, especially when he smiled and revealed that charming dimple in his cheek.

Behind him, Lord Darcy glowered.

"Lady Bridget! I was hoping to see you this evening."

"Hello, Rupert." She smiled and thought she sounded coy and womanly. Or not.

"Hello, Rupert," Amelia mimicked softly. Bridget smiled and made a point of stepping on her sister's foot. "Ow!"

"Lord Darcy." Bridget nodded.

"Lady Bridget." He did not smile.

"Have you saved a dance or two for me?" Rupert asked, leaning over to glance at her dance card. "I hope so."

"I daresay I have," Bridget said.

"If I may have the pleasure . . ." Rupert penciled in his name to not one, but two dances.

He smiled.

She smiled.

Darcy did not smile, not even when Bridget looked at him. For a moment she thought that he might ask her for a dance. A long moment. A long, awkward moment, full of agonies. But there was no offer forthcoming. Well then.

Any hurt feelings were soothed when Rupert lifted her hand to his lips and promised to see her soon. He took a few steps before Darcy joined him, which meant there was a moment when Darcy gazed at Bridget as if he wished to say something.

But he only gave her a perfunctory nod and joined his brother.

That kiss, then, meant nothing. They would

never speak of it and it would never happen again. Well then.

Rather than delve into an examination of her innermost thoughts and feelings pertaining to Darcy, Bridget fixated all her attentions on Rupert.

During their first waltz they chattered away . . . except for the moments when she happened to see Darcy. Standing against the wall. Like a wall-flower. Glowering. Honestly, she could not understand the man. What did he have to be so morose about? Was life really so difficult for a handsome, wealthy, powerful man who knew how to kiss a woman until she was weak in the knees?

She would be so bold as to ask him, but he kept his distance. Even so, she was still aware of his attentions fixed upon her. He watched her as she muddled her way through the quadrille with Rupert. His gaze was dark as she returned from a stroll on the terrace with Rupert. She was aware of his eyes on her as she and Rupert made their way through the crowds to the lemonade table. She caught his gaze, dark, while taking a sip. Her hand shook and she spilled a little on her dress.

Still, he watched, his expression dark and thunderous. He must disapprove of her . . . with Rupert.

I find myself drawn to Darcy now, ever so curious as to what he is thinking or, dare I say it, feeling.
                                        LADY BRIDGET'S DIARY

Darcy had done his best to avoid her all evening. Rupert had received another letter from the blackmailer and thus was more determined than ever to put a stop to it—and to make any rumors seem absolutely implausible. His life depended on it. So he wooed and courted Bridget.

And Darcy watched, dying.

He saw that they would be happy together. Rupert did genuinely seem to like her. And her adoration of him was all too apparent. They laughed together frequently. Anyone could see how they were at ease in each other's company. If he cared for them both, he would stay away and banish all memories of a heart-stopping kiss in a rainstorm. He would take his lust and shove it deep down inside, along with the other feelings he refused to feel.

Later, much later in the evening, he found himself standing with her and his brother.

"Is anything the matter, Loooord Darcy?"

He wanted to smile at the way she drawled out his name. But he was only reminded that the one woman who dared to speak to him like a human was going to marry his brother. That wasn't amusing at all.

"No," he said flatly.

Yes. Everything. You are pretty.

"Because you seem very . . ." Rupert's voice trailed off as he searched for precisely the right word to describe the inner turmoil inadvertently revealed in his expression.

"Morose," Bridget said.

"I daresay I would go with dour," Rupert replied, thoughtfully.

"Or perhaps broody," Bridget said, evaluating him.

"I know! Cantankerous," Rupert suggested with a little too much glee.

"Only very old men are cantankerous," Bridget said. "And Darcy isn't quite there. Yet."

"Good point. Despondent?" Rupert mused. "But then what does my dear brother have to be despondent about?"

"The trials and tribulations of being a wealthy, titled, respected, handsome man," Bridget said with a sigh.

She thought him handsome. Also, he loved the rise and fall of her breasts when she sighed. Somehow that only made him feel worse.

"I am none of the above," he snapped.

"You are not wealthy, titled, respected, or handsome?" Bridget asked, being deliberately obtuse.

"I am not morose, dour, broody, or cantankerous."

But he was. He was tortured with lust for Bridget. He was agonizing over his self-sacrifice, denying his desires for the sake of his brother's need to take a wife with whom he'd probably enjoy a long, amiable marriage, while Darcy burned with lust for his sister-in-law.

Because family came first. None other than Lady Bridget herself said so. And family certainly trumped lust.

Unless it was more than lust.

Unless he put himself first for once.

"On second thought, perhaps he *is* cantankerous," Bridget mused.

"Perhaps it is none of your concern." He brushed her aside, ignoring her obvious shock, as he stalked off into the night.

Chapter 19

Just another day of lessons. Just another day of reviewing household accounts with the duchess and the housekeeper. Just another day of practicing sitting up straight, conjugating French verbs, and not having dessert. Being a Lady of Quality is not all it's cracked up to be.

LADY BRIDGET'S DIARY

The following day, Darcy sat behind his desk with a large stack of papers before him and he found it impossible to concentrate. A mad idea had occurred to him last night: if he desired Bridget so strongly, perhaps he ought to express that desire. Or relieve it. Or do something other than feel massively frustrated by it. Then he could carry on with his perfectly ordered and planned life.

But if he were to do something about it, a marriage proposal and wedding ceremony would have to take place. It was only logical: if he wished to bed her, he would have to marry her. That was the catch with gently bred ladies. Especially ones related to dukes. And most especially ones with the Duchess of Durham as a chaperone.

But it was a mad idea all the same. A mad, insane idea that would not leave his brain. He couldn't drink it away; the three whiskeys he drank last night had proven that. It was there when he went to bed and the first thing on his mind when he opened his eyes this morning.

It would be a terrible match. That was a fact.

A week ago he would have said the match would be terrible—laughable, even!—because Lady Bridget was hardly an ideal countess. A countess had to be graceful, refined, polished, re-served. She needed to know just what to say and how to properly address the person to whom she said it.

Lady Bridget was too outspoken, too emo-tional, too prone to things like a tumble in the lake at a garden party. A man of his position had to consider such things. A man of his position had to consider so much more than himself.

A man had to think of his family as well.

Rupert's blackmailer was still out there, in possession of a secret that would destroy him. Them. Their only prayer was to have enough powerful allies to protect his brother and their reputations. And sadly, Durham and his sisters hadn't quite conquered the ton just yet.

Rupert's plan to save his reputation—and po-tentially his life—through a marriage was the right thing to do. And Darcy was thinking about ruining it.

He ought to marry Francesca as planned; her brother and his best friend was a marquis. Their uncle was a close friend of the king. It would be an excellent connection to have.

But excellent connections did not warm a man's bed, or satisfy his rampant desires, or wink at him across a ballroom. They did not tease a man, or unlock long dormant parts of him.

Darcy stood, frustrated, and began to pace. What if he dared to think of himself, just this once? Desire was a strong and demanding creature, seducing him with such ideas.

As he paced, he occasionally looked up and saw his father's portrait. The damn thing glowered at him in soul-crushing disapproval as if it knew the direction of his thoughts. Darcy lived under that perpetual frown, that constant glare.

He stopped short. Recognizing that same expression upon his own face. And it wasn't that he hated everything and everyone, or found the world not quite up to his standards. It was because it took such an enormous effort to remember one's place, one's duty, one's Noble Purpose . . . when a pretty girl fell over in front of you and then stood up and cracked jokes.

Darcy called for his hat and gloves. He was going out.

Darcy had the good fortune to find Lady Bridget alone at Durham House. She was in the garden.

She smiled, and seemed happy enough to see him. He dared to exhale the breath he was holding. His heart was pounding in his chest as if he'd sprinted from London to Dover and back again. She, this slip of an American girl, made *him*, a peer of the realm, nervous and speechless.

"How are you today, Darcy?"

A proper reply would have been "Very well, thank you, and you?" An acceptable answer would have been "Fine."

He did not say either of those things.

"I cannot stop thinking of you, Lady Bridget. In spite of my struggles, my valiant efforts, my thoughts constantly stray to you."

Her lips parted. Shock, probably. He was shocked as well. These words. Were being spoken. Aloud. By him. To her.

"You, Lady Bridget, *you*. I don't know what it is about you . . ." He paused, trying to collect his thoughts, slow his racing heart. "God knows there are plenty of reasons I shouldn't want you and yet I have been tormented by desire for you these past weeks. I have fought against my better judgment, expectations for my marriage, Rupert's interests, the reputation of you and your scandal-plagued family, but I can bear it no longer. I crave you, your kiss, your touch."

He ached to reach out to her, touch her cheek.

She said nothing. Her lips parted, but still, she didn't speak. It seemed he had brought this constantly chattering woman to silence and he desperately need her to say something.

Anything.

Or he would.

"I think I might love you, Bridget. You are hardly the kind of woman I had imagined making my wife. But I fear I will never find happiness with anyone else. I beg you to put me out of my agonies. Will you do me the honor of becoming my countess?"

"I . . . I . . . don't know what to say."

One thing was becoming abundantly, terribly clear: this was a disaster. Because of this impulsive idea from his lust-addled brain to *propose marriage*, he was now stuck in this nightmare of a scene, playing the role of absolute idiot.

If she said yes, it would be worth it.

"Say you will be mine. My happiness depends upon it." *And my pride. And my lust.*

"And what of my happiness?" she demanded. He was taken aback by the sharpness of her tone.

"I want nothing more than to be the one to make you the happiest woman."

"You might begin by not insulting me, or my 'scandal-plagued' family, or confusing love with lust."

She might as well have slapped him.

The fog cleared from his brain. Sense and reason returned. She was right; he had insulted her horribly by revealing all the things he was forced to consider, by virtue of his position. But he had to. He wouldn't be who he was, otherwise.

She could not love him as he was.

Who was he, anyway? Was he this man? Or

had his father succeeded in wiping away any trace of Colin Fitzwilliam Wright, who had once loved to laugh, chase girls, and even dance?

"I apologize."

"For what? For holding yourself and others to impossible standards? For being all lordly, as you are supposed to be? You probably cannot even help it."

She had it all right. No, all wrong. This was not who he was, deep down. He hoped she could unlock the cage he'd found himself in. But no.

"I apologize for insulting you. That was not my intention. I wished only to give an indication of the turmoil I am experiencing with regard to you."

"I am sorry for your struggles. But I cannot accept your proposal."

"Right." He nodded. Dying. He was dying inside. God, how had this even happened? "This is not how I . . ."

Words. Not available to him at the moment. He started to go. But one question remained. He stopped, and turned.

"Is your refusal because of Rupert?"

"No," she said, eyes flashing in anger. "It is because you are an ass."

"Good." He paused, carefully weighing the words he was about to say. "He will never love you. He will never love any woman the way she ought to be loved," he said. "Do you understand me, Bridget?"

She nodded yes, but he saw the confusion in her eyes.

"But he will love you, in his own way. I only mention this because I wish you to be happy. And loved. And I regret that I dared to think I was the one who could make you happy."

There was nothing else to say. He turned and walked back to his house at a much slower pace than when he had rushed headlong into disaster.

He was worried about ruining her, but the truth was she had ruined him. He always said the right thing, until today, when every sentence he uttered was worse than the last. And he had felt nothing until he made the acquaintance of Lady Bridget and he reluctantly had begun to allow himself to feel. And now he felt too damn much.

> *I have received my second marriage proposal and I can't quite decide if it's worse than the first. Darcy—DARCY!—asked me to be his wife. Even though I am not what he wants in a wife, which he made ABUNDANTLY CLEAR. Even though my family is "scandal-plagued" in spite of my BEST EFFORTS. Even though marriage to me is against his better judgment. Well. WELL THEN.*
>
> *I have refused him, naturally.*
>
> LADY BRIDGET'S DIARY

The logical thing to do now was to numb all and any feelings of rejection, despair, and self-loathing. Not to mention a physical and mental sensation he might have described as heartsick, if he had been less of an Englishman.

Darcy proceeded directly to the sideboard in

his study and poured a large tumbler of whiskey. The first drink did nothing. He could still recall everything, from the way Bridget tasted when he kissed her that day to the horrified expression on her face when he proposed. After the second whiskey, he could still recall everything, but he didn't feel it as intensely. Everything went to hell after the third.

At some point, Rupert strolled in, took one look at him, and asked, "Who died?"

"My hopes and dreams," Darcy said flatly.

"Mine as well," Rupert said grimly. "Read this."

Rupert tossed a crumpled sheet of paper into Darcy's lap.

He set down his now empty glass, alas, and fumbled with the paper. The words blurred before his eyes.

Two thousand pounds by Tuesday or I'll tell the ton about you and you know who.

"I don't know what to do anymore, Colin." His brother rubbed his eyes wearily. Pushed his fingers through his hair. Paced around the room before collapsing into a chair.

"This is very vague," Darcy said, puzzled. "Are you sure this person even has the information with which to blackmail you?"

"Are you suggesting that someone simply goes around sending such letters, assuming everyone has skeletons in their closet they'll pay to hide?"

"Genius, if you ask me."

"Evil genius. And no, he—or she—knows. A lot. The first letter was very detailed and specific." Rupert paused, debating whether to say more before finally confessing. "It was about Frederick and me, and the times we visited Ivy Cottage."

"Do you still have it?"

"No, I burned it. I burned them all."

"Do you remember anything? Were they sealed? Was the handwriting the same?"

"No, I saw nothing but the threats. It was small amounts at first. And then more and more over time. As if they knew I would pay."

He had paid. Someone had illegally obtained a fortune.

"We have to put a stop to this once and for all. I've been meaning to go to down to Ivy Cottage anyway. There was some trouble with the housekeeper and other things. In the meantime—"

"—I'll propose to Lady Bridget." Rupert thought he was finishing his brother's sentence. But he wasn't. Not at all.

"No." Darcy said this firmly, but softly. Rupert didn't seem to hear.

"We'll marry and that will ensure any rumors don't gain a foothold if they should emerge. We'll get along, Bridget and I. It could be worse, I suppose."

God, Darcy would give anything to be able to love Bridget, to marry her, spend his life with her. And here was his brother, thinking it wouldn't be the worst fate, when compared to social ostracization, possible deportation, or death.

Bridget deserved better than that.

"No." Darcy spoke louder now, but Rupert was lost in his own world. He stood, and started pacing around the room, muttering.

"Frederick won't like it. But *c'est la vie*. If this is what I must do to protect us, well then I must. And I am rather fond of her. She makes me laugh."

Darcy stood.

"No."

The match would be one of convenience, but it would make them all miserable.

"What do you mean, no?" Rupert stopped abruptly, having finally heard his brother. "Have you lost your mind?"

"Perhaps. Probably." Darcy shrugged. And exhaled. "Absolutely."

"You've been after me for years to wed. And now I've finally decided to settle down with a perfectly amiable girl and—"

She wasn't a perfectly amiable girl. She was a woman. A complicated, confusing, confounding woman who wanted to be loved for herself, not in spite of stupid, perceived obstacles. She wanted to belong. She was a woman whose kiss made him forget himself—or find himself, he wasn't sure. He just knew that she was more than merely *amiable*.

Darcy couldn't take it anymore. Before he knew what he was about, his punched his brother. In the face. Right in the eye, to be precise.

"What the bloody hell?"

Rather than wait for answers, Rupert retaliated.

A scuffle ensued. Punches were thrown—and missed their intended target. Or any target, really. Their battle quickly devolved into a juvenile scuffle, complete with slaps, kicks, and hair pulling. Chairs were overturned. At one point, a volume of Shakespeare's tragedies was used as a weapon.

It was utterly undignified.

"What the hell has gotten into you?" Rupert asked, panting.

"Don't speak of her that way," Darcy replied, breathing hard.

"Why?" Rupert asked, confused and enraged. He held his eye, in pain. Darcy doubled over, trying to catch his breath. But he looked up and saw comprehension dawning in Rupert's eyes. "Oh. Oh my God."

> *Marriage proposals: 2*
> *Accepted proposals: 0*
> *The hour: late*
> *Cake: lots*
>
> LADY BRIDGET'S DIARY

The duchess would undoubtedly be horrified to learn that the duke and his sisters were frequently in the habit of sneaking down to the kitchens in the middle of the night. The cook, however, had reluctantly accepted the practice and had taken to leaving out plates of cakes, pastries, and the like, where hungry Cavendish siblings might find them without too much fussing around in her kitchen.

It was shortly after midnight when Bridget found plates, a freshly baked vanilla pound cake, and the company of her brother.

"Has Amelia told you where she went on her big adventure?" James asked, pouring them each a glass of milk.

"Not yet," she mumbled, having just bitten into a heavenly slice of cake. Vanilla. With lemon frosting. They did not have cakes this good in America. If they returned home, Cook would certainly have to come with them. "Have you?"

He shook his head no. "This is officially the longest she has ever kept a secret."

"Usually I would think that's a good thing—a sign that she's growing up," Bridget said between mouthfuls of cake. "Not that I am in any position to speak of growing up. But . . ."

"But . . ."

Bridget took another bite of cake. Yes, they were growing up. The duchess was seeing to that. But to what end? Yes, she had snared a proposal from Darcy but it was one he was obviously reluctant to issue because she didn't measure up. She and her scandal-plagued family didn't belong.

"What are we doing here, James?"

"Opportunities like this . . ." He shrugged and waved his hand in the general vicinity of the kitchens, the house, the city of London, the country of England, and all the bits of it that he personally owned.

Funny, that.

"I know, I know. Opportunities like this don't come along often or ever. Are you happy here? Everyone always does what you say. And you can go out without a chaperone and have as much cake as you like. All the girls fancy you."

"The dukedom is not without its charms, I'll grant you that," he said with a grin. "But they don't want me here."

"They don't want any of us here," Bridget said.

"But I wonder if we would find more of a welcome if we tried to belong more," James said.

"Speak for yourself," Bridget mumbled. "That's what I thought and I have made every effort to do so and it is not enough. So don't bother. Even if someone comes to care for us, all they will see is our endless stream of scandals."

"And what if one of us finds a reason to stay?" James asked, glancing at her, hair falling in his eyes. He was serious. Gravely serious. And he seemed to be holding his breath waiting for her answer. And just when she was about to ask who the lucky girl was, he said, "That Darcy fellow isn't so bad."

"I refused him today," Bridget said. Her voice cracked and she half laughed, half cried. Hours later—and some tears, and pages upon pages in her diary, and more tears—and she still wasn't sure if it was funny or a complete tragedy. She thought he hated her and disapproved of her, but no . . . he might love her.

Well, he did still disapprove of her. He had said as much.

"What? Why?"

"I am not perfect enough. We are not perfect enough. He insulted us, and then declared his love for me." She took another bite of cake, something sweet to counteract the bitterness.

"Wait—what is the problem?" James asked, genuinely perplexed, leaving Bridget to wonder if all men were utter fools. "Insults trump love?"

"Yes," she said resolutely.

"Insults trump a title, heaps of money, and a declaration of love?"

"Obviously."

"Women." He rolled his eyes.

"Women! How is this *my* fault and the fault of my entire sex?"

"He said he loved you, Bridge." Her brother gave her a sad smile. "I think he was probably trying to say he loved you in spite of all his stupid reasons not to. He was probably trying to convey that love trumps all other considerations."

She hadn't thought of that. She had only heard Perfect Lord Darcy fling insult arrows right into her heart, one right after another.

He loved her, but she was embarrassing.

He loved her, but her family was embarrassing.

He loved her, even though he shouldn't.

And now her brother was suggesting that a

simple "I love you" mattered far more than all the grave insults that would make it impossible for them to have any real, equal marriage.

Well, she had always questioned her brother's wits.

"Whose side are you on, anyway?" she questioned. "Can a girl not count on familial loyalty in a trying time like this?

"Yours, of course." He reached out, tousled her hair, and gave her another one of those sad smiles that did nothing to soothe her heartache.

"It is lust he feels, not love," she said, scowling.

"Something every brother wants to hear about his sister," James said, groaning.

Bridget laughed, a little.

"What am I going to do?"

"Well, obviously you're not going to plan a wedding," he said, stealing a bite of her cake while she sighed and glanced heavenward. Ugh, brothers.

"For a minute there you were helping. And now . . . not so much."

"If you think having a brother is vexing, trying having three sisters."

"And with that, I bid you, and this cake, good night."

Chapter 20

I asked James what Darcy meant when he said Rupert would never love me the way a woman ought to be loved. He turned red and said one does not speak of such things, so now I am left to make all sorts of assumptions.

LADY BRIDGET'S DIARY

A fortnight had passed since Darcy proposed. A fortnight had passed since he left London and presumably took Rupert with him—she had learned this from her lady's maid, who heard it from a downstairs maid, who heard it from a footman. Bridget's life carried on; a mixture of deportment lessons, trips to the modiste, and an endless round of balls and soirees. On Wednesdays she wore pink and trailed after Lady Francesca, Miss Mulberry, and Miss Montague, but it wasn't quite the same. Her friends, if they were ever really her friends, seemed distant. Bridget found she lacked the heart to fret over it.

At the breakfast table, a fortnight after Darcy had proposed, Bridget was perusing the shipping timetables in the newspaper, searching for the next ship to America, when the duchess cleared her throat, requesting everyone's attention.

"Lady Wych Cross has invited us to dine."

"Your best friend," Bridget said.

"So we are attending," Claire said.

"And arch enemy," Amelia added with a wicked grin.

"So we are not attending," Claire replied.

"Oh, we are most certainly attending," Josephine said. "I don't suppose one of you will make a match in the next few hours? Otherwise, Lady Wych Cross will have something to gloat over."

Bridget sipped her tea and eyed her siblings. James shifted uncomfortably in his chair. Amelia pushed food around on her plate and took a small bite from a piece of toast. Claire's cheeks were pink.

"Has Lady Francesca made a match?" Bridget inquired, trying very hard to sound utterly disinterested in the answer.

Josephine gazed shrewdly at her.

"Are you asking if Darcy has proposed to her?"

"No?"

"That means yes," Amelia replied.

"I would not be surprised if they did invite us over to announce the news." What Josephine said next surprised Bridget. "She has seen you as a rival from the beginning."

"Oh, the drama," Claire said.

Shortly thereafter, everyone except the duchess left the breakfast room, but Bridget remained. She reached over and, etiquette be damned, took a piece of bacon from Amelia's plate.

"You cannot be serious," Bridget said, eyeing the duchess. "There is no way that Lady Francesca—beautiful, elegant, sleek-haired, and perfect—has seen me, the girl who fell, as a rival."

"Have you known me to jest?"

Bridget sighed. That was such a Darcy thing to say.

"Lady Francesca has been counting on a proposal from Darcy since her debut; longer perhaps. And then you arrive and slip and fall right into his heart."

"That's very poetic of you."

"The study of poetry is one we haven't had time for yet. But that is neither here nor there at the moment," the duchess said with an elegantly dismissive wave of her hand. "She has done everything right . . ."

". . . And I have done everything wrong, I know."

"Oh hush! Lady Francesca may walk with a certain air, know all the finer points of etiquette, but she is also mean-spirited. And you, Bridget, are a kindhearted girl. And that is what makes a true lady." The duchess clasped her hand and Bridget blinked away tears. "Don't lose that," she continued. "Don't let me crowd it out with rules and dancing lessons, and don't lose it trying to fit in with the likes of Lady Francesca."

Gah, she felt something like tears in her eyes at the duchess's kind words and at the thought of what it would be like to stop trying so hard to fit in or to impress people who did not wish to be impressed. What if she could just . . . be?

Tonight we shall dine with Lady Witchcraft and Lady Francesca and I am looking forward to this evening as much as one would look forward to having their teeth pulled out, one by one, without so much as a splash of whiskey or laudanum to ease the pain.

LADY BRIDGET'S DIARY

Of course *she* would be here. Darcy was standing by the mantel, bored by Lady Francesca's conversation, when Lady Bridget walked in with her family. When he'd been invited to an intimate dinner party, he'd never imagined that Francesca would invite the Americans. If he had known . . .

. . . he would still be here. There was no denying the way his breath caught when he saw her, like he'd been caught unawares and punched in the gut.

He'd been away for a fortnight, traveling between his estates, tending to matters at each one, avoiding Bridget and tracking down Rupert's blackmailer. The problematic housekeeper at Ivy Cottage, one of their smaller properties, gave her notice, saying she had come into a fortune. Given that middle-aged housekeepers rarely came into fortunes, Darcy made some inquiries. In a short conversation he had made her aware of the punishment for blackmailing a peer of the realm and mentioned the option of returning the money. He also mentioned that Australia was lovely this time of year. He said these things in his I-am-Darcy-do-as-I-say voice. Mrs. Keyes was on a ship in the Atlantic at this very moment, and Rupert's secret was safe.

Darcy had come to realize that his motives were not purely altruistic, either. Of course he thought of the family's reputation, his brother's life, the wealth of the estate, etc., etc. But if this threat of discovery were removed, then Rupert would have no reason to wed Bridget.

The threat of discovery had been removed.

Now there was nothing stopping Darcy's marriage to her, other than the fact that she didn't love him and he had insulted her so tremendously that it would be impossible that she should forgive him, let alone love him.

"I've missed you," Lady Francesca cooed, resting her hand on his arm. He glanced at her; she was gorgeous. And he hadn't thought of her once. But the woman on the other side of the drawing room, obviously talking about him with her brother, he'd thought about her constantly.

I simply do not know if I can carry on in my quest to be a True and Perfect Lady. I wonder what

would happen if I threw caution and polite man-
ners to the wind and said whatever was on my
mind.

LADY BRIDGET'S DIARY

Dinner was a disaster. There was not one particular moment that was horrendous; it was simply an onslaught of tiny indignities, one right after the other. Bridget was miserable by the time they arrived at the soup course and had a difficult time concealing it. Matters only became worse.

"And how are your prospects, Lady Bridget?" Lady Wych Cross asked. Bellowed, really, from the other end of the table.

Bridget paused, halfway through lifting a spoonful of turtle soup to her lips.

Of course she was acutely aware that one of her rejected prospects was seated at this very table, avoiding her gaze.

"Yes, Bridget, do tell us," James said, and she kicked him under the table.

"My prospects are fine, thank you for asking," Bridget replied. The polite thing, the done thing would be to leave it at that. She could go back to her soup and count the minutes until they could leave. But she could see her and Lady Francesca smirking—in a ladylike way, of course—as they tried to embarrass her. In front of Darcy. Because they thought her a rival.

Maybe she was. Maybe she wasn't. There was really nothing she or Lady Francesca could do about that; it was up to Darcy. All she could do was be herself.

Bridget decided then and there that she was finished with trying to shrink herself so that she might fit in and gain the approval of the likes of Lady Francesca. Or even Darcy.

And so, because she saw where this conversation was going if she played along, she decided to turn the tables. "And how are your prospects, Lady Wych Cross?"

Josephine gave Bridget A Look.

For a moment, the old woman looked shocked. "Dead," she said bluntly.

"I overheard Lord Burbrooke say that he thought you amusing, Bridget," Lady Francesca said. Lord Burbrooke was a slow-witted fellow who monopolized most conversations with stories of his pack of hounds.

"I am so charmed to have attracted the notice of someone who exemplifies the English aristocrats I have met thus far."

"It would be a pity if such lovely girls were left too long on the shelf," Lady Wych Cross said, her voice tinged with sarcasm, glancing from Bridget to Amelia to Claire before settling on the duchess.

"Indeed. My girls are only on their first season, though. Perhaps Lady Francesca can tell them about the plight of women who have had three seasons without wedding."

"But not for lack of offers," Lady Francesca said with a sharp smile.

Darcy took a sip of wine. Bridget did the same.

"And what makes you think my girls haven't had any offers?" The duchess smiled a catlike smile.

Darcy took a long swallow of his wine. Bridget took another sip of soup. Oh, she did *not* like where this was going.

"Quite a few offers, in fact," James drawled.

Darcy motioned to the footman for more wine.

"Congratulations. Shall we have champagne to celebrate?" Lady Wych Cross inquired. Then, dropping her voice, she asked, "Or were the offers unsuitable?"

"The offer was suitable, though my sister is undecided on the gentleman in question," James said.

Darcy wouldn't meet her gaze. This could be interpreted only one way, she thought. He was mortified to have proposed to her and lived in a holy terror that the ton should find out, especially Francesca.

Bridget drained the wine in her glass.

Josephine gave her another look of dismay. True Ladies did not overimbibe at the dinner table.

"And the other one? You made it sound like you had a few."

"My other offer was unsuitable," Bridget said.

"Most unsuitable," Amelia agreed.

"Very unsuitable," Claire added.

"I think you should have accepted one of your offers," James said with a pointed look at her, while tipping his head in Darcy's direction. Gad, her brother had the subtlety of an invading army. She would never confide in him again.

"What is done is done," Bridget snapped.

Darcy took another sip of wine.

"It is deplorable how long girls are taking to wed these days," said Lady Wych Cross.

"Is it the fault of the ladies for refusing proposals or the gentlemen for not offering?" Josephine asked, with a pointed look at James.

"Who says the gentlemen do not offer?" James inquired.

"Perhaps they do not make attractive offers," Amelia said. "Perhaps they natter on about all the wrong things."

Well, Amelia was reading her diary again. Bridget would probably murder her after supper.

"I'll tell you what the problem is," Lady Wych Cross declared. "It is these newfangled, foolish notions of marrying for love instead of sensible reasons like lineage, connections, or how one will be supported. Far too many girls are led astray by irrational and lofty ideas about romance and whatnot. Now we have young men and women unwed, causing all sorts of trouble."

"And how happy were you in your marriage, Lady Wych Cross?" Bridget asked.

"Bridget . . ." the duchess warned.

"Oh, Duchess, let the girl ask her impertinent questions," Lady Wych Cross said. "Marriage is not about happiness, girl. It is for the purpose of accumulating wealth, prestige, and passing it to the next generation. It's utterly foolish to enter a marriage without considering such things. Happiness has little to do with it. Love, even less."

Darcy had said as much in his mangled, insulting proposal to her. It was impossible not to glance at him, quickly, though, so he would not catch her looking. She saw that he had developed a sudden fascination with a silver spoon. It so happened that hers was quite interesting as well. She would have to compliment her hostess on her silverware.

"Perhaps some people do not wish a lifetime of misery whilst accumulating wealth they will not even get to enjoy and titles that serve no purpose whatsoever other than to make a parade out of walking in to dinner," Bridget replied.

"Of course the Americans would say that," Lady Francesca said dismissively with her sharp little laugh that felt like it could cut glass.

"I may not know all your silly rules, but I do know who won the war," Bridget said, pointedly, with reddened cheeks. She'd had enough discussion of her prospects—or lack thereof. She'd had enough of being made to feel foolish for who she was: American, interested in love, impertinent. "Excuse me," she said, and quit the table.

She could not get to the foyer fast enough. From there she would inquire about the ladies' retiring room. Or perhaps she should just take the carriage home and send it back for her family. She just needed to be alone.

Heavy footfalls sounded behind her, echoing on the marble tiled floor.

"Bridget."

She knew that voice. That low voice that issued orders, that expected to be obeyed, and that also made heat pool in her belly. She stopped, but required a moment of deep, controlled breathing before she could turn around and face Lord Darcy.

Nothing had changed. Everything had changed.

Darcy still wanted her. Wanted her with yearning that shocked him. And he was finished with trying to fight it.

Bridget had had multiple offers of marriage, both of which were unsuitable and one of which was his. His competitive instincts had flared— and were promptly drowned with wine.

Bridget who, he now realized, cared nothing of wealth, status, duty to one's title, etc., etc. All the things he had been raised to care for above all else.

She cared only for love.

How modern. How American. How luxurious.

How *that* made him jealous.

He did not know what mad force propelled him to follow her from the dinner table. It would be commented upon, probably. But in spite of her refusal, his time away, he still craved her.

He found her in the foyer.

"Bridget."

It was a moment before she turned around.

"If you have come to chastise me for being rude to the hostess, or drinking too much wine with supper, or otherwise forgetting my manners, you needn't bother. I already know that."

"That is not what I came to say at all."

In truth, he had no idea what he had come to say. This business of speaking of one's feelings was foreign to him.

"I enjoyed your conversation at the table," he said, finally.

"Did you?"

"Enjoyed is perhaps not the right word. It was . . . enlightening," he admitted. It had made him see where he had gone wrong and it made him see how he could possibly, maybe make things go right. "It was interesting. And admirable that you challenged old, tired, ingrained notions."

She looked at him with disbelief.

"And here I thought that my outspokenness was one of my lamentable qualities that you were willing to overlook," she replied. "I thought my foreign values were incompatible with the world you live and breathe in."

He took a few steps to be closer to her.

"I have made a wreck of things, haven't I?" Darcy said softly.

"No, Lord Darcy. There was never anything to wreck," she said, and he wondered just how much pain a man could take. Funny, that he should have spent his whole life trying to avoid this feeling. Or any feeling. And that was precisely what led him to this agonizing moment.

"I have hurt you, and that was not my intention. I have said some foolish things about your family's reputation, your tendency to speak too much, and how you are not what I had always looked for in a countess."

"Do go on," she said dryly. "I love that you think that I am unaware of all my faults when you, Josephine, the gossip columns, and the likes of Lady Wych Cross and even Lady Francesca have spelled them out so clearly. Repeatedly."

"I am one of the best orators in Parliament. But you would never know that, given how inarticulate I become around a pretty American girl who drives me to distraction. What I mean to say, Bridget, is that I like you just the way you are."

"That is very polite of you to say, but you really needn't worry about me, Lord Darcy. It is very clear that I do not belong in English society. Perhaps I shall convince my family to return home with all the heathens and savages where we belong."

She turned to walk away. He grabbed her wrist. She stopped and looked down at the sight of her gloved wrist in his hand. She lifted her gaze to his, curious. He ought to apologize and release her.

He did not.

He did no such thing.

Darcy pulled them into the butler's pantry, just off the foyer, and shut the door behind them.

* * *

Oh my Lord. Oh my *Lord*. Bridget's heart started to beat at a frantic pace. The room was empty; a candle burned, provided the barest hint of illumination. Her back was against the hard wooden door and Darcy stood before her. Tall, proud, proper Darcy.

She could barely see his expression but she knew it wouldn't matter if she could; he was always so inscrutable. He must have gone mad, to pull her into a closet at a dinner party. *This* was all kinds of impropriety and he was the King of Proper Behavior.

Or was he?

"Don't go," he whispered fiercely. "Please do not run away."

And then his mouth claimed hers for a kiss that was rough with pent-up passion, frustration, and longing. She felt her knees buckle beneath her, but his strong arms held her up.

His scent enveloped her and she breathed him in deeply. She ought to protest. How dare he just drag her into a darkened closest and proceed to kiss her senseless! Just because everyone did his bidding and bowed down to him, he thought he could simply ravish her with kisses in a butler's pantry!

It was positively barbaric.

It was also devastatingly romantic.

It was hardly the behavior she expected of the tightly reined in Lord Darcy, who was now pressing hot kisses along her neck. But it was wonderful all the same. His hands skimmed along her hips, and he pressed against her, as if he could not get enough. Of *her*.

"I love your mouth. The way you kiss, the way you taste, all the shocking things you say," he whispered.

"Oh." She had nothing to say now, shocking or otherwise. Her head and heart were a tangled knot of feelings. There was surprise, and there was something like her heart breaking open, and then there was desire. Hot, wicked desire. Certain parts of her had not received the message that she loathed him.

"I love how you feel against me," he whispered, skimming his hands along her waist, her hips, everywhere. She felt just how much he loved it. And she felt herself lean into his every touch.

Then he pressed another hot kiss along her neck. Sparks. She felt sparks.

"I'm too plump," she mumbled. "I'm too . . ." She was going to list all the reasons he couldn't possibly want to do this with her.

Darcy pulled away from her. Held her face in his hands. Looked her in the eye.

"No, you are not," he said in his I-am-a-lord-I-am-right voice.

"Oh," she sighed. Oh, why hadn't anyone ever said that to her before? Oh, why hadn't she known? Oh, why did it have to mean so much to hear *him* say it? Oh, why did he have to make her feel like this?

Like she couldn't remember why she had re-fused him, even though she'd had very good rea-sons, she was certain of it.

"I have longed to kiss you here," he whis-pered, pressing his lips to the delicate skin just above the line of her bodice. Sparks. She felt more sparks. In a hoarse whisper he continued, "I long to kiss you everywhere."

She felt his words. Everywhere.

"Bridget . . ." Her name was a plea, a question, in a voice laden with longing.

Then he kissed her.

She could taste how much he wanted her. He was confounding. Maddening. But dear Lord above, did the man know how to kiss a woman. The more he kissed her, the more she forgot about slights, perceived or real. She forgot about lady-like rules of behavior. Nothing mattered any-more except this strange, new wonderful feeling of his lips against hers. A tingling of her skin. A heat in her belly. A feeling of being wanted, des-perately wanted. She couldn't get enough of it.

She kissed him back. She touched him, feel-ing his hard chest beneath her palms. His heart pounded. He wanted her and there was no pre-tending otherwise. Thinking soon became im-possible, save for one thought: *Yes. More.* Bridget felt hot inside. She wanted more, and yet the more he kissed her, the more she wanted.

Then he gently pushed aside the sleeves to her gown and dropped a kiss on her bare shoulder. Sparks. His hands rested on her shoulders, slowly sliding the silk away, moving lower. Smolder.

There was just enough light to see him gaze up her, asking with his eyes for permission. She sighed. That was all, just a little sigh of pleasure.

"I wanted to do this ever since that day in the lake."

He teased the centers of her breasts with his thumb, lightly, back and forth. She sucked in her breath as her nipples stiffened under his touch and the cool air.

Then when he did the same with his mouth, she gasped, and something in her core tightened. She moaned in pleasure. And forgot to breathe. She'd had no idea that he had wanted her like this, and had wanted her for so long.

And that was *almost* as arousing as that wicked thing he was doing with his mouth. To her breast. In the butler's pantry. How so very un-Darcy.

"Bridget . . ."

He kissed her again. She pulled him in close, savoring the sensation of his body against hers. She felt him, hard, pressing into the vee of her thighs. She couldn't help but move against him, driven by instinct and desire. "Yes . . ." he rasped. "Please . . ."

His hands skimmed up her thighs; she felt his hands pause where her silk stockings ended and her bare skin began. This was dangerous territory now, wicked territory, unknown territory. Whatever it was, every nerve in her body was aching for more of his touch.

"Yes," she whispered.

As they kissed, his fingers pressed upon her secret place and she moaned softly. He knew just what to do, just how to touch her, to fuel her desire, to make that maddening tension within become tighter and tighter. Here, just as she was, bare to him, there were no rules to follow. She gave in to instinct and surrendered to her desire for this man.

And then it was all a blur of sensations: the feeling of his soft hair between her fingers; his lips upon hers; his fingers, there, driving her mad in the most wonderful way; the sound of her skirts rustling as she moved; the sound of his breath; the pounding of her heart.

And then she could take it no more. She cried out in pleasure; he captured the sound with a kiss.

Bridget melted against him, breathing hard, trying to comprehend what had just happened to her. Something had changed. Everything had changed.

"Bridget . . ."

Desire for his touch, his kiss, for *him* was making her lose her wits. Gone was the woman who demanded love. Gone was the woman who had tried to hold herself to higher standards, and who played by the rules, even if she didn't understand them. This potent kiss, that exquisite pleasure, made her forget herself, but it couldn't just change everything.

That he loved her mouth didn't change the fact that he didn't think she would make a good countess. A good *wife*.

Bridget broke away.

"You cannot just kiss me in the butler's pantry and expect . . ." She didn't know what else to say. And it was more than just kissing that they had done.

"I have no expectations. I just . . ." He stepped away from her and pushed his fingers through his hair. Then, slowly, he turned. "You have an effect on me, Bridget."

"My apologies."

"Don't apologize. I think you are what I need."

She needed to catch her breath. She needed her heart to slow down. She needed to think. And she could not do any of these things while he was so close, so bare to her.

"We should return to the others."

She turned and opened the door and stepped out into the foyer. Darcy did not stop her.

The good thing about having hair that never looked quite done was that if someone were to mess it up in the throes of a passionate encounter in a closet, no one would be any wiser.

Or so Bridget hoped.

Lady Francesca was standing there, in all her elegant glory. She tilted her head curiously.

"I should be surprised to see one my guests emerge from the butler's pantry," she said. "But with you, Lady Bridget, I'm not surprised at all."

Gad, now she would have to lie about trying to steal the silver—anything was better than the truth.

"Bridget, wait—" Darcy said, having thrown

open the door and rushed through it. He stopped suddenly as well. Bridget didn't need to turn and look at him to know that.

Lady Francesca's eyes widened. She opened her mouth but closed it quickly, for once at a loss for words. Well, there was *one* guest she was shocked to see emerge from the butler's pantry in the middle of the dinner party.

Bridget held her breath, waiting for a reaction. Then Lady Francesca, having collected herself, smiled. Oh, this was terrible.

"Don't worry Lady Bridget. You can be assured that I won't breathe a word of this to anyone. Come, Darcy, the gentlemen are having their port. Bridget, all the ladies are in the drawing room for tea, wondering what has become of you."

The carriage ride home was agony. While their carriage was large, luxurious, and well sprung, it was also packed with the family, all of whom had burning, unspoken questions about the state of her coiffure (a mess), her lengthy disappearance during dinner (no comment), her silence (Darcy had left her speechless. Still.).

Finally, it was Amelia who broke the silence.

"What did Darcy want with you, Bridge?"

Oh, just to ravish me in a closet. Just to bring me to such pleasure as I have never known. As one does.

"I don't know what you're talking about," she replied, staring out the window, not that she could see very much at this late hour. She hoped, desperately, that no one could see the hot blush on her cheeks as she thought about what Darcy had wanted with her. Just the way she was.

It was Claire who explained, patiently. "You left the table. And then he left the table. And then time passed. And then you were both out of sorts and, dare I say, slightly disheveled, for the rest of the evening. Everyone noticed."

"I don't know what you are talking about," Bridget repeated.

"Darcy would be an excellent match for you," Josephine said. But she also thought Mr. Collins would be a good match.

"Except that it wouldn't be," Bridget replied. And she could not explain that while he might love to kiss her and do other wickedly wonderful things with her, he would be embarrassed to call her his wife. He might value family, but he would be embarrassed by hers, scandal-plagued as they were. He lusted after her, and would come to regret it. "I could not be happy married to a man who valued reputation and wealth and estates above all else."

"You don't know him at all, do you?" Amelia asked softly. *Amelia!* Bridget turned to her, incredulous.

"And you do? I have not seen you exchange more than a few sentences with him."

"He is the reason I returned home after I ran away."

The silence had gone from awkward to stunned with this revelation. This was the first

Amelia had spoken of her great escape since she returned.

"He's not the *only* reason but he did find me, and reminded me what I was missing, should I not return soon. He did not speak of what the ton would say or what a lady ought to do. He spoke of love, Bridget. You all ought to thank him."

"Do you mean to say you would not have come home?" James said, sounding bewildered and possibly heartbroken.

"The possibility crossed my mind," she admitted. "But I won't be leaving you anytime soon. I shall plague the lot of you for years to come."

Then she turned to look out the window.

So Darcy had gone to rescue her sister. He had done a great service to her family to bring her home safely and not breathed a word of her disappearance. And he hadn't mentioned it. If he were really the man she thought him, he would not have tried to salvage Amelia's reputation; he would have left her to the consequences of her actions.

"It sounds like he is quite the hero," the duchess remarked.

He had saved *her* sister for no reason other than they had asked for his assistance. He kissed her like he was a drowning man and she was air. And he liked her, just the way she was. In fact, he loved her.

If he was not the man she thought, then perhaps she was not the woman she believed herself to be. She had clung to her own stubborn view of him, warped by her insecurities. She had not tried to understand him, but dismissed him as another judgmental English lord and simply rejected him out of her wounded pride. Bridget choked on a sob. She had been such a fool.

Chapter 21

The dinner party was horrible, save for the part where Darcy nearly ravished me in the butler's pantry. After he declared that he likes me just the way I am. What does this mean? WHAT DOES THIS MEAN?

LADY BRIDGET'S DIARY

The revelations about Darcy continued the next morning, making it impossible for Bridget to ignore how very wrong she'd been about him. She'd been alone in the drawing room, writing in her diary, when Pendleton interrupted.

"You have a caller, Lady Bridget."

"Who is it?"

Darcy? Her heart leapt at the possibility. Or did it lurch? She was expecting to see him this morning. After what had happened last night . . . there were things to be said. Questions to be asked. Honor demanded it. But so did love.

Love?

"Mr. Rupert Wright."

"Please show him in."

The butler returned with her guest a moment later, and then stepped away, leaving the door to the drawing room ajar.

"Rupert! It's so good to see you. It has been so long."

It had been a fortnight, in fact.

She crossed the room and clasped his hands. It was so good to see her friend. But it was also . . . strange. She and Rupert shared something and yet she had indulged in all sorts of liberties with his brother, just last night. And in a butler's pantry, no less.

"It has indeed. I have been traveling. With Darcy."

"Oh." She faltered at the mention of his name. "Yes, I saw that he is back in town. I saw him at dinner last night."

I felt him at dinner last night.

"Well, that explains his dark mood," Rupert said.

Oh God, what does that mean? She wanted to grab Rupert by the lapels and demand he tell her everything about Darcy's dark mood, and how dark was it, and did he happen to say anything about her? But then again, perhaps it was all nothing. Darcy was always dark and brooding.

"I'm sure I don't know what you mean," she said, joking. But Rupert didn't catch her meaning.

"I know you don't," he said, utterly serious.

She suddenly became aware of the beat of her heart and the temperature in the room. She had never seen Rupert serious. "And that is why I'm here. There are some truths you must be made aware of, Bridget."

"I'll just sit down then," she said in a small voice, and sat on the settee.

Rupert paced.

"For the past few months, I have been blackmailed."

She gasped dramatically because the news shocked her and the situation seemed to call for it. Rupert continued to pace back and forth, taking long strides across the carpet.

"Someone possessed knowledge about me that would have ruined me," Rupert said. She immediately thought of murders or robberies or other heinous crimes. But she could not picture Rupert engaged in such nefarious activities. It was . . . Rupert. "I would have had to leave the country. Indefinitely. I would have had to leave behind my friends, my beloved brother, my life here."

"Is this what you needed the money for? I thought it was for gaming debts."

"Yes."

"But Darcy wouldn't give it to you."

"Oh, he did. For most of the year, he gave me the funds I required, no questions asked." Oh. Bridget clasped a handful of fabric from her skirts, needing to hold on to something. She had wrongly accused him of refusing to help his own brother, saying it was the worst thing she could imagine. She felt, in that moment, quite awful. "I had to let him believe that it was for gaming debts. But eventually, he cut me off and I cannot blame him. He wanted me to be responsible for my own actions. But once he learned the truth, he did the Darcy thing."

"What is the Darcy thing?" Bridget asked, a hitch in her voice. She suspected she knew.

"Ride in. Issue orders in that lordly, commanding way of his. Save the day. Take care of everyone, except for himself."

She turned away, to look out the window into the garden, but saw nothing of the scenery outside. If anything, she saw a scene from days, weeks earlier when she had accused him of being cruel to his own brother. *If that is what you are determined to believe . . .* She had been blind.

She recalled Amelia saying, *You don't know him at all, do you?*

So very, very blind.

But then again, he'd never let her see these things.

"But you see, Bridget, I don't think he put a stop to the blackmail because of the money, which matters little as we have plenty of it," Rupert continued. "I don't even think he did it entirely just for me, even though I know he would lay down his life for me unblinkingly. I think he did it for you."

"I don't see how this has to do with me."

"I was going to propose to you," Rupert said.

Her breath caught. "I needed to wed for the sake of my reputation. I care for you greatly. I thought we would get along. But I would never make you happy the way a man ought to make a woman happy."

"Whatever do you mean?" She had asked James about this and he'd hardly been forthcoming with an answer.

Rupert's cheeks turned red and he looked away.

"I do not have . . . romantic inclinations toward women."

She knit her brow, confused.

"It is not something to be spoken of," he said. "And it was the reason for the blackmail."

And then her heart broke for him as much as for her. While she had written their names over and over in her diary, he was dealing with grave life or death matters. She had been blind to that, too.

Rupert quit his pacing and dropped into the chair opposite her. He leaned forward, gaze locking with hers.

"Can you imagine what torture it would have been for him to be in love with his sister-in-law? And to know that I wasn't making you happy? Or how unfortunate for you to be wed to a man who loved you only as a friend?"

She thought to protest that he would have made her happy. But then she thought better of it because if she was understanding him correctly, Rupert would never, say, become overcome with passion for her in a butler's pantry. Or at a gazebo in a rainstorm in the afternoon. He might love her, but only as a friend. Not the wild, tumultuous, confusing, maddening, yet wonderful, falling-head-over-heels kind of love she wanted . . . the kind of love she might possibly feel for Darcy.

"I care for you deeply," Rupert continued. "Which is why I am telling you this. And why I will not propose to you, or any woman. You deserve real love and true happiness. And so does my brother."

"This is . . . unexpected."

That was the understatement of the year. She found herself shocked, confused, and terrified of the implications of what he was telling her. She might have been gravely wrong about Darcy. And thus, she might have thrown away her chance at true happiness.

"Our father raised him to think only of his duty to the estate and to the family name. There was no Colin, there was just Darcy. If that makes sense."

He wasn't pushing her away because he was embarrassed by her, but because of his own desire. His offer of marriage was so tortured because he was, in effect, potentially sacrificing his brother to make it. His battle wasn't between lust for her and what everyone in the haute ton thought, it was between everything he'd been raised to believe and to value and his love. For her.

"I see," she said. Two little words. I. See. But it was everything.

"I think he loves you," Rupert continued. Then, looking into her eyes, and possibly the depths of her heart, he added, "And I think, Bridget, that you might love him, too."

> *I have been wrong about Darcy. Here I thought he was [unladylike word crossed out] but it turns out he is a hero. But what am I to do about it? What can I do about it?*
>
> LADY BRIDGET'S DIARY

Bridget had half a mind to utterly disregard propriety and dash over to see Darcy and . . . say something. She owed him an apology for misjudging him. She ought to thank him for saving her sister. But then how to explain how her eyes and heart had been opened. *I see.*

Should she throw herself at him?

What if she apologized and explained and groveled and kissed him passionately and he turned away, coldly? If he did not forgive her, if his love for her was not strong enough, then she had most certainly, well and truly, ruined her life.

But it was their day to receive callers and Josephine wouldn't hear of Bridget crying off for any reason at all, whatsoever. *Especially* not if said plan involved a lady calling upon a gentleman. It was not done. She would have to wait and see when—*if?*—Darcy came to call.

He was the sort of gentleman who would feel compelled to issue a marriage proposal to a woman after nearly ravishing her in a pantry and then being caught doing so. And yet, Pendleton did not announce his arrival.

It was, as one might imagine, incredibly difficult to maintain a cheerful demeanor after one had quite possibly and very foolishly destroyed one's best chance at a lifetime of happiness, all while being exposed as a judgmental, silly person whose priorities were not in the correct order.

It was the sort of anxiety that could only be soothed by a declaration of love and a promise of forever from Darcy. Who still had not come to visit. He had not even sent a note.

In the meantime: pastries. Bridget helped herself to one and then, ignoring Josephine's raised eyebrow, another.

She no longer cared about trying to emulate Lady Francesca or any woman like her. No matter how many lumps of sugar she refused or biscuits she didn't eat, she would never grow five inches taller and find herself lighter with a willowy figure. It was a hopeless endeavor and she might as well enjoy food and drink and sunshine on her face, freckles be damned.

She was American born and bred, raised by a father who fled the life in the haute ton and married for love. She would never reorganize the priorities she'd been raised with. And if that meant she never quite fit in with all the fancy English people? So be it.

She had her siblings. And, if she hadn't lost it, she had the love of a good man. No longer would she try to be something, or someone, she was not.

"Put your diary away, Bridget," the duchess said.

"Yes, Your Grace." She set the blue leather volume on a side table.

They had barely taken their seats when the first callers, who were not Lord Darcy, were announced. The Duchess of Ashbrooke and her friends had called; Claire had become friendly with the Duke of Ashbrooke over some mathematical whatnot that made her head spin. Bridget actually liked the duchess and her friends, particularly Lady Radcliffe. She liked them far more so than their other callers who mostly consisted of fortune-hunting third sons or marriage-minded mothers desperate to foist their daughters onto James, who was not interested in the slightest.

Pendleton announced the arrival of more guests, who were not Lord Darcy. Bridget was dismayed to see the calling cards of Lady Wych Cross and Lady Francesca.

"I don't suppose we can tell them we are not at home," Bridget muttered.

"We are not cowards, Lady Bridget," Josephine told her.

"So you admit this is a battle."

"If so, then it is also war. And the outcome of one battle matters little if one ultimately wins the war."

"Has anyone ever told you that you are unbelievably terrifying?"

"All the time." She smiled, patting Bridget's hand. "I take it as a compliment."

She was glad to have the duchess on her side when facing Lady Wych Cross, whom she had probably gravely insulted and irritated terribly at dinner. That was to say nothing of the terror she felt facing Lady Francesca, who had caught her emerging from the butler's pantry with Darcy and who had, surprisingly, not said anything.

But why should she? Then Darcy would have to marry Bridget, and she knew Francesca had been waiting for his proposal for some time now. Her secret was safe, was it not? For some reason, Bridget was far from relieved by the silence.

"Lady Wych Cross, it's excellent to see you," said the duchess. "And you are looking well, Lady Francesca."

"As always," she quipped with a little laugh.

"Modesty is *such* an overrated virtue," Amelia remarked.

"So is self-righteousness, my dear," Lady Wych Cross said. "Anyway, we have come to call and thank you for attending our dinner party the other evening. What stimulating conversation you all provided."

"Yes, our guests were certainly stimulated," Lady Francesca said with a pointed look at Bridget.

"Well *someone* must provide the stimulation," she replied, holding Francesca's gaze.

"What are we talking about?" Claire asked. "I find myself terribly confused."

"Why, the dinner party, of course," Lady Francesca said, with a wicked smile. "Unless you were speaking of something else, Lady Bridget?"

"Of course not," she murmured.

The conversation then turned to focus on the weather, Lady Benton's upcoming ball, the latest opera, and other things Bridget did not pay attention to. Because, Lord above, Lady Francesca had information that could ruin her, especially given that oh-so-proper Darcy had not come to propose again after kissing her.

She was now the sort of woman who dallied with lords in butler's pantries and did not receive proposals after. She would be ruined if word got out. Oh bloody hell, Bridget thought. Suddenly her fate and future happiness were held in the hands of a viper like Lady Francesca.

She could hardly expect Darcy to come to her rescue with another proposal. Or could she? The butler interrupted just then to announce more callers who were *not Lord Darcy*.

"It was lovely to see you all, but we must be going," Lady Wych Cross said. "We have an appointment at the modiste."

"For my trousseau," Lady Francesca said, smirking.

Bridget felt a sinking feeling in her stomach. Trousseau meant marriage, which meant someone had proposed or was about to. It had to be Darcy. And if he was marrying Francesca, then he wasn't marrying Bridget, which meant that she had lost the love of a good man and had no other prospects and would die alone, a spinster, in a cottage by the sea.

"Please do come call again. It is always a pleasure to see you both," Josephine said, lying through her teeth.

After they left, an influx of new callers, none of whom were Lord Darcy, arrived. And then Bridget endured another hour of company, the tedium and torment eased by an appalling number of biscuits. The duchess even gave up with the chastising looks, as they obviously had no effect. Finally, calling hours came to an end. Darcy hadn't called. Bridget had ruined everything.

Where the devil is my diary?
LADY BRIDGET'S INNERMOST
PANICKED THOUGHTS

Later that evening, while waiting for her sisters to get ready for dinner, Bridget thought she'd take a few moments to write in her diary. But it wasn't on her bedside table, or anywhere in her room. Sigh. Amelia. Again.

She crossed the hall to her sister's bedchamber. Amelia was sitting before her vanity table, whilst her maid was trying to tame her curls. It was a losing battle.

"Amelia, what have you done with my diary?"

"Why do you always blame me when you cannot find it?"

"Because you have a habit of picking it up,

taking it someplace to read, even though it is private, and leaving it somewhere else."

"I hardly see how that signifies."

"Are you daft? Amelia, where is my diary?"

"I told you. I don't know," Amelia ground out.

"Just tell me where it is and I won't be mad that you've read it," Bridget promised. It was a lie. She was already furious that her sister took it and read it and lost it.

"Fine, I shall admit to reading it in the past—and being bored to tears by it—but I have not removed it or read it recently."

"Claire—" Bridget called out to her sister, also getting ready for supper in her room.

"I haven't seen it either," she called back.

Bridget burst into James's study. He and Miss Green jumped apart, which might have raised questions in her mind if she weren't so focused on finding her diary. Oh God, the things she had written!

About Darcy. About Rupert. About Amelia. About *everything*.

"My diary," she gasped.

"A riveting tale of a young woman's entrance into high society," James said. "In which two brothers vie for the hand of an exotic American—"

"Does everyone read my bloody diary?" she cried out.

"Honestly, I have not, since I have neither the time nor interest in the inner workings of your mind. Sorry. I guessed that is what you wrote about and apparently I was right."

"Have you seen it?"

"No," James said, wincing. "Sorry."

God, her stomach was beginning to ache now. It seemed well and truly lost. If it fell into the wrong hands . . . She closed her eyes and moaned. She would have to leave England and return to America and spend the rest of her life answering the question, "Why did you give up living with a duke to return to America as a tragic spinster?"

"I'll help you look for it, Lady Bridget," Miss Green offered kindly.

"Thank you, Miss Green. I appreciate your assistance as well as your understanding of my great distress."

"Where did you see it last?"

Bridget took a deep breath and thought back.

"In the drawing room this morning. I was writing in it before calling hours."

"Then let us begin our search there."

It was not in the drawing room. It was not on any of the tables. It was not shoved under a chair cushion—and she knew because she flung them all aside, onto the carpet. It was not under the carpet either. Nor was it under the settee. She was in the process of looking there when Josephine's voice cut in.

"What is the meaning of this?"

Bridget froze on her hands and knees, with her bottom high up in the air. Well, this was an inelegant position to be in. As gracefully as she could, Bridget rose to her feet.

"I have lost my diary. It is a great tragedy and possibly an unprecedented disaster."

"Is it really?" Josephine raised one brow.

"I have faithfully detailed my time in England, which means that I have written many compromising things about myself and members of this family. I have also written insulting things about at least half of the haute ton."

Bridget watched the duchess carefully as her expression paled as she thought back over all the things that could possibly be recorded: Amelia's unchaperoned journey to God only knew where, Bridget's refusal of two eligible gentlemen.

And those were just the things Josephine knew about, to say nothing of Rupert's secret or what she'd done with Darcy in the gazebo. And the butler's pantry. Oh God.

If she held out any hope that she was overreacting or blowing things out of proportion, the duchess's horrified expression confirmed that yes, this was a disaster of unprecedented proportions. Yes, she should go to her room and pack her bags and prepare a return voyage to America.

But even in this time of utter terror and certain ruination, the duchess was strong, determined, and ready to fight.

"Well then, let us call in the troops," she declared. Then she dramatically pulled the bell cord once, twice, thrice, and a bevy of housemaids and footmen came running.

All the servants were enlisted in the search efforts for Lady Bridget's diary. No pillow was unturned, no bookshelf left unexamined. Long after midnight they were forced to face the truth: the diary was gone. Missing. At large. Absent. Unaccounted for. Lost.

A very somber group of Cavendish siblings gathered in Claire's bedroom. Amelia lounged at the foot of the bed, Claire and Bridget leaned against the headboard, and James sat in a chair next to the bed. It was a long moment of excruciating, heartbreaking silence before Bridget felt obligated to say something. And not just anything.

"I have ruined us all I am so, so sorry."

And she was. It had nothing to do with all the embarrassing things she wrote about herself and everything to do with the way she had embarrassed her family. If the contents of her diary were known, it wouldn't complicate things for just her.

"I'm sure it is not that bad," Claire said consolingly, resting her hand on Bridget's.

"It is that bad," Bridget said glumly. "In fact, it is probably worse than you can even imagine."

"Bridget is right," Amelia agreed. "I have read it. She writes about my escapades. And how Darcy compromised her."

"It was one kiss in a rainstorm," Bridget retorted. Event though, gah, it was so much more than that.

"One devastatingly romantic kiss so perfect that Amelia will think I'm making it up," her sister quoted, verbatim.

"Amelia!" Bridget lunged for her annoying, plaguing little sister, and Claire grabbed a handful of her nightgown, restraining her.

"Amelia," James said in his I-am-the-head-of-this-family voice.

"We'll be ruined if word of this gets out," Bridget lamented.

"So we shall be spinsters together," Amelia replied with a shrug. "We can get a cottage by the sea and a dozen cats and eat cake for breakfast. Besides, Claire and James won't tell anyone. They're *family*, Bridget. And if everyone is going to find out, they deserve to hear it from us."

Bridget banged her head against the headboard. *Thud. Thud. Thud.* It was really the only thing to do in a crisis like this.

"I think what our dear sister means to say is that if we know what we're dealing with, then we can figure out how to help," James said. And she felt terrible because this wasn't his fault, but he would do whatever it took to fix it. "And it sounds like we are dealing with two scandalous Cavendish sisters."

"Which shall reflect on us, James," Claire said softly, with a pointed look at her brother.

"I know." His mouth settled into a grim line. He was thinking about something . . . or someone. Even if James and Claire weren't mentioned explicitly, the scandal would still complicate their lives.

Worst of all, the family did not have the clout to weather this sort of scandal. Someone like, say,

Darcy, with his unblemished reputation and the respect of his peers, could possibly withstand it. But the upstart, outsider family who had forged very few connections with the ton were not in the best position to emerge unscathed.

"I'm so sorry," Bridget said for the thousandth time.

"We know you are. And it was your private diary, that you didn't expect anyone other than Amelia to read," Claire said. "And it's not as if you were careless and left it somewhere public. It was stolen right out of our home."

That was the other thing. It was very likely stolen. During calling hours. Bridget kept quiet about her suspicions of *who* had taken it.

"You mentioned Darcy was, er, implicated?" James asked, glancing at her.

"Yes," she muttered. He was, along with his brother.

"So he stands to have his own reasons to find the diary and ensure its contents are kept confidential," James said, and Bridget did *not* like where this was going but she was in no position to protest. "Do you think he might help?"

She thought of what she had written about him. *No.* But then she thought about what she'd written about Rupert. "Yes," she said. "He would probably help."

It would not be because of her. He might have loved her once, but certainly not anymore, and absolutely not after this. She hadn't just lost her diary, she had lost the love of a good man and her hope for future happiness.

> *It is after midnight. The house has been searched.*
> *My diary has not been found. I do believe this is the*
> *correct time to panic.*
>   LADY BRIDGET'S INNERMOST THOUGHTS

It was nearly midnight and the hour for making social calls and marriage proposals had long since passed when Rupert strolled into the library. Darcy was at his desk, a mountain of account books that required his attention today and correspondence that demanded responses immediately spread out before him. He hadn't even begun to review the documents that would be discussed in Parliament on the morrow.

Just focus. But the truth was, he could not. And he didn't need to. Accounts, correspondence, and Parliament could wait. What could not wait: the marriage proposal he was honor bound to issue Lady Bridget.

After the last one, he was in no hurry to repeat the experience.

And as for what came after, he imagined the worst. He would love her in his own restrained way. She would make herself miserable trying to conform to what she thought a countess ought to be.

It would be a disaster. He did not rush headlong into disaster. Not twice, anyway.

Rupert, being unfamiliar with crushing amounts of responsibility and work and a determination to avoid thinking about a woman, poured two brandies and set one down on Darcy's desk.

"What do you think is going on at Durham House?" Rupert asked.

"I'm sure I do not know," Darcy said, not even looking up from his work.

"I walked past and saw that the whole house is lit up. Upstairs. Downstairs. I can see people rushing about all over the place."

Rupert seemed concerned, but Darcy wouldn't allow himself that feeling. For all he knew, it was a bizarre American practice to light every candle and have an entire household rush about at a late hour. Perhaps it was one of their holidays.

"I hope no one is ill," Rupert said, worried.

"No one is ill."

"Miss Comte came down with the tuberculosis just last week. And I saw her and Lady Claire speaking close together. What if she has contracted it?"

"Your imagination is running away with you."

"What if *all* the sisters get it?" Rupert asked in a horrified whisper. Darcy didn't miss his sidelong glance and emphasis on *all*. He might as well have just asked, *What if Bridget is dying?*

"I'm sure that in the unlikely event that one sister has contracted tuberculosis, they will take every precaution to prevent its spread," he said in his calm, measured tone that did not belie his true feelings inside.

"Are you not worried about Lady Bridget at all?"

Yes. No. Yes. Darcy sighed. Set down his pen. He would have to do that Darcy thing, where he pretended to ignore his feelings to death.

"Why would I be worried about Lady Bridget?"

"Because you are in love with her," Rupert said flatly. He raised his glass in cheers. Darcy only scowled at him. Then he downed the contents of his glass in one sip, setting the glass heavily on the desk.

"You do not deny it," Rupert pointed out. Was that a note of glee is his voice? Was this torturous state of unrequited love somehow *amusing* to him?

"Lady Bridget has made it perfectly clear that she has a low opinion of me and is not interested in furthering our acquaintance."

"Lady Bridget might have revised her opinion," Rupert said cryptically.

Darcy was certain she had done no such thing. She was trying so hard to be a lady and he had not treated her thusly last night, in the butler's pantry of all the places in the world. Good God, he had gone after her as if he were a panting schoolboy and she was a lovely milkmaid known to be generous with her favors. He hadn't given the slightest care for her reputation; he had cared only for her soft sigh of pleasure when he kissed her.

And then today, he did not call on her. Did not speak to her brother about his intentions and marriage contracts. Did not even send a note saying, *I shall take care of this situation. Yours, Darcy.*

It turned out that he wasn't perfect after all; he was just a man in love, tortured by lust and terrified of being refused by the woman he loved. Again. For the second bloody time.

He expected to be refused. In fact, he was so certain that she had *not* revised her opinion that he was shocked to find her on his doorstep at an ungodly early hour the next morning.

Chapter 22

I'm afraid only Darcy can save me now.
LADY BRIDGET'S INNERMOST THOUGHTS

*B*ridget had spent a sleepless night in a state of acute heart-pounding, stomach-aching anxiety. Her diary was missing, and after a thorough search of the house with the assistance of twelve maids, eight footmen, two sisters, one duke, and even the duchess—there was no denying it.

Worst of all, she knew what had happened to it. Well, she didn't *know* beyond a shadow of a doubt but she had her suspicions. And if she was right . . . they would all be ruined. She and her siblings would have to return to America, failures. The duchess wouldn't be able to face society and would have to retreat to one of her six country estates to live out her days in shame.

With a disaster of this magnitude, Bridget would need help, beyond what her family could provide. There was only one man to turn to. Only one man would certainly just resolve the matter with a minimum of fuss. Only one man could do the Darcy thing where he rode in and issued commands until everything was sorted.

He just so happened to be the *last* person in the known universe that she wished to ask for help right now. She hadn't had an opportunity to apologize for misjudging him or to thank him, and now she would have to beg for a favor. But if she didn't . . . and if the contents of her diary were known . . . she did not think it an overreaction to already deem it The Scandal of the Century.

To be clear, Bridget did not care one whit about everyone knowing the embarrassing things she recorded about herself. No, she was thinking of the things that could ruin the reputations of people she cared about deeply. Amelia. Rupert. Darcy. And for them she would have to swallow her pride and call upon Lord Darcy (even though young unmarried ladies did not call upon gentlemen) and request his assistance in Saving Them All from The Scandal of the Century (even though it was all her fault).

Early the next morning. Very early.

If the butler was shocked to see a young lady on the doorstep, he did not give any indication. It was impressive, that.

Her fears that Darcy would not be at home to

her were quickly assuaged. The butler showed her into his study. Though it was early, Darcy was already impeccably dressed and seated at his desk. She noted a cup of coffee near his left hand, along with neatly organized stacks of papers and a small mountain of correspondence.

So this was where he spent his time, being lordly. Stepping into his private chambers— without a chaperone—felt so intimate, almost as much as a kiss.

He stood when she entered, and stepped in front of the desk. She searched his gaze for a clue about his feelings but he was as inscrutable as ever. Drat the man.

"Lady Bridget, this is most unusual."

"But hardly surprising," she said.

"I wouldn't say that," he said softly. She wasn't sure what he meant by that, and given that they hadn't a moment to waste, she decided to get right to the matter at hand.

"I hope I can still count on your discretion," she said nervously.

"Of course." He spoke as if it were that simple. And to him, it was. She knew then that no matter what she did to hurt him, he would never, ever betray her. Because he was good. Because it was the right thing to do. And he always did the right thing. Nothing else mattered.

Her heart cracked open a little then. Was it breaking? Or was that just the love starting to burst out? Whatever it was, it scared her . . . almost as much as the portrait above the mantel that had just caught her eye. Ah, a blessed distraction.

"That is a terrifying portrait," she remarked, eyeing it warily.

"My father."

"Oh! I am so sorry for saying he is terrifying," she said, cursing inwardly. Of course she had to go and say something vaguely insulting when she imposed upon him. "But I do hope that is not his likeness."

"It is a tame version of it," Darcy replied dryly. Bridget dared another glance at the furious old lord in the picture.

"Oh my."

She gazed at Darcy with new eyes now. She could just imagine what it was like growing up with a father who glared menacingly like that. How one would always strive for perfection to avoid that look, to mask one's feelings, to try to escape notice. Her own father had been laughing and smiling more often than not, and always encouraging his children to think and feel freely. She understood now what Darcy meant when he said he *needed* her. It hadn't just been about lust.

"I'm sure you did not come to discuss my art collection or my father," Darcy said stiffly.

"I just cannot imagine living with that expression staring down at me. It would make me so nervous. It *is* making me nervous." She laughed. Nervously.

"I plan to have it removed to the attics. I have tired of looking at it."

"What shall you replace it with?"

"I haven't given the matter much thought."

"Perhaps a nice pastoral. With dogs, and horses . . ."

"Lady Bridget, I suspect that you did not come here to discuss paintings or pastoral landscapes with me," he said impatiently.

Right, then. To the disaster at hand. Time to explain how the diary of a young woman was about to destroy lives. She sighed and summoned her courage and launched in.

"I need your help," she said. "My diary has gone missing. And I know you would never *say*, 'Who cares about the silly diary of a silly young woman' but you might be thinking it. And in case you are, I must tell you that the diary could ruin me. Us. Rupert. Amelia. Everyone and everything."

Darcy was silent, regarding her.

"It will be The Scandal of the Century," she added in a whisper. It sounded a bit ridiculous when said aloud.

He lifted one brow. "Is that so?"

How dare he mock her now! How dare he make light of this!

"I wrote about Amelia's mysterious and extended absence." He frowned and looked down at the carpet. "I wrote about the time you kissed me in the rain. And the butler's pantry. I wrote the truth about Rupert."

His head snapped up, eyes flashing.

"How do you know?"

"Between what you said, and what he told me . . . I figured it out. Well, I asked James to explain it and *that* didn't exactly go well." That had been an awkward conversation for both of them, to say the least.

Darcy closed his eyes, took a deep breath, and if he tried counting back from ten, he made it only to six or seven. When he finally looked at her again, his eyes were full of sorrow.

"Bridget, Amelia would be cut from society. In fact, none of you would be welcome. And Rupert could be hanged if that were revealed. Or he might have to leave the country. Forever."

And Darcy would be left alone, with no one. She so badly wanted to say, *You will have me.* But that wasn't the same, it wasn't enough, and it wasn't the right moment.

"I know. I am so sorry. I thought that the worst that would happen would be Amelia reading it. She's a snoop, but she doesn't gossip. I care greatly for Rupert. And my sister. And *that* is why I'm here seeking your help. I don't care at all about everyone finding out how many hours I spent practicing the quadrille, or how many desserts I refused over the past few months."

"Record of your dessert consumption aside, this is indeed a disaster," he said flatly. And calmly. And that was why she loved him.

He strode across the room and poured himself a glass of brandy.

"Brandy?"

"It's quite early for that, don't you think?"

"We are facing a crisis."

"Ladies don't drink."

"Please don't try to be a perfect lady," he said softly. He glanced over at her.

She bit her lip. Her efforts to Be a Lady had some good effects: she was no longer confounded by a formal table setting, she knew most of the steps to the quadrille, and she knew how to address most peers. But it had also made her miserable as she tried to fit into some mold that wasn't her. To please a man who liked her just the way she was. After the other night, she simply didn't have the patience or the energy to keep trying.

"Oh, that ship has sailed. And I am not on it."

"Right." He set the drink down and started pacing. She watched his long legs, long muscular legs, take powerful strides across the carpets. *Focus, Bridget.*

"Where did you last see it?"

"Yesterday, in the drawing room. Before calling hours. We have searched the house all last night."

"That explains it," he muttered. And then, "I told him it wasn't tuberculosis."

"I beg your pardon?"

"Nothing. Do continue."

"I am afraid that Lady Francesca stole it during calling hours."

He stopped short and turned to face her, his dark gaze narrowing. It occurred to her now that Lady Francesca was having her trousseau made and Darcy hadn't proposed to her. She did not like what those two things added up to.

"That is a bold accusation."

"This is true. Any one of our dozen callers yesterday could have picked it up and walked off with it. But I am not oblivious. I know she doesn't like me. I would not be surprised if she wished to ruin me."

"Why?"

Bridget sighed. "I'm given to understand that she has been expecting a proposal from *you* for quite some time. And then the other night . . ."

"Right. I see."

If he wished to roll his eyes and groan, *Women!* he gave no indication of it.

"I am asking for your help because I know you care about Rupert, if not me. I would hate for something to happen to him. And I know you have already assisted Amelia—yes, she finally told us you had encouraged her to return to us and we cannot thank you enough—so I wonder if you might perhaps help protect her again. I am not concerned with anything else, not even that I will be ruined if everyone learns that I am the sort of girl that kisses men in rainstorms and closets. I'm not worried about myself at all, although it will be tremendously embarrassing to have the haute ton know how desperate I was to fit in. Why, I kept track of my sugar cube consumption and the number of dance invitations I received . . ."

Darcy stood there for a moment, willing his pounding heart to slow down. She rambled on, as she was wont to do, about this and that and

God only knew what. And he loved her. Loved the sound of her voice and her strange American accent. He loved all the ways she endeavored to be better, each and every day. Even though she was lovely just as she was. He loved that she was facing utter ruin and tremendous ridicule, but her concerns were focused upon others. He loved that she had come to him, because he wanted to save the day.

Because that was what he did.

There was no denying that this was a disaster.

"I wrote about Rupert's blackmail and the reason for it," she said in a strangled whisper and horrified expression. "I wrote all about Amelia's disappearance. I mentioned how long she had been gone, and that we did not know with who, so everyone will assume the very worst."

He did not deny that this was a disaster. One of epic, unprecedented proportions.

"Oh God, I called Lady Wych Croft Lady Witchcraft." She fumbled to sit down in a chair by the fireplace. "Oh, she will never give me a voucher for Almack's. Which shan't matter because I will be ruined."

It was a disaster, but it was also his chance to save her and to show her that he loved her, and that was all that mattered. He had no expectations of his success or, should he succeed in locating the diary and keeping its contents confidential, that it would change anything between them. But there was no way he wouldn't try.

He ought to recoil from her company now

but that was the last emotion he felt as he gazed down at her, flung back in the chair, wincing as she recalled what she had written.

"And Darcy?"

"Hmm."

"I'm so sorry."

"What for?"

"For calling you Dreadful Darcy, and writing about that proposal, and my refusal. And how we kissed in the butler's pantry and how we are not betrothed."

Oh God. So this was what it felt like to have the blood drain from one's face. His reputation would be damaged as well.

"You'll be wrecked and it will be all my fault. Though I did mention how pleasurable it was."

Oh God. Were those tears in her eyes? He could handle anything—except for a woman's tears. In all his training, this was never dealt with. He dropped to his knee before her.

"What good are years of perfect behavior and a spotless reputation if I can't cause a scandal every once in a while?" He gave a slight smile. She looked at him curiously.

"And for the rest of us?"

"I will find the diary, Bridget," he vowed. "And furthermore, I will ensure that *no one* is ruined by this potential scandal."

"How?"

"This is what I do, Bridget," he said. "Saving everyone from total ruination and certain disaster is one of those lordly things I do all day."

A little laugh escaped her.

"You should return home. I will take care of everything." He rang for Danvers and requested his hat and carriage.

"Darcy, wait . . ."

He turned, and she lingered there nervously, and impatiently. As if she wanted to say something but was being held back. Which was unusual. Even more unusual—he knew, without speaking, what she couldn't bring herself to ask.

And he knew how to answer without saying a word.

Darcy closed the distance between them in two quick steps. He cradled her face in his palms and lowered his mouth to hers. This kiss was not enough, no, but it was promise of more.

As Bridget started to walk home, she foresaw a day of sitting in the drawing room, in a state of anxiety, eating loads of biscuits and pastries, and regretting everything. She wouldn't even have her diary to write in, to help soothe her. That was the thing about men dashing off to save the day: it left one little to do other than sit home and fret. This was hardly appealing, especially when one was in an advanced state of emotional agitation.

Besides, perhaps he would need help. Two heads were better than one, weren't they? They had a history of searching for lost things together. First her sister, now her diary.

Oh, whom was she kidding? Bridget just wanted to be with him. So she turned and dashed back, where Darcy was waiting for his carriage to be brought around.

"Darcy, wait!"

He turned. If he was surprised that she would dash after him in public, hollering his name, he did not show it. He was probably not surprised in the slightest. He didn't even seem embarrassed by her display.

"I'll go with you," she said, slightly out of breath from having run. Corsets were not helpful in such endeavors (running or breathing).

"Where?"

"Wherever you are going."

"I am planning to visit Lady Francesca. If what you said is true, do you really think it will help your cause if you were to call on her with me?"

"I'll just wait in the carriage whilst you go in to see her," she said, preparing to climb into the carriage.

"I don't think this is a good idea," he said. He offered his hand anyway. She placed her hand in his. Their gazes locked. She felt sparks. And shivers.

He then joined her in the open carriage.

"What is your plan for when you call on Lady Francesca at this early hour? It is too early for calling hours."

"I thought I might clarify our relationship," he said. And before Bridget could whip herself into an emotional frenzy, he continued, looking straight ahead, "She should feel at liberty to accept one of her other suitors."

"Oh," she said softly. It wasn't a proposal of marriage to her, but it was an indication that one was forthcoming. *"Oh."*

They rode on in silence for a moment.

"Do you think she will just hand over the diary?" Bridget asked. She was under no illusions about whether Lady Francesca would read it. If the situation were reversed, Bridget would absolutely ring for a pot of tea and a slice of cake, and settle in for a long, thorough read. If she were a more motivated person, she would perhaps take notes.

"I'm hoping that she will have carelessly left it lying about somewhere so I could just take it," Darcy said.

"That would be theft," Bridget said, relishing the thought of Darcy committing a crime on her behalf. "Darcy, you would be breaking the law."

"Laws do not apply to men such as myself," he said. And honestly, it was probably true.

"It is small volume, bound in blue leather," she said. "I wrote *Lady Bridget's Diary* on the front page and the rest is full of my 'hideous scrawl' in the words of Amelia, who still manages to read it."

"Family," Darcy lamented, shaking his head. But he also cracked a smile.

It was a very short drive to the stately home that Lady Francesca shared with her brother, Lord Fox, and her chaperone, Lady Wych Cross. As the carriage rolled to a stop, Bridget's heart lurched into her throat. The den of vipers, she had called it in her diary, as Lady Francesca was now undoubtedly aware.

"Wait here," he said in that I-am-a-lord-and-I-will-be-obeyed voice of his. And truly, she did wait. For a moment. A long moment, even. She had every intention of staying right there in the carriage until he returned.

But as she waited, she got to thinking. What if Darcy was shown into the dining room and invited to join Lady Francesca for breakfast? She probably wouldn't have the diary with her for meals. No, it was probably in the drawing room, or on her bedside table. If it were in the drawing room, how was Darcy to discreetly take it? How on earth was he supposed to get it, should it be in her bedchamber? If he were caught, it would be an immediate marriage and . . .

. . . she wanted him for herself.

Besides, a lady probably oughtn't be alone in an open carriage on the road, even if said carriage was parked outside the home of a woman of her acquaintance and a bevy of footmen were standing round. That settled it. Bridget could not remain in this carriage. She would have to enter the den of vipers and assist Darcy in locating and absconding with the diary.

She immediately formulated a plan.

It was one that struck terror into her heart, but she could see no other choice. It would be risky and downright embarrassing if she were caught.

But she could not sit in this carriage for another minute, waiting on her fate and future happiness. She would have to take matters into her own hands. She would even rescue Darcy for a change.

Bridget exited the carriage and rang the bell.

The butler opened the door and stared at her in that stony way that butlers did. She had been there just the other night and yet he gave no indication that he'd ever laid eyes on her before. That suited her purposes just fine.

"I am here to see Lady Francesca," she said in her best English accent, which was terrible.

"Who may I say is calling?"

Oh hell and damnation. She couldn't very well give her real name and she hadn't planned on a pseudonym. She blurted out the first thing that came to mind.

"Lady Fogbottom."

The butler lifted his brow curiously but did not crack a smile. Not even a little. Not even at all.

"Very well, Lady Fogbottom. Please wait here and I shall see if Lady Francesca is at home to callers."

Meanwhile, in the drawing room

In spite of the early hour, Lady Francesca had other guests. Her faithful companions, Miss Mulberry and Miss Montague, were with her. The three ladies surrounded a decimated tea tray.

"Darcy! What a surprise."

"Good morning. I hope I am not intruding."

"Not at all. Do join us." She gestured to the nearest chair for him and arranged herself prettily on the settee. "I have been so bereft of your company."

"We did just see each other the other evening," he pointed out. Stupidly.

"The less said about that the better, don't you think?" She gave him a smile that he could only describe as foreboding.

"What happened the other evening?" Miss Mulberry asked.

"Nothing," Darcy and Francesca said at the same time.

He could see now that all the reasons he'd thought Lady Francesca would make a perfect wife were all the reasons she was the last woman he needed. She was graceful, elegant, and so smooth. She knew how to control any situation. She gave no hints as to her thoughts or feelings.

She did not twist his insides up in knots, do strange and potentially dangerous things to his heart, or make him think deeply about what really made him happy. He wanted—no, needed—a woman who made him feel all those things, for better or for worse. Sometimes it felt like worse. But overall it was worth it.

"I was just telling my friends about the most sensational book I've been reading," she began. He glanced around the room for said sensational book and didn't see it lying about. "I cannot quite decide if the author means it to be a tragedy or a comedy."

"What is the book?" he asked, carefully maintaining an expression of vaguely polite interest.

"Oh, a man like you would never have heard of a book like this," she said with a little laugh. That laugh.

"Silly female stuff I suppose," he said dryly.

"Exactly. You wouldn't find it interesting at all . . . the trials and tribulations of a debutante during her first season. She is a bit plump and terribly awkward. It would be amusing if it weren't so heartbreakingly pathetic. "

So Bridget was right. Lady Francesca had stolen her diary. And was reading it. And talking about it with her vapid friends.

"I am, actually . . ." He coughed, choking on the words he had to say. ". . . interested. Very interested."

She lifted one brow. Miss Mulberry and Miss Montague giggled.

"Is that so, Darcy?"

Of course she did not believe him for a minute. He did not believe it for a minute. Dying of embarrassment inside, he said in his haughtiest lord voice, "Yes. I would be very interested in, ah, seeing such a book."

The things a man said and did for love. He would have to act interested. And he would have to provide a remotely plausible reason as to why a stuffy, self-important earl would be interested in the diary of a young woman.

"I cannot imagine why you have taken a sudden interest in the musings of an awkward, unmarried girl."

"You see, I am endeavoring to better understand women. And reading a book such as this would be an excellent, uh, addition to my course of studies."

Three incredulous females stared at him. And then they burst out laughing.

Meanwhile, upstairs

Bridget raced to the top of the stairs, only to be confronted with a lengthy corridor with dozens of doors to the left, dozens of doors to the right.

Oh Lord, how was she ever going to find Lady Francesca's room? What if she *never* found her diary and had to live her life knowing that all the secrets of people she loved were Out There, waiting for the worst possible minute to be revealed?

Focus, she told herself. Then as quickly and quietly and methodically as possible, she started opening the doors, one after another, and peeking in.

Finally she spied one that seemed like it might be Lady Francesca's. She recognized the pink gown lying on the bed as one she wore to Almack's on Wednesday evenings.

Bridget closed the door softly behind her.

Then she began to snoop, quickly but thoroughly and without leaving any evidence of her activities. Having grown up with two sisters, she had acquired this skill at a young age.

On Francesca's bedside table she found a stack of issues of *La Belle Assemblée* with pages folded down, presumably on the pages of beautiful dresses she wished to have and would have. There was a small vase of pink tea roses. There were a few conduct books and collections of sermons; Bridget had a few of the same titles. She found a sheet of paper with names written and crossed out; it seemed to be the guest list from the dinner party the other night and the order in which everyone was to go in to supper. So even Lady Francesca didn't just know everything off the top of her head. She had to look it up and study ahead of time, just like Bridget.

In the drawer she found more books.

"Well, well, well," Bridget murmured, picking up *The Dreadful Duke* and *The Mad Baron*, along with a few other gothic romances. Who would have thought she and Francesca shared a love of the same titles? If only she'd known; they might have had a real conversation or even a real friendship.

She did not find her diary.

It was not under the bed, under the pillows, or in the armoire. It was clearly not on the vanity table, though Bridget took a moment to note all the creams, potions, and face paints there. There was a pot of red rouge, suggesting that Francesca's lips weren't usually so red. There was kohl, suggesting that she darkened her lashes. There were creams to lighten spots and even an ointment for warts.

Even though she really ought to hurry, Bridget paused for a moment, looking down at all the evidence that Lady Francesca didn't wake up flawless. The perfection was carefully applied with lotions and potions.

That meant that perfection—or something like it—was attainable for Bridget after all. She could soothe away her imperfections with ointments and creams or disguise them with powders and paints. A little rose oil here, a tighter corset there . . . She could adhere strictly to her reducing diet.

She could improve her skin by staying inside, out of the sun, and applying goopy moisturizing and lightening creams. She could touch up her lashes, redden her lips, pinken her cheeks.

She could spend hours each day putting herself together, having her hair done just so and her face done just right, so she wouldn't feel bad about herself when she stood next to Lady Francesca.

Or she could enjoy herself, just as she was. She could eat. And feel the sun on her face. And redden her lips by passionately kissing Lord Darcy.

There was really only one choice.

Certain that the diary was not in the bed-chamber, Bridget turned to go. Getting upstairs was one thing; now she had to get back outside.

Meanwhile, in the drawing room

The three women laughed heartily for a good long minute at his admission that he wished to read a young woman's diary for the purpose of improving his understanding of the fairer sex. Darcy died a thousand deaths knowing that these women were going to dine out on this scene for months—along with all the revelations in Lady Bridget's diary.

He shifted uncomfortably in the chair.

The butler interrupted just then, for which Darcy would be eternally grateful. That is, until he heard who was calling.

"A Lady Fogbottom is requesting an audience, Lady Francesca."

Darcy stifled a groan.

"Who?" Lady Francesca was very perplexed. Naturally.

"Lady Fogbottom," the butler repeated. That he maintained a straight face whilst saying the name twice was laudable indeed.

"Tell her to leave her card."

The man nodded and returned to the hall, leaving the drawing room doors open.

Oh bloody hell. Darcy did not believe for a second that Lady Fogbottom was calling. He rather suspected that it was Lady Bridget Cavendish, of the American Cavendishes, up to some sort of scheme that could only go awry and create a bigger mess than the one she was already in.

"Now where were we?" Lady Francesca asked, resting her palm on his forearm and gazing into his eyes. "Ah yes, your educational reading material so that you might better understand the mind of a young woman. I cannot imagine why."

Rather that meet her eye, he looked around the room, seeking a blue leather volume. Nothing.

"Darcy?"

Darcy looked her in the eye and weighed his words carefully. He would do best to just get this over with.

"Perhaps we might have a moment of privacy?"

"Oooh, I bet he's going to propose," Miss Mulberry said.

"We'll just be in the foyer. Eavesdropping," Miss Montague added.

"I think that we should be clear with one another," he started, once they were gone. He shifted in his chair. Damn, this seat was uncomfortable.

"You are here for a serious conversation."

"Am I known for any other kind?"

"Touché," she replied, unsmiling.

"We have known each other for quite some time," he said. They practically grew up together, in fact. "And we have had an understanding for the past season or two. And it is now time for me to make my intentions clear."

"Yes," she whispered breathlessly. God, he'd given her the wrong idea. He was terrible at proposing *and* at not-proposing. And people thought he was perfect. Ha.

"Lady Francesca, if there are other suitors you admire, I think you should encourage them."

It took her a moment for the truth to sink in. He had always prided himself on being reliable, and now he was letting down a woman who had been counting on him. Not to mention angering his good friend. He did not want to marry her, but he also did not like having to have this conversation.

"Do you mean to say that I should not expect a proposal from you?"

"I'm afraid not, Lady Francesca."

"Does Fox know about this?"

"I have not spoken to him, no." Of course he had not found the time to mention to Fox, an expert swordsman, champion boxer, and crack shot that he would not, after all, marry his sister as planned. "I thought I would speak to you first."

"Well, I can't say that I'm surprised. You have not seemed yourself lately."

"Yes, well, I have been doing some thinking."

"About a certain American girl, I suppose," she said witheringly.

Speaking of a certain American girl, he saw

a flash of something—someone—in the hall. Probably Lady Bridget, in the midst of a scheme that would only make things worse. Fortunately Lady Francesca was angled away from the doors.

Darcy might have felt a flare of panic, not that anyone would ever know because he always took care to appeal inscrutable. He did not wish to discuss any Americans with her, but he was at a loss for what to discuss with Lady Francesca during the most awkward social call in the history of social calls. He had a hunch that he needed to distract her for a little longer while Bridget finished up whatever trouble she was currently engaged in.

"No, nothing like that," he lied. Then, inspiration struck. "I am very focused on my work in Parliament. Allow me to tell you about it."

Meanwhile, in the library

Bridget had lingered at the top of the stairs while Miss Mulberry and Miss Montague eavesdropped shamelessly outside the doors to the drawing room.

"Oh, he's not proposing," Miss Mulberry said with unconcealed boredom.

"How dreadful. Let us take our leave. We can go buy that cunning little hat we saw on Bond Street yesterday."

"Let's! I'll wear it Tuesdays and Thursdays . . ."

They chattered away, determining a schedule for the sharing of the most cunning little hat while donning their bonnets and gloves. Finally, they left. The butler returned to his pantry, the very same one where she had done wicked things with Darcy. The foyer was empty.

Bridget had managed to dash downstairs undetected. She had sought refuge in the library, with doors just opposite those to the drawing room, but now she was trapped. Trapped! The butler was in the foyer, near the door, doing butler-y things, and blocking her exit. Further complicating matters, the drawing room doors were open and she could see Darcy and Francesca in there. She could hear them. He was droning on about Parliament. She listened for a moment before dismissing it as the dullest thing she'd ever heard.

She examined her options and found a second set of double doors that led to another room, which also opened into the foyer.

Perhaps she could create a distraction that would draw the butler's attention. Then she could sneak out and resume her place in the carriage and act as if she'd been there all along. It was the perfect plan.

Bridget glanced around and looked for something breakable. She passed over the porcelain figurines on the mantel, or the full decanter of brandy, or the lovely china teacup left out, suggesting that someone would be back soon. *Oh my Lord, someone would be here soon!*

Bridget looked around wildly and her attention settled on a rather unremarkable and plain vase of flowers. She picked it up and crept into the adjacent room. Then she softly opened the doors to the foyer. Then, after raising the vase high above her head, she brought it crashing down on the marble floor.

Meanwhile, in the drawing room

Francesca managed to appear vaguely interested in his deliberately tedious description of his current reform projects in Parliament. This was why she would make an excellent political wife. But he had since reprioritized.

"Darcy, darling," she interrupted after a good ten minutes. "If we are being honest with each other, you should know that I haven't the slightest interest in your work in Parliament."

Oh thank God. He was beginning to bore himself and he actually enjoyed his work.

"I do apologize, Lady Francesca."

"I know why you are here."

"You do?"

"I do."

The awkward silence that ensued was abruptly halted by the sound of glass shattering in the foyer. Wordlessly they both ventured to see what the commotion was.

Darcy stepped into the hall only to find a broken vase of flowers at one end, with the butler staring down at it, puzzled. Darcy just happened to look at the opposite end of the foyer—at the front door. He just happened to see Bridget dramatically creeping out. She made a show of shaking her head: *I'm not here.* She lifted her finger to her lips: *Silence. Say nothing.*

Lady Bridget would be the death of him.

He turned back to the scene of the crime.

"How odd," he murmured, pretending to be fascinated by the shards of glass, spill of water, and stems of roses in a mess on the floor.

"Hardly," Francesca scoffed. "Lady Bridget, I can see you."

Francesca, Darcy, and the butler all turned to see Bridget right by the door with her hand on the knob. Caught.

"Oh, hello! I was just arriving. I saw Lord Darcy's carriage outside and thought I'd pop in to say hello." She paused and, turning to him, said, "Hello."

"Spare us all the tall tales," Francesca said with a wave of her hand. "I've had enough ridiculous stories for one morning. I know why you are here."

"Oh?"

"You're right, Bridget. I do have your diary," Francesca said smugly.

"Oh! Funny that," Bridget said. "I wondered if it got misplaced. Into your possession. Though it doesn't belong to you. How careless of me."

Francesca just shrugged.

"Actually I'd like to have it back, if you don't mind," Bridget said. "That is, if you're finished reading it."

What Francesca said next surprised them all.

"Of course. Come with me."

They followed her into the drawing room and she pulled the book from under a chair cushion. In fact, it was the chair he'd been sitting in. No wonder it was so deuced uncomfortable.

"You need only to have asked," Francesca said, making them feel foolish for the lengths they went to in order to retrieve it.

"You already read it, didn't you," Darcy said flatly. It was not a question.

"Shall I recite from the ongoing list of things Bridget hates about Dreadful Darcy?"

"Well I hope you found it entertaining and edifying," Bridget said sharply. He saw tears in her eyes. As always, it was so easy to read her: embarrassment, frustration, fear.

Francesca was either oblivious or unconcerned with her distress. "Oh, I learned all sorts of things that I suppose you both would rather I didn't know."

"We would appreciate your discretion," Darcy said, which was akin to a baby gazelle telling a starving lion it would prefer not to be eaten.

"There is one way you can be certain that I won't say a word." She paused for dramatic effect, knowing they were in no position to decline her request. She knew too much. Not one but two families would be destroyed by the revelations.

"Marry me, Darcy."

Francesca smiled.

Bridget gasped.

His heart stopped.

He had only just determined that he desperately did *not* want to marry her. He had only just decided to consider his own desires, and not put everyone else first, second, and third. But protecting those he loved was something he did, like breathing. He'd die if he didn't.

"Marry me, or I shall tell all my friends about Amelia's unchaperoned escapade and I will whisper rumors about your dear brother's proclivities. Marry me, and I won't breathe a word about how you've compromised Lady Bridget, twice. Marry me, and all your secrets will be safe. Tell me what you decide, Darcy. Tell me at Lady Esterhazy's ball tonight."

Chapter 23

Lady Francesca is devious and has issued an impossible ultimatum. My heart aches to consider the choice Darcy must make. Actually, my heart aches because I know the decision he will make.

LADY BRIDGET'S DIARY

Darcy needed to think. And he needed to drink. And he needed to be in public, where he would never allow himself to fall to pieces. Because there was a good chance he might fall to pieces. Thus, he went to White's and ordered a whiskey and took a seat in the back corner.

But then Rupert showed up and Darcy reconsidered the virtues of solitude when a man needed to brood.

"Ah, my dear brother Darcy. Brooding, as always. Honestly, I have no idea what you have to be so morose about. You are young, in good health, wealthy beyond belief, don't have the ugliest face I've ever laid eyes on, you are fairly intelligent . . ."

"Are you finished?"

"I could go on about your charmed life, if that would cheer you up. The multiple country houses, the bevy of servants to see to your every need, the love of a wonderful woman . . ."

"It would not. And it is no longer charmed."

"Well, now I'm intrigued."

Rupert pulled up a chair, collapsed into it, and motioned for a drink. Darcy didn't know where to begin. He decided there was no time to beat around the bush.

"My life is ruined. Or yours is. I must decide."

"I'm so grateful for the consideration. You might want to start at the beginning."

"Lady Bridget's diary was stolen."

"Let me guess. You recovered it for her, because you do the Darcy thing where you ride in and save the day. But then even you could not resist snooping through it and you discovered that she called you Dreadful Darcy and made lists of things she disliked about you and now you are heartbroken."

Did everyone know about that? Good God. He took a sip of his drink.

"It is far worse than that, I'm afraid." Darcy dropped his voice very low. "She wrote about you, intimating exactly what we'd hoped to keep quiet." Rupert paled. Darcy continued, "She wrote about her sister not being ill at all; she was out in the city for four and twenty hours. And

Bridget wrote about how I have compromised her."

"You? Compromising a gently bred young lady? I am shocked." Rupert gasped dramatically. Darcy scowled. "Truly," Rupert said, seriously, "I am indeed shocked. When did this happen? And where?"

"You needn't be so surprised. I'm as red-blooded as the next man. Even I have moments of weakness, apparently. And she is very . . . desirable." This was a vast understatement. "I would marry her except Lady Francesca has obtained the diary, read it, and threatened to reveal everything unless I marry her."

"You mean unless you do the thing that you've been meaning to do for years now?"

"Things have changed."

They had changed so drastically he hardly recognized himself. While he wasn't happier all the time, he certainly felt more alive because of all the feelings Bridget unlocked with him. He knew joy, and heartache, and the pleasure of a passionate kiss in the rain. And that was everything.

A lifetime of matrimony with Francesca now seemed like a death sentence. He didn't know if he could stuff all those feelings back into the box, buried deep. And he would have to if he were to wed her.

"I might have become aware of a certain feeling of devotion to Lady Bridget and a fondness for her. As such, I am no longer inclined to marry Lady Francesca."

Rupert burst out laughing. He threw his head back and howled. Slapped his knee. Heads turned in their direction. Heads belonging to peers of the realm, who were discussing gravely important matters of state and such until they were distracted by Rupert laughing. At Darcy, in his hour of need.

Brothers.

"Do shut up. This isn't funny and you're causing a scene. You know how I detest scenes."

"You could just say that you are in love with her. Like a human."

He could. Maybe. But things had gone very badly the last time he said those three little words, and he was terrified of repeating that scene.

And in the event Darcy thought things couldn't get worse, Alistair Finlay-Jones showed up, settling into an empty chair, also looking morose.

"What is so funny?" he asked.

"Darcy attempting to express his feelings," Rupert told him. "It's like a baby bird, trying to fly."

"I should like to see that," Jones said. "And what feelings? Hunger, thirst, annoyance, and a vague sense of disappointment with the entire world?"

"Love," Rupert said proudly. "He is in love."

"Have you not heard anything I said?" Darcy asked, indeed annoyed. "We could all be ruined. We shall be cast out of society."

He gave a sharp look to his brother, who finally seemed to grasp the gravity of the situation.

"All of us?" Jones questioned.

"Lady Bridget. Rupert. Myself. Her sister."

Jones's eyes flashed. "Which sister?"

"Lady Amelia."

And then Jones swore under his breath. Darcy gave him A Look.

And then Fox showed up, because apparently this situation could indeed become worse.

"What are we discussing? I hesitate to ask, because it looks very serious and you know how I feel about serious things," he said, pulling up a chair and settling in.

"We are discussing whether Darcy will marry your sister or not," Rupert answered with a distinct lack of subtlety or tact.

"I thought this was decided ages ago," Fox asked, yawning. "Have you still not popped the question? Gad, Darcy, what are you waiting for?"

"She proposed to him. In a manner of speaking," Rupert said.

"When is the wedding?" Jones asked.

"That's the thing. He would rather there wasn't a wedding," Rupert explained uneasily.

Fox turned and leveled a stare at Darcy. "Are you saying that you've strung along my sister for years and now you aren't going to marry her?"

"Yes. Precisely that."

Fox stood, drawing himself up to his full height of well over six feet. Darcy sighed and stood as well, not at all eager for what was about to happen but knowing it was inevitable and his duty as a gentleman to take it.

Fox promptly punched him in the face. Darcy stumbled back, clutching the side of his face where he'd been hit. Fox shook out his hand.

"I deserve that," Darcy muttered. "But bloody hell, you can throw a punch."

"Apologies mate, but I had to do that. Family honor, etc., etc. I could use a drink while you tell me what she has done now."

"She is blackmailing Darcy," Rupert said.

"God she's devious," Fox said, grinning. "Got all the brains in our family."

No one contradicted this.

"Well, there goes my plan to enlist your help," Darcy said dryly.

"Could you explain the problem? I'm confused," Fox said.

"Francesca is threatening to expose information that would ruin Amelia, myself, and Bridget unless he marries her," Rupert explained. "But he no longer wishes to marry her, as he discovered that he does in fact possess a heart and it yearns for Bridget."

Darcy rolled his eyes at such a treacly way of phrasing it.

"That's quite the dilemma."

"Thank you, Fox, for bringing that to my attention."

"We can do something. We can fix this," Jones said. "After all, it is not every day that Darcy admits to feelings, especially of the romantic variety. Rupert, was there concrete information about you? Whatever it is about you?"

"It was just rumors," Rupert said dismissively. "There isn't really any proof. Not anymore. Thanks to Darcy."

"Well if there is no proof, then I would think that between the lot of us, we'd be able to dismiss any rumors. Should they surface," Jones said.

"What kind of rumors?" Fox asked.

"Nothing," Darcy and Rupert said at the same time.

"I will only say this," Rupert continued. "Lady Francesca would damage her own reputation should she speak of it."

"Now I'm intrigued," Jones said. And Fox said, "I as well."

"You shall have to live with your curiosity," Rupert said. "Besides, we have more important matters to attend to at the moment. Such as my dear brother's future happiness."

"Right," Jones said. "I may have been out of society for some time, but won't Lady Amelia and Lady Bridget's reputations be protected if they are wed?"

"Yes."

"I should think the solution is damn obvious," Jones said. "We marry them."

"Clever . . ." Fox mused.

"It seems too easy," Darcy said.

"Have you proposed and been accepted?" Jones asked, with a lift of his brow and a distinct rise in his voice. "Have you tried to convince one of those women to pledge her troth to you?"

Darcy sipped his drink and winced. Or winced

and sipped his drink. He wasn't sure what burned more—the whiskey or the memory of Bridget's rejection. While he thought that her feelings might have changed, he had no proof. And he knew that she would want to protect her sister and Rupert above all else.

He knew what he had to do.

> *There are no words to describe the utter despair*
> *I feel in my present state.*
>
> LADY BRIDGET'S DIARY

Bridget set down her pen. She closed her diary. Her cursed, wretched diary that had ruined everything for everyone. She had half a mind to throw it across the room. Or burn it.

But there was no point now. Lady Francesca had so much devastating information—and was the sort of mean-spirited person who would deliberately use such information or share it with the biggest gossip of London. Bridget wouldn't be at all surprised to read about it in *The London Weekly* tomorrow morning.

Or to have it all flung in her face at the ball tonight.

There was only one thing to do. Bridget threw herself on her bed, and stared up at the canopy. She closed her eyes. She could not go out tonight.

She could not go out ever again. She would have to return to America, in disgrace. Just when she had found a reason to stay.

She opened her eyes at the sound of a maid entering the room.

"Good afternoon, Lady Bridget," her maid said. "Which dress would you like me to press for this evening?"

"None of them. I will not be going out."

"Of course," her maid agreed, and quietly left the room.

But there was no "of course" about it.

A moment later, Josephine entered the room in a swish of silk skirts and closed the door behind her.

"What is this nonsense about not attending the ball tonight?" she demanded.

"It is not nonsense," Bridget said, still lying on her bed, staring at the canopy, still desolate. "I am ruined. In fact, I have ruined us all. I'm very sorry, Josephine. I did try to be a True Lady. I tried to follow the reducing diet and to learn whether the third son of a duke outranks the firstborn of an earl. I meant to practice the pianoforte and learn French. I want to know how to do things with a certain air, but I have no idea what that even means. I shall never be an accomplished woman. And because I wrote about my struggles to be one and to fit in here, I have ruined myself and everyone I hold dear."

"Bridget."

"Yes?"

"Shush." Josephine gingerly sat down on the edge of the bed and arranged her skirts. She gently, and a bit awkwardly, to be honest, stroked

Bridget's hair. Bridget remembered her mother doing this when Bridget was in a fit of despair over a fight with her sisters, or upset about something in school. She found it comforting now.

"As you know, I never had children, which meant that I have never given one of these consoling and encouraging speeches before. Bear with me." The duchess paused. Gathered her thoughts. Cleared her throat. "You are a lovely young woman. I have been impressed and heart warmed by your efforts to fit in here when it cannot have been easy for you. Now why are you so convinced that we are all ruined? You have your diary back. And I understand Lord Darcy helped you."

"I do have it back. But it doesn't matter. Lady Francesca already read it. She already possesses the information to humiliate me and, worst of all, ruin the lives of people I love."

"I see," Josephine said calmly. She was silent for a long moment. Then, matter-of-factly, she said, "Well, everyone has their price."

"Hers is Darcy."

"Whatever do you mean?"

Bridget sat up to explain.

"She issued the most dreadful ultimatum. If Darcy doesn't marry her, she will tell everyone everything."

"Well, she and Darcy had been meaning to wed for some time now. It's about time he came up to scratch with her. Your secrets will be safe. See, there is nothing to worry about at all. Now which dress would you like to wear tonight? Perhaps the pink?"

"We both know that I look terrible in pink. But that is beside the point."

Bridget sighed a mighty, heartfelt, aching sigh. She flung herself back against the pillows. And then Josephine finally understood.

"Ah. I see. You are in love with him."

"Yes."

"Well, this *is* a wretched dilemma," Josephine mused. "Destroy those you love or lose the man you love."

"If it were up to me . . ." Bridget began. But then she stopped because it wasn't up to her. The choice was Darcy's and she knew what he would do. He would sacrifice himself to protect those he cared about. She wanted to hate him for that, but she found she loved him for it instead.

But the duchess, that clever, sharp, terrifying duchess, had other ideas. "Who says it isn't?"

Chapter 24

The duchess and I have a plan . . . I would write more, if I weren't so terrified that this volume will fall into The Wrong Hands. Again.

LADY BRIDGET'S DIARY

Bridget was informed in no uncertain terms that ladies—especially Cavendish ladies—did not hide in their bedchambers whenever something went the slightest bit wrong. While she hardly thought the situation counted as the slightest bit—she truly believed it was The Scandal of the Century, even if she felt silly saying it aloud—she was nevertheless done up and on her way to the ball.

"You look beautiful, Bridget," Claire said, smiling at her younger sister. The duchess had insisted on the blue silk, and it really did flatter her. The color of the silk highlighted the blue of her eyes, and the cut of the dress did marvelous things for her figure.

Even James said she "cleaned up well," which was high praise from an older brother.

She was glad to be looking her best when facing Lady Francesca, the haute ton, and Darcy. It was only now, at this impossibly late hour, when they were arriving at the ball, that she realized she had never told him "I love you." He would be making a decision that would influence the course of their entire lives and she hadn't given him that crucial bit of information. She loved him, just as he was.

"Now tonight," the duchess began, drawing her charges in closer, "we will abandon our usual plans to mingle with suitors."

"I never thought you'd say so." Claire sighed happily.

"We are to ensure that Lady Francesca holds her tongue. James, you'll need to claim at least two dances with her. We'll enlist some other gentlemen to keep her similarly occupied. The rest of us will need to hover over her, shamelessly eavesdropping on her conversations and prepared to intervene, if necessary."

"By any means necessary?" Amelia inquired.

Josephine replied immediately. "Whatever it is you're thinking—no. Just no."

They began with an ambush at the lemonade table, where Lady Francesca stood conversing with Miss Mulberry, Miss Montague, and a few others. Josephine engaged Lady Wych Cross in one of their insult-laden conversations whilst James enacted the first part of their plan.

"Lady Francesca. May I have the honor of a waltz this evening?"

She looked between him and the rest of the Cavendish clan. She was not stupid and seemed to suspect something. But young, handsome, eligible dukes were never to be refused.

"Of course, Your Grace. I would be honored."

He penciled in his name on her dance card. Twice.

"Until then," he said, with a perfunctory bow.

"I am looking forward to it," she murmured with a devilish smile.

James turned away and muttered to Bridget, "The things I do for my sisters."

She patted his arm affectionately. "There, there. It is a difficult task being a young, handsome, healthy, wealthy gentleman with a loving family. But somehow you manage, James. Somehow."

And thus began the second part of their plan: the Great Hovering of 1824.

While Lady Francesca conversed with her friends at the lemonade table, Bridget and her sisters lingered nearby, sipping champagne and obviously eavesdropping on her conversation lambasting the fashion choices of half the ladies of the ton.

When Lady Francesca stepped out for air on the terrace with Lord Ponsonby, there was the

Cavendish family, also desperately in need of fresh air. Bridget wondered if it were possible to push them both into the bushes, then discover them in a compromising position, thus forcing them to marry.

"Whatever you are contemplating—no. Just no," Josephine said, again.

When Lady Francesca took a trip to the ladies' retiring room, Bridget and her sisters found they needed to do so as well. Funny, that.

"I daresay this is the most fun I have had at a ball," Amelia said as they returned to the ballroom at a respectable pace behind Lady Francesca. "If only we had thought of this sooner."

"Speak for yourself. I am a nervous wreck," Bridget muttered.

"Have you seen Darcy yet?" Claire asked in a low voice.

"No," she said darkly, with a Darcy-esque scowl.

No, she had not seen Darcy yet. And that was causing acute problems in the region of her heart. There were things she needed to say (namely, that she loved him) and things she needed to hear (oh, what choice he made). Their fates would be decided tonight and he wasn't even here. Anxiety mingled with annoyance, longing tangled with heartache. And so she decided: she would slip away and find him.

Darcy had only just arrived—late, he hated being late—and he hadn't even entered the ballroom when he encountered Bridget in the foyer. She looked beautiful in that blue dress. Breathtaking, really. The minute he laid eyes on her, he knew. He knew what he had to do, what had to happen. A sense of urgency overwhelmed him.

"Come with me," he said, taking her arm and ushering her away from the ballroom, away from the crowds, away from the scandal that awaited them.

"Good evening to you, too," she said.

"We need to talk," he said quietly.

"Yes, I have to tell you—"

"Shh."

Just a few more steps and they were at Lord Esterhazy's library. Darcy opened the door, ushered in Bridget, and when he was certain they were alone, he shut the door.

And locked it.

"What is—"

Things gentlemen did not do: interrupt a lady when she was speaking. But he could not wait a second longer to kiss her. He, the master of self-control, could hold back no longer. He needed to taste her, to feel her, to *know* her. With her back against the door, and blocking her in with his large frame, he kissed her.

She tasted sweet, like champagne. Her lips were soft. Her body warm and tempting. If he could have one thing, one moment, forever, it would be this one stolen moment.

"I have to tell you something," she gasped. He paused, heart pounding. "I love you," she said simply. "I love you just the way you are."

"I know."

"Modesty, much?"

He grinned. And kissed her again. And wanted *this* to be the moment that lasted forever. Because someone loved him not for his station or status, or any favor he could bestow. It wasn't about money or manners or popularity . . . none of that. She encountered the raw, flawed, aching parts of him and loved him anyway. He knew that she also saw the sacrifices he'd made for those he loved. And accepted them.

It made his heart pound hard in his chest.

Darcy slid his fingers though her hair, cradling her head and kissing her deeply. And she sighed and wrapped her arms around him, pulled him close so that he was hard against her soft, luscious curves, and then he forget about what else might transpire this evening. There was only this moment, with the woman he loved in his arms, sighing with pleasure.

Bridget had said it once: *I love you.* She had said it again: *I love you just the way you are.* She wanted to say it again and again—but later. Because this kiss . . . oh, this kiss! A girl could get lost in this moment. She could forget the impossible bargain, forget that hundreds of people were just down the hall, forget that this could ruin her.

It would be worth it. This kiss, the feel of his hands caressing her, the heat in her belly, the weakness in her knees . . . it was all worth it.

"I want you to know, no matter what happens tonight . . ." he said, and her heartbeat slowed. It pounded in her breast, heavy and slow, as if bracing itself for bad news. ". . . I think you are beautiful."

Oh, she sighed. He kissed her neck. *Oh*, she moaned.

"You are kind, and funny and wonderful. You are just what I need." His voice was rough. Bridget started to worry that this wasn't a romantic speech but *goodbye*. She tightened her grip on him, grabbing a handful of his shirt fabric. It would be wrinkled horribly and everyone would see it. *Good*. She didn't want to let him go, not even a little, not at all, and especially not when he whispered, "I love you."

In the dark, they fumbled, finding each other for another kiss.

This kiss was fierce and urgent from the very first second their lips touched. She just knew, from the way he gasped and tasted her and pulled her against him, that he had wanted this, and wanted her, for a long time now. That feeling of being so *wanted* set her afire.

"I love you," she gasped. "I wish I could tell you all the time."

What a gift that would be, to be able to tell someone that you loved them any time, whenever the mood struck: at the breakfast table, in the afternoon, late at night, and later still, then early in the morning. And stealing kisses here and there, in the corridor or in the carriage, before calling hours or late at night after a ball. *That* was what she wanted.

And if she couldn't have it—even now, she still feared she couldn't have it—then she would revel in this moment when the whole world was shut away and there was nothing but her and the man she loved. She knew him to be a good man, but it so happened that he was more than a little bit wicked after all.

God, he had her up against a *door*. A public door with a few hundred people on the other side of it. In a house that didn't belong to him. Darcy was reminded of this when the sound of someone twisting the knob interrupted them. Even though he had locked it, he pulled Bridget away, darker in the shadows. She tripped on the carpet and stumbled into his chest. Her hands curved around his biceps. He wrapped one arm around her waist, holding her flush against him.

She writhed a little against his hard cock and he groaned. From there it was the matter of a few stumbling steps before she was lying on the settee and he was gazing down at her.

One more kiss, just on her lips, turned into a dozen more, each one lower and lower. He kept waiting for her to say no, or stop, or some nonsense about ladylike behavior. But the only sounds she made were soft sighs of pleasure.

He tugged down her bodice. She threaded her fingers though his hair, holding him close. Her breasts were gorgeous, full and . . . That was the first crack of his self-control. He teased the centers of her breasts until they were stiff peaks and then he teased her with his tongue until she was writhing and whispering, *Darcy yes, Darcy more.*

His self-control cracked a little more.

He shifted lower still, pushing aside blasted skirts and petticoats, skimming his hands along silk stockings, past her garters and higher still. And then he kissed her at the soft part between her thighs. She gasped. Then she moaned. And then he kept going.

Oh God. Oh my *God*. Bridget had never imagined this pleasure. With his tongue he teased her, taunted her. Darcy—Darcy!—was doing the most wicked things with his mouth to her most achingly sensitive place.

He slid one finger inside; her core tightened and her breath caught. She couldn't breathe. Yes, this. She wanted so much, so badly. Her hips moved of their own volition, finding a rhythm and moving with him. And the sounds she made—she didn't recognize them.

None of it compared to sensations building within her. There was the heat in her belly, an unrelenting tension. There was pressure—ever increasing, spiraling almost out of control pressure. The things he did with his mouth . . . his hands . . . his fingers . . . She arched up off the settee, crying out.

And that was only the beginning.

* * *

Gentlemen did not ravish young women on flimsy bits of furniture. So Darcy pulled Bridget down to the plush carpet with him. He pulled her into his arms. There were kisses. The soft rustle of fabric being pushed out of the way. There were moments he just breathed her in. And then there was the way her hips rocked against him. She arched her back, pressing her hips against his hard cock.

Never mind where they were and all the rules they were breaking. They were in love. And when she said things like "I want you, make me yours," even *his* self-control shattered.

When her hand brushed against his breeches and fumbled with the buttons, even he could not restrain himself. He touched her and found her wet, ready.

"Bridget . . ."

She kissed him. And whispered one word. "Yes."

Bridget looked up at him in the dark, recognizing the intensity of his gaze and the depths of his wanting. His blatant desire for her sparked a surge of her own. *Yes, Darcy. More, Darcy. Cannot get enough, Darcy.*

Stupid bits of fabric were moved out of the way—his breeches, her skirts—and she longed to feel his bare skin against her own. Perhaps another time . . . when they weren't at risk of discovery . . .

She sighed at the sensation of his weight bearing down on her. But that was nothing compared to the feeling of him, hard and hot, there. She felt him slide inside her, inch by tantalizing inch, giving her time to adjust. But she didn't want to wait and she didn't want to go slow. Darcy then began to move inside her and the whole world was reduced to her, to him, and to this moment when they became one.

Oh God. He thrust into her once, twice, then he lost count, lost his head completely and just allowed himself to feel. There was lust, burning-up-need-more-more-more lust. But there was also love . . . like a profound connection, like . . . like he didn't even know. It just felt right. And intense. And everything.

Heart pounding. Moving inside her. Frantic, fumbling kisses.

A cry. A shout. A sigh.

A kiss. His heart was slowly beginning to resume something like a normal pace. She lay in the crook of his arm, her head on his chest. His cravat was . . . somewhere. His attire would be wrinkled, to say nothing of the damage he had done to her hair and gown.

"This is where I belong," she said softly.

"On the floor of Lord Esterhazy's private study?"

"No, silly. Here. With you. In your arms."

Chapter 25

No, Amelia or anyone else who is reading this,
I will not relate the details of what transpired between Darcy and myself.

LADY BRIDGET'S DIARY

*B*ridget had done her best to repair her appearance but there was no hiding how Darcy
ruined her . . . coiffure. Just as there was no
hiding the telltale signs that she'd been kissing
someone: reddened, plump lips and pink cheeks.
Oh, and that sparkle in her eye; there was no
hiding that.

She slipped out of the library—Darcy would
follow in twenty minutes—and into the ladies'
retiring room. It was there, standing in front of
the mirror, noticing how ravished she looked,
that she realized she did not know what Darcy
had intended to do: marry her, or marry Francesca.

A true lady—or any woman with half a care for her reputation and future—might have determined that before offering up her virtue. On the floor. Of someone else's library. But she, Lady Bridget Cavendish, was overcome with passion, in love, and didn't regret a thing.

Nevertheless, she rushed back to the ballroom.

She found her family in conversation with Lady Evelyn Fairfax and her sister, Miss Eileen, a pair of sisters who had been kind to the Cavendishes from the beginning. Nearby, of course, was Lady Francesca.

When she caught the entire Cavendish clan, and their friends, looking her way, Lady Francesca's polite smile faded swiftly into a plainly furious expression. She stalked over, leaving a bevy of suitors behind, curious.

"I know what you are doing," she said sharply.

"Oh? We are just enjoying this lovely soiree," Bridget said. No one had any idea just how much she had enjoyed it thus far.

"Isn't it lovely? I daresay Lady Esterhazy outdid herself with the decorations," Claire remarked.

Francesca ignored them.

"You are hoping to ensure that I won't say a word about the contents of your precious diary. You think that if you just hover nearby, then you will prevent me from gossiping about everything that I know." She dropped her voice. "Everything."

"Now Lady Francesca . . ."

"Well, you are gravely mistaken, Lady Bridget.

Unless Darcy finally proposes to me. Do you know how long I have been waiting?"

"I do not."

"Years," she hissed. "I turned down a marquis, two earls, and a few barons. Not that barons truly signify. Now you think you can just come along and steal my intended, and I am quite nearly on the shelf."

"I didn't want to. I didn't mean to," Bridget said softly. Oh Lord, did she really need to feel pangs of empathy for this woman who was threatening to ruin her? No. But she felt them anyway. How dreadfully inconvenient. "Say whatever you wish about me, Lady Francesca, but don't drag anyone else into it."

"It depends on Darcy, does it not?"

Aye, it depended on Darcy, who stomped around being lordly, saving the day and sacrificing his happiness for silly things like reputation. Darcy, whom she loved. Darcy, who was presently nowhere to be found.

Unless it depended on her.

Perhaps she could save the day.

Bridget's heart started pounding at the thought of what she was about to do.

"Actually, Lady Francesca, it does not depend on Lord Darcy. You see, if I were to tell everyone all the secrets in my diary, then you would have no leverage with which to force Darcy's hand."

The look of shock on her face revealed that she had not considered this. Then she considered it. And scoffed.

"You wouldn't dare," she said menacingly. "You would ruin your sister."

"Not necessarily," Amelia cut in. Bridget caught her eye. What the devil did that mean? Amelia winked, leaving her even more confused.

"You ran away unaccompanied and told the ton you were ill," Francesca said in a quiet, lethal voice. "I daresay you would be ruined if anyone knew about that. And Bridget, you will also be ruined if everyone knew what you did with Darcy. And I don't see a betrothal ring on your finger and I certainly don't see him by your side, coming to your rescue."

And then, there he was.

Lord Darcy.

Both she and Lady Francesca sighed and turned to watch him walk through the crush in their direction.

She tried to read his expression: determined? Angry? Ravished? Vexed to be embroiled in a fraught standoff between two gently bred ladies over a diary? It was impossible to tell. She suspected it was all of those things.

And then he smiled at her. The one time he had to smile at her, in public, across a crowded ballroom, and it was a mistake. Lady Francesca understood something in that smile, directed toward Bridget. It meant she had lost. She turned to address the ballroom, clapped her hands for attention, and spoke loudly.

"Attention, everyone. I have an announcement to make."

Darcy stopped short. The crowd around them fell quiet, and slowly a silence descended upon the ballroom.

"This is so dramatic," Amelia whispered.

"Thank you for stating the obvious," Claire replied. She had come to stand with her sisters in what by all accounts appeared to be their hour of need.

"Honestly, isn't your heart just racing?" Amelia asked.

"Honestly, I feel like I might cast up my accounts," Bridget said softly. "On your shoes."

But she wasn't nervous about what Lady Francesca was about to say. Bridget was nervous about the declaration she was about to make.

Francesca stood there, poised, reveling in having all the attention in the ballroom fixed on her.

"I also have an announcement to make," Darcy declared. He knew how to speak to make himself heard. His low, strong voice made her heart start to pound. She didn't know what he was going to say. She only knew he loved her. But was that enough?

"Ladies first, Lord Darcy," Francesca chided him. "Or would you like to make the announcement together?"

There were audible murmurs and gasps in the crowd. Everyone would now be expecting a betrothal announcement. Bridget's heart began to pound in earnest now. Breathing suddenly became an impossible task. And why hadn't she noticed how many people were here? Hundreds and hundreds of people who were standing around, sipping champagne, and about to watch her make an arse of herself. Again.

"And now I feel faint."

"Don't swoon now, Bridget. Things are just getting interesting," Claire said.

"You have no idea how interesting," Bridget said. She took a deep breath, as much as she was able. She stood up straight, as Josephine had instructed her to (or nagged, really). She ignored the pounding of her heart and the dampness of her palms; instead she thought about love and happiness and summoned every last ounce of courage she possessed.

"Actually I have an announcement to make," Bridget said loudly, which stole all the attention. "And I do believe I outrank you, Lady Francesca, so I shall go first."

She found Josephine's face in the crowd; the duchess's look of pride and satisfaction gave her the encouragement she needed. Then she looked for Darcy. She saw Rupert with him, too. Both brothers nodded at her. *Go on*, they seemed to say.

"Good evening, everyone. I am Lady Bridget Cavendish, of the American Cavendishes. I am also known as the girl who fell . . . in love." She paused, as there was a ripple of kind laughter through the room. "I wrote all about it in my diary, as a young lady is wont to do. And it so happens that my diary has fallen into the clutches of a person with . . . unladylike intentions. Someone threatens to reveal all my innermost secrets to embarrass me."

Here Bridget paused as a shocked, collective murmur stole through the crowd.

"But you see, I may not be very good at walking across a ballroom without falling on my backside, or remaining in a rowboat without crashing into the water, but I am quite good at embarrassing myself in public."

There was more laughter. Was it friendly or mocking? She could not be sure. This was a terrible idea. This was the worst idea in the history of bad ideas. But she could not stop.

But then her gaze found Darcy.

And she felt even more nervous. Because, as usual, he was gazing at her with that dark intensity. Watching her now the way he'd watched her at all the other balls . . . with devotion. Purpose. He hadn't disapproved at all, she realized. He'd been captivated. That realization kept her going.

"I wrote about how I struggled to fit in here: everything from my inability to learn French and the pianoforte to how I didn't know when I was allowed to walk in to supper. I wanted so badly to belong here. I also wrote about falling in love." Here she paused not just for dramatic effect but to catch her breath. "With Lord Darcy."

She dared to look at him. She couldn't look away, really. After all, what she was about to say wasn't for the benefit of the ballroom, but for him. There just happened to be a few hundred people listening in.

"It turns out that he is not as dreadful as I once thought. In fact, he is not dreadful at all. He is the best man I know. He will do anything for other people's happiness. But I would like the chance to make him happy."

It was just as well that Francesca interrupted then, as Bridget really did not know what else to say. She had been counting on Darcy to step forward and declare his everlasting love, or propose, or something that made the risk worthwhile.

"I cannot believe this. You can't possibly make her your countess."

The way Francesca said "her" revealed so much more: her, the clumsy girl who fell; her, the woman prone to public displays of mortification; her, the girl who didn't know the ins and outs and roundabouts of English high society; her, the girl who was always making a cake of herself.

Finally, thank God, finally Darcy said something in that low, powerful I-am-the-lord-and-master voice.

"I can make her my countess. And I will."

The crowd erupted in noise then—gasps and aws and "Can you believe it?" And "Did he just say . . . ?" If she weren't so keen to hear what he would say next, Bridget might have swooned.

"When I first learned that a pack of horse-farming orphans from the colonies would be inheriting one of our finest and most prestigious dukedoms, I shared the same sentiment as many in this room: disappointment, dismay, and a morbid curiosity to watch this family stumble and fall. And indeed, I watched them stumble. And fall."

Bridget bit her lip.

"And then I watched as Lady Bridget—and her family—stood back up, and endeavored to make the best of what must have been a trying situation with hope and humor. The more time I spent with them, the more I was reminded of what truly matters. Family. And love."

It seemed so very hard to believe that Darcy was standing up and saying such things in front of, oh, the entire haute ton. The man who said very little and certainly nothing about emotions. The man who was always right was confessing that he sometimes made mistakes. And the man spoke to just a few hundred of the finest, most prestigious, and snobby families in the country. Just a gathering of people who had dismissed her and her family out of hand. But Darcy saw her, really saw her, and liked her just as she was and wanted everyone to know it.

"And, while I am demonstrating more emotion than I have in my three and thirty years, allow me to finish with this: I love you, Lady Bridget."

He smiled slightly, nervously, at her as the crowd in the ballroom burst into applause and cheers. Bridget thought her heart might explode with love for this man. She waited impatiently for him to make his way through the crowd to her.

And just when she hoped the worst was over, there was Lady Francesca before her.

"Are you not forgetting something? About your sister? I'll tell everyone. I may not be able to make an announcement but I can whisper here or there . . ."

"Can we discuss it later? I am in the middle of a devastatingly romantic moment," Bridget said. Darcy was standing before her now and she very badly wished to feel his arms around her.

"I shall handle this one, Bridget," Amelia said, coming to stand beside her. "You go off with your Looord Darcy."

"And what about your brother?" Lady Francesca challenged, turning to Darcy.

He reluctantly turned to face her and gave her the Darcy stare, the one that would probably cause God to question his own righteousness.

"What about my brother? I daresay you wouldn't compromise your own reputation to whisper about unfounded rumors of things which proper young ladies oughtn't know or speak of."

Francesca was speechless. But then again, Darcy had made it plain that there was nothing more to say. And then Lord Fox was there, linking arms with his sister. "I'm sure my dear sister has nothing to say about our good friend Rupert."

Chapter 26

*Darcy loves me. Darcy. Loves. Me. And every-
one knows it.*

LADY BRIDGET'S DIARY

The next day, the duke summoned Bridget to
an interview. It sounded so dramatic and forbid-
ding. An interview. With the duke. In truth, her
dear brother, James, said, "We need to talk," and
she followed him not to his study but down the
stairs and into the kitchens.

Luncheon had already been cleaned up and
the preparations had not yet begun for dinner, so
the place wasn't overrun with activity. They took
seats around the large prep table and availed
themselves of the cake Cook had left out. Bridget
even made them a pot of tea.

"Darcy was just here," James said after she
had settled in with a cup of strong tea with two

sugar cubes and a generous slice of cake. She was ravenous after last night.

"I know," she replied. "I watched from the window. I also knew he was planning to see you."

"I presume you also know why."

James looked at her and she couldn't help but blush, partly with happiness and partly with embarrassment. God, if her brother knew . . . Best not to think about that and focus on what truly mattered.

"He wishes to marry me," she said softly. It was so strange and magical to say those words, and even better to know them to be true. Even sweeter because she was happy about it, deliriously so.

"And what about you, Bridge?"

"I wish to marry him as well," she said. Of course after last night, she now had to, but truly, she was well aware of the consequences— marriage, or spinsterhood—and she decided he was worth the risk. She wanted to marry him with all her heart.

But James was looking at her intently now, as if trying to discern if she really meant it—or worse, if he was going to allow it. Or, Lord above, was she supposed to have a talk with her brother about feelings and why she truly must marry Darcy? She'd much rather not. "So now that we have agreed to the match, I best let Josephine know. She'll want to start planning."

She stood to leave. James grabbed a handful of her skirt.

"Not so fast, little sister."

She slunk back into her chair and nervously met her brother's gaze.

"Ever since we arrived, you have called him Dreadful Darcy and thought he was the embodiment of everything you despised about England. Amelia said you kept an ongoing list of things you disliked about Dreadful Darcy in your diary."

"Amelia! It's one thing if she reads my diary, but she's not supposed to gossip about it!"

"Never mind that now. You also fancied his brother. So much so that you asked me to lend him a thousand pounds. I'm just curious; what has changed?"

Very well, that was a fair question.

"It so happens that he is not the worst. Not at all. And I hadn't known until it was almost too late," Bridget explained. "You know how he went out and found Amelia. He is so protective of his brother. And he helped me find my diary when it was missing. He is so good."

He was also a good kisser, amongst his other talents, but her brother didn't need to know that.

"And he needs me. And I love teasing him—I'm the only one who does. It's such a trifling thing, but it isn't really and—" Fortunately James cut her off. She was rambling, trying to find a way to explain that she and Darcy fit together, and balanced out their strengths and weaknesses.

"You know what this means, don't you?" James asked.

"I'm sure you're going to tell me."

"We need the rest of the family."

He found a maid who could go find Amelia and Claire and tell them the duke had summoned them for an emergency meeting in the kitchens. Meanwhile, James and Bridget ate cake and drank tea while she tried to guess What This Means.

Finally, her sisters arrived, stomping loudly down the stairs, bickering over something or other.

"Oh, cake!" Amelia exclaimed.

"Is there any more tea?" Claire inquired.

James cleared his throat. "We have an important matter to discuss."

"Yes, yes, Your Grace," Claire said dismissively. "If it's important, then I need some tea."

"And I need cake or I shall perish," Amelia replied.

James sighed wearily and did that thing where he gazed toward the heavens (or in this instance, the first floor) and muttered a request for the Lord to save him from his plague of sisters. Finally everyone was seated with slices of cake and hot cups of tea.

"Bridget is in love and wishes to marry," James declared.

"I think that was made quite clear last evening," Claire said. "The entirety of English society knows that she is in love and wishes to marry."

"Darcy was here this morning requesting

permission to wed her. Of course I have granted permission because I'm not an ogre. But . . ."

"If she marries, she stays in England," Claire added.

"And we must stay together," Amelia finished.

"But I could never choose between you or Darcy," Bridget cried.

"We wouldn't ask that of you," Claire said, resting her hand over Bridget's.

"But," James said, pausing dramatically. "Do we all wish to stay in England, or does someone wish to return home?"

There was a long moment of silence as each one considered it. They had come to England expecting perhaps nothing more than an extended visit, for it was laughable that James would be a duke. But he was growing into the role more and more each day. If they stayed, it meant goodbye to America and hello forever to life in England.

Bridget wanted to be everywhere at once, and she wanted her siblings and Darcy by her side. She did not wish to choose.

She loved him, loved him in a way that was so right and good that nothing else mattered. And no one else would ever love her as Darcy did, completely and just the way she was. And he needed her. They balanced each other out, perfectly so.

"We could always take trips back to visit," Amelia said in a small voice, breaking the silence.

"That is always an option," Claire said.

They would stay.

"So it's decided then," James said, glancing at each of them.

And that was when Josephine arrived, resplendent in a rose silk dress that contrasted greatly with her simple and dim surroundings. Of course the sight of her down here stunned the siblings into silence. With her was Lord Darcy, looking perfectly out of place but determined to fit in, all the same.

"We have a vast house full of proper meeting rooms and I find you all in the kitchens," she said.

"Cavendish family tradition," James said. And then to Darcy he stood, offered his hand, and said, "Welcome to the family."

Darcy gave a half smile and nodded, and was clearly out of sorts to be below stairs. Bridget found it adorable.

"Well you weren't wrong about our informality," she said to him. "Though we shall see if it is the downfall of civilization."

He smiled, and took her hand, and kissed her palm. "As long as we're together for it."

Claire interrupted the moment with an offer of cake.

"Don't mind if I do," the duchess said grandly. And then to their surprise, Josephine joined them at the table for tea and cake and chatter about wedding plans. In the kitchen. With servants milling about.

"I do believe this occasion calls for champagne," the duchess declared. James rummaged around and found a bottle and some flutes.

They all toasted to family and love and happily ever after.

Epilogue

It was the morning after their wedding and, as one would expect, Darcy and Bridget were to be found in bed. Tangled up in soft white sheets, tangled up in each other. There were kisses and soft sighs, quiet moans and gasps as they made love in the lazy, leisurely way of a couple who had the promise of a lifetime together and no need to rush.

It was only when the sun was high in the sky that husband and wife deigned to leave their bed, dress, and go down to breakfast. There were freshly ironed newspapers by Darcy's place at the table, and a present near Bridget's.

"What is this?" She glanced over at him and smiled in that mischievous way of hers.

"It is a present for you," Darcy answered, nervously. He wanted to give her something that would not only please her, but demonstrate that he loved her, just the way she was. Needless to say, he'd agonized over finding exactly the right thing. "A wedding present, to be precise."

"What is it?"

"I should have known," he said, shaking his head, closing his newspaper, and setting it aside.

"What should you have known?"

"I should have known that you are the sort of person who asks what is in a present rather than just opening it." He couldn't help it. He grinned.

She laughed. "And I suppose you are the sort of person who oh-so-slowly and oh-so-carefully unwraps gifts so as not to wreck the wrapping. As if *you* needed to save it or economize."

"You say that as if there were something wrong with that method. It is a very dignified way of unwrapping a gift."

"Ha! I knew it."

"Are you going to open it?" he asked impatiently.

She unwrapped in a manner that was the opposite of his, which was to say not neatly or carefully at all. She dropped the crumpled paper by her place at the table.

"Oooh," she sighed. "It's beautiful."

It was a book. To be specific, it was a book full of empty pages, waiting to be filled with Bridget's thoughts, feelings, and observations. It was a thick, leather-bound volume in "the prettiest shade of lilac," according to the shopkeeper. The thick pages had silver edges, and a silver filigree design was stamped into the leather.

"And look at this, it has a lock," Bridget said, smiling. She glanced up at him and batted her dark lashes. "Are you tempted to see what I shall write?"

"Not in the slightest. I would never read the private writings of another person."

"I suppose it is in the event that my diary once again falls into the clutches of a nefarious creature with malicious intentions. Don't those words just give you shivers?"

"No. I told you grown men don't get shivers," he replied. "I thought a lock would be appropriate for the times when Amelia is here for a visit."

She laughed. "How well you know the Cavendishes now! It is perfect, Darcy, I love it. I love *you*. Thank you."

She swept over to him, leaned over, and kissed him. He tugged her down into his lap, dismissed the servants, and they did things at the breakfast table that gentlemen did not discuss.

Later that afternoon Bridget sat at the delicate writing desk in her private drawing room at Darcy's house. Correction: the home she shared with him. She traced her fingers along the leather cover of her new diary, thinking of all the wonderful things with which she hoped to fill up the pages.

On the first page she wrote:

Lady Bridget's Diary, Volume the Second

But that didn't seem quite right. This was her first day as a married woman, the first day of the rest of her life. This wasn't another volume about her trying to fit in, but what she would do now that she found the place where she belonged. Oh, there was so much she could do now that she wasn't fretting over silly little things, like how her hair didn't hold a curl or whether she had too many sugars in her tea.

So she crossed out the words

~~Lady Bridget's Diary, Volume the Second~~

And instead she wrote

Lady Darcy's Diary

She turned the page and began to write.

Things I love about my Dear Darcy
I love that I can say MY dear Darcy.
I love the way he always does the right thing and protects those he loves.
I love the way he kisses me.
I love the way he would become adorably embarrassed if I were to write any more about that.

Bridget caught herself staring into space with a dreamy smile on her lips and wicked thoughts in her head. Thoughts of kisses and more than that.

I love that when I have thoughts of kisses and more than that, he is just downstairs and I only need to go knock on his door . . .

She set down her pen. That would do for now; she had a whole lifetime with him to add to the list and a desperate need to go kiss him, immediately, because she could. But before she shut the book she flipped through the pages and noticed something—there was writing on a random page in the middle. It was not her handwriting. In fact, it looked like . . . Darcy's.

Things I love about my wife
I always know what she is thinking.
I love that she stands back up when she falls.
I love that she makes me feel alive and reminds me what is important.
I love things that I am too much of a stuffy English gentleman to put into words, but she knows what they are . . .

With that, Bridget laughed, closed the diary, locked it, and put it away. Then she went off in search of Darcy, to interrupt whatever vital work he was doing, with something far more important: a kiss.

Keep reading for a sneak peek at

the next title in bestselling author

Maya Rodale's hilarious

Keeping Up with the Cavendishes series,

CHASING LADY AMELIA

Available July 2016

*In which our hero and heroine should
not be meeting like this*

*I*t was a warm summer night in Mayfair and
Alistair Finlay-Jones sang an old drinking song
as he walked back to his flat after a night pleas-
antly spent drinking and wagering with his old
friends at White's.

At this late hour, the streets were empty.

Except for . . . a woman?

He slowed his pace and observed.

She strolled slowly and stumbled slightly. As
he drew closer, he heard something like singing,
but she was slurring her words and it was hard
to discern what she was saying. Or singing. But
she did have a lovely voice.

A lovely figure, too, from what he could
glimpse from behind. Women with lovely fig-

ures and voices oughtn't be strolling the streets of London, not even in Mayfair, at this late hour.

He caught up with her.

"Madame."

She whirled to face him, nearly falling flat on her face as she did so.

"Good evening, sir. Or is it lord? Or mister or right honorable? I do apologize for not knowing." She tried to curtsy, which was a terrible idea, given her difficulty standing. He propped her up. "I am delighted to make your acquaintance. You must be the man with the song."

In the moonlight, he could see that she was young. Far too young and far too female to be out on the streets alone, never mind that she was out at night. Never mind that she was clearly three, possibly five sheets to the wind.

Given that this was Mayfair, a neighborhood populated by the marriage minded mamas, the most dangerous subset of human for the common rake, Alistair had half a mind to rush away from her, in the event that this was some marriage trap.

But then he looked into the dark pools of her eyes, fringed with dark lashes and thought *it could be worse*.

He put the thought out of his mind.

Madness, that.

"I have been looking for you," she told him. At least, that's what it sounded like.

"May I escort you home?" Better him than, oh, anyone else she might encounter. Besides, it's not as if he needed to be up in a few hours for an interview so important he was summoned from another continent for it.

"No, thank you. But it is so kind of you to offer."

She tried to dip into another curtsy and thought better of it. She swayed slightly, leaning in toward him.

"May I escort you elsewhere?"

"No, thank you. I prefer to walk."

"It is not safe for a lady on the streets alone, especially at night."

"It isn't safe for a lady anywhere, ever. But now I have you to protect me from the dangers." She nestled up to him, resting her cheek on his chest. Then she yawned. "You will, won't you?"

"Yes," he said softly. Because honestly, what else could he say when a lovely young woman pressed against him like that?

"Let us walk," she said, quickly stepping away from him and pitching forward. He quickly darted forward and linked arms. She leaned heavily against him and they took a few slow steps. "And do carry on with your song. It tempted me to come out. Like the sires."

"The sires?"

"You know, from the odessisseusness."

"I beg your pardon?"

"The Greek story."

"Ah," he said, comprehension dawning. "The sirens. From the Odyssey."

"That's the one! That's you."

"I can assure you, I'm not luring you to your death. Quite the contrary, I would like to see you home safely. Where do you live?"

"America."

Wrong. Impossible. Try again.

"Where do you live?"

"One of these big old drafty houses." She waved her hand in the general vicinity of the approximately twenty houses lining the street.

If he had stayed in England, he would know who she was, who she belonged to, and which house was hers. She was obviously a person of quality if she was referencing The Odyssey and lived in a drafty old Mayfair house. Or perhaps she was merely a governess. Either way, the last he checked, the young ladies of England of any social class were not encouraged to drink themselves into a stupor and wander the streets alone.

The girl was leaning more and more heavily upon him. Her footsteps were slowing. He probably had precious few moments before she blacked out entirely.

"Miss, where do you live?"

She slumped against him. Yawned loudly. She rested her cheek against the wool of his jacket and her hands slid against his chest.

"Oh bloody hell," he muttered.

She mumbled something that sounded like, "Ladies mustn't use such language."

"Good thing I'm not a lady."

"Wish I wasn't."

She nestled even closer against him. He could feel that she was very much a lady.

He suddenly, keenly regretted not accepting Darcy's offer of a ride. At this very moment he could be back in his lodgings, loosening his cravat, removing his boots, and falling into bed to snatch a few precious hours of sleep before the baron told him why he'd been summoned back after six years abroad.

But no, he was on Bruton Street in the middle of the night, in a hellish predicament. Somehow, he was in possession of a drunk or drugged woman who probably had rich and powerful relatives who would make him pay for his role in this farce.

Alistair considered his options. He could knock on each door and make inquiries: "Does this girl belong to you? No? Do you know whom she belongs to?"

He couldn't just leave her on the street.

Perhaps he could leave her on a doorstep of one of these houses, ring the bell, and run, thus making her someone else's problem. A butler would know what to do with her. Butlers always knew what to do.

But that would certainly ruin the girl.

And she seemed like such a sweet girl, with her dark eyes and tumble of curls and mentions of ancient Greek literature. Drunken, unchaperoned, slightly flirtatious antics notwithstanding. He wanted no part in her ruination.

But Alistair didn't exactly want the responsibility of saving her from such ruination either. He wanted to collapse in his own bed and snatch a few precious hours of sleep before what promised to be a life altering interview with the baron. And to do that, he needed to get rid of this girl.

Alistair grabbed her and shook her warm, limp shoulders.

"Where do you live?"

Her head lolled to the side, dark curls tumbled out of her coiffure. She muttered something completely unintelligible. Oh, bloody hell.

Alistair glanced around at the dark night and desolate streets. There was only one thing to do: he would have to take her home.

Next month, don't miss these exciting new love stories only from Avon Books

All Chained Up *Sophie Jordan*

Some men come with a built-in warning label. Knox Callaghan is one of them. Danger radiates from every lean, muscled inch of him, and his deep blue eyes seem to see right through to Briar Davis's most secret fantasies. But there's one major problem: Briar is a nurse volunteering at the local prison, and Knox is a paroled inmate who should be off-limits in every way. But a single touch can lead to a kiss—and a taste . . . until the only crime is denying what feels so right . . .

Six Degrees of Scandal *by Caroline Linden*

Olivia Townsend is in trouble and out of options. Pursued by a dangerous man in search of a lost treasure she doesn't possess, she's got only two things in her favor: her late husband's diary, which she was never meant to see . . . and James Weston, the man who was her first—and only—love. But when he comes to her aid and vows to stand by her, no matter what, she can't help but hope things will be different for them this time.

A Better Man *by Candis Terry*

Hockey star Jordan Kincade wasted no time ditching Sunshine Valley and everyone who mattered for a career in the NHL—a truth Jordan confronts when his parents' deaths bring him home. Now he's back to make amends, which begins with keeping his younger sister from flunking out of school. It's just his luck that the one person who can help is the girl whose heart he broke years ago, and whom he could never quite forget . . .

Discover great authors, exclusive offers, and more at hc.com.

REL 0316

THE SMYTHE-SMITH QUARTET BY #1 *NEW YORK TIMES* BESTSELLING AUTHOR

JULIA QUINN

JUST LIKE HEAVEN

978-0-06-149190-0

Honoria Smythe-Smith is to play the violin (badly) in the annual musicale performed by the Smythe-Smith quartet. But first she's determined to marry by the end of the season. When her advances are spurned, can Marcus Holroyd, her brother Daniel's best friend, swoop in and steal her heart in time for the musicale?

A NIGHT LIKE THIS

978-0-06-207290-0

Anne Wynter is not who she says she is, but she's managing quite well as a governess to three highborn young ladies. Daniel Smythe-Smith might be in mortal danger, but that's not going to stop the young earl from falling in love. And when he spies a mysterious woman at his family's annual musicale, he vows to pursue her.

THE SUM OF ALL KISSES

978-0-06-207292-4

Hugh Prentice has never had patience for dramatic females, and Lady Sarah Pleinsworth has never been acquainted with the words *shy* or *retiring*. Besides, a reckless duel has left Hugh with a ruined leg, and now he could never court a woman like Sarah, much less dream of marrying her.

THE SECRETS OF SIR RICHARD KENWORTHY

978-0-06-207294-8

Sir Richard Kenworthy has less than a month to find a bride, and when he sees Iris Smythe-Smith hiding behind her cello at her family's infamous musicale, he thinks he might have struck gold. Iris is used to blending into the background, so when Richard courts her, she can't quite believe it's true.

New York Times Bestselling Author
LISA KLEYPAS

Somewhere I'll Find You
978-0-380-78143-0

Julia Wentworth guards a devastating secret:
a mystery husband whom she does not know,
dares not mention . . . and cannot love.

Prince of Dreams
978-0-380-77355-8

Nikolas burns to possess Emma Stokehurst, but the proud,
headstrong beauty is promised to another.

Midnight Angel
978-0-380-77353-4

Enchanted by her gentle grace and regal beauty, widower
Lord Lucas Stokehurst impetuously offers "Miss Karen
Billings" a position as governess to his young daughter.

Dreaming of You
978-0-380-77352-7

Curiosity is luring Sara Fielding from the shelter
of her country cottage into the dangerous
and exciting world of Derek Craven.

Then Came You
978-0-380-77013-7

Lily Lawson is determined to rescue her sister from an
unwanted impending marriage to the notorious Lord Raiford.

Only With Your Love
978-0-380-76151-7

Abducted by a man who has paid a king's ransom for her,
Celia despairs for her safety.

**Available wherever books are sold
or please call 1-800-331-3761 to order.**

LK3 0215

At Avon Books, we know your passion for romance—once you finish one of our novels, you find yourself wanting more.

May we tempt you with . . .

- **Excerpts** from our upcoming releases.

- Entertaining **extras**, including authors' personal photo albums and book lists.

- Behind-the-scenes **scoop** on your favorite characters and series.

- **Sweepstakes** for the chance to win free books, romantic getaways, and other fun prizes.

- Writing **tips** from our authors and editors.

- **Blog** with our authors and find out why they love to write romance.

- **Exclusive content** that's not contained within the pages of our novels.

Join us at
www.avonbooks.com

AVON
An Imprint of HarperCollins*Publishers*
www.avonromance.com

Available wherever books are sold or please call 1-800-331-3761 to order.

FTH 1013

*G*ive in to your Impulses!

These unforgettable stories only take a second to buy and give you hours of reading pleasure!

Go to *www.AvonImpulse.com* and see what we have to offer.

Available wherever e-books are sold.

AVONIMPULSE

IMP 0811

AVON BOOKS

The Diamond Standard
of Romance

Visit AVONROMANCE.COM

Come celebrate 75 years of Avon Books
as each month we look toward the future
and celebrate the past!

Join us online for more information about our
75th anniversary e-book promotions,
author events and reader activities.
A full year of new voices and classic stories.
All created by the very best writers of romantic fiction.

Diamonds Always
Sparkle, Shimmer, and Shine!